PRAISE FOR *THE OTHER HALF*

"A wickedly funny ménage à trois." —*Cosmopolitan* magazine (UK)

"Compulsive enough to have you walking into lampposts."
—*Company* magazine (UK)

"An all-too-likely tale of marriage and infidelity." —*Express*

THE OTHER HALF

Sarah Rayner

 ST. MARTIN'S GRIFFIN ≋ NEW YORK

This is a work of fiction. All of the characters, organizations, and events portrayed in this novel are either products of the author's imagination or are used fictitiously.

THE OTHER HALF. Copyright © 2014 by Sarah Rayner. All rights reserved. Printed in the United States of America. For information, address St. Martin's Press, 175 Fifth Avenue, New York, N.Y. 10010.

www.stmartins.com

Designed by Anna Gorovoy

Library of Congress Cataloging-in-Publication Data

Rayner, Sarah.
    The other half / Sarah Rayner. — First U.S. Edition.
        p. cm.
    ISBN 978-1-250-04210-1 (trade paperback)
    ISBN 978-1-250-04559-1 (hardcover)
    ISBN 978-1-250-03472-4 (e-book)
    I. Title.
    PR6118.A57O88 2014
    823'.92—dc23

                                    2013046241

St. Martin's Griffin books may be purchased for educational, business, or promotional use. For information on bulk purchases, please contact Macmillan Corporate and Premium Sales Department at 1-800-221-7945, extension 5442, or write specialmarkets@macmillan.com.

A different version of this title was published in the United Kingdom by Orion in 2001.

First Edition: April 2014

10 9 8 7 6 5 4 3 2 1

THE MISTRESS. THE WIFE.

EACH HAS HER OWN STORY.

THE OTHER HALF

1

There were three men opposite her, all hard at it. One had been going for ages and had worked up a real sweat. Every stroke was accompanied by a noisy "ooof." The other two seemed more blasé. Chloë struck up her own rhythm, feeling self-conscious.

There's something sexual about rowing machines, she thought, with their rhythmic propulsion backward and forward. Particularly the machines at this gym, which are set up facing each other, toe to toe.

As she realized this, it seemed the men did too. They appeared to be looking at her, and trying not to. For the briefest moment, she knew what it might be like to have sex with them all. Simultaneously.

The "ooof" man was the fittest—a muscular, ruddy-cheeked, rugby type, determined to go faster than anyone else. He'd be crap in bed, she decided, governed by his own ego. To his right, a nice guy. He smiled at Chloë when she caught his eye and looked skyward, as if to say in camaraderie, Why are we putting ourselves through this? Yet it was the man on the far left who looked the most appealing: a slender, long-distance-runner's body, a poetic face. And inevitably—once he'd given her a cursory glance—no interest in Chloë whatsoever.

However hard she worked out, Chloë would never have the kind of physique that was attractive to all men, which, of course, was what she wanted. Instead she was lumbered with a voluptuous appeal that a few found irresistible but many far too much. She had a bosom, hips, a tummy. And whereas some women seemed to gain a certain something when they "glowed" in the aftermath of exercise, Chloë simply looked dishevelled and hot. Momentarily she worried that this was how she looked during sex—a nightmare thought, best not contemplated.

I'm at that point in life, thought Chloë as she left the gym, where men don't wolf whistle as much as they used to. And although publicly she liked to dismiss whistling as animal behavior at its vilest, privately she found it galling to be no longer readily appreciated.

A short walk up Battersea Rise and she was home. Experience had taught her that unless a gym was on her doorstep she'd find any excuse not to go.

"Hiya," she called. As the front door banged, the whole place seemed to shake.

"Hi there," came a familiar voice. "Do you want a glass of wine?"

A delicious smell was wafting toward her. Chloë dumped her bag on the chair kept in the hall because one of its legs was broken and there was no room for it elsewhere, and went into the kitchen.

"Love one," she said, picking at the spaghetti.

"Stop it!"

"Oh, Rob." She leaned her head on his shoulder and messed his blond hair. "What would I do without you?"

He passed her a glass of red. "Starve."

Chloë Appleton was hurtling toward thirty years of age with a speed that made her feel compelled to get a move on with her life. Thanks to an impatient and demanding nature, in those decades she'd already experienced a great deal to distress and irk her. Born to an affluent intellectual couple in comfortable West London, vexation had started at three with the arrival of a younger sibling, a round-faced, fat-limbed baby whom everyone—especially her parents—adored. She didn't like sharing them, yet she was also wooed by her new brother, and photos of the time showed her veering between anxiety and sisterly affection; one of her father cuddling her while she squinted worriedly at the camera, another of her leaning over Sam and stroking his apple cheeks.

Over the years they'd grown closer, united by the adversity of their parents' divorce. Now he lived in California with an affable Australian who, Chloë acknowledged, was probably his soul mate. The patterns of old reemerged: on one hand she envied their relationship, on the other she enjoyed their company. Above all she missed Sam. So after supper she sat down at the desk in her bedroom, shoveled her way through a mountain of papers, and turned on her laptop to type him an e-mail.

To: Sam Appleton
Subject: Spaghetti

How goes it? Has our dreadful cousin gone yet? Did you do that Couples' Weekend Michele had her heart set on? (I have a bizarre vision of you both sitting naked banging drums in the desert as you bond with your Native American souls—correct me if I'm wrong . . .) Or did your English cynicism win through and see you pull out at the eleventh hour?

At this end all is much the same—still got the bargain apartment, the job at *Babe*'s going well, and I'm hardly Chloë No Mates—yet occasionally I wonder if something's missing. Rob and I are getting on fine, but I'm beginning to think there's a limit to how long we can carry on sharing the same space. Sometimes my head feels like a plate of spaghetti (and that's not because he's just cooked me some—he's great in that way) that could do with unraveling.

I suppose this mood will pass. Anyway, I haven't time
to worry—I'm presenting that proposal I told you about
tomorrow. And if that takes off, I'll have heaps to keep me
amused. On that note, I must finish it before I go to bed, so
best stop procrastinating and crack on.

Love,
Chloë
Xox

By the time Chloë had finished, Rob was already brushing his teeth in the bathroom.

"All done then?" he said, mouth full of toothpaste.

"Yup." She struggled to squeeze the last remnant from the tube. He gargled while she brushed, sharing the basin. Although she occasionally griped about Rob, she loved these moments of intimacy. There was no one she felt more able to relax with, even after so many years.

In many ways I'm lucky, she thought. We rarely argue, we give each other unconditional support, and our friends get on like a house on fire. Some married couples do a lot worse.

Ablutions completed, it was time to hit the sack.

"Night, then," said Rob, disappearing into his room and closing the door.

"Night," said Chloë. She stripped off her clothes, throwing them onto the floor where they added to the growing pile. Exhausted, she climbed into bed and turned out the light.

The alarm went off at seven forty-five. Chloë checked she was okay after her workout. "Good, don't seem too achy," she muttered. (First sign of madness, talking to yourself.) She listened to *Thought for the Day*, gleaned a sound bite of spirituality, and threw back the duvet.

Kettle on, swift rinse of a dirty mug to make it fit for coffee, feed the cat.

That's the last of the Whiskas, she thought, I must remember to buy more—and toothpaste. Why do I never have time to go to the supermarket? I always seem to end up paying over the odds at the corner store.

Rob, dead to the world, wouldn't be up for another hour. Chloë envied his ability to sleep that soundly.

So, what to wear? She had a meeting with the new publisher at ten thirty. Her Whistles suit. Shit! She'd splodged Bolognese down the skirt last night. A riffle through her closet revealed nothing appropriate was clean.

I'll never make it to editor at this rate, she thought. What I need is a wardrobe of natty little numbers, all interchangeable, carefully ironed and perfect for impressing one's superiors.

Over the years Chloë had commissioned numerous articles about the merits of coordinating colors and capsule wardrobes, yet she was still more inclined to buy clothes when she fell in love with them rather than because they fulfilled a useful purpose. This left her no choice other than to wear a dress that Rob had brought back for her from New York bearing the label *Spunky*. According to Rob, its bright floral print and vampishly low cleavage made her look cute yet cool, but it wasn't ideal for a meeting with someone she had to impress. Still, it was the only thing that was vaguely presentable, and if she pinned the neckline it wasn't too revealing.

What the hell? she thought. It's flattering, and it's more my style than the suit any day.

"Loving the oufit," said her assistant, Patsy, when Chloë arrived at work.

"Thanks," said Chloë, flattered. With her sparrowlike physique, savvy fashion sense, and incredible eye for detail, Patsy was the style barometer of the office. Given that the competition in the world of magazines was intense, this position carried some kudos.

"Is it for James Slater's benefit?"

"Whose?"

"The new publisher. You're meeting him this morning, aren't you?"

"Oh, yeah," said Chloë, trying to sound as if it wasn't that important to her. "Make sure to walk him past my desk," said Patsy. "He's *gorgeous*."

"Really?" Gorgeous men in women's monthlies were a rarity.

"And married," Jean, the editor, interrupted, "to one of my best friends. Chloë, did you finish proofing that article? The copy editors are waiting."

"Of course, of course," said Chloë, fishing in her handbag for the hard copy she'd taken home. Where was it? She emptied the contents onto the desk. There was her purse, her makeup bag (held together with an elastic band as the zipper was broken), a packet of chewing gum, numerous receipts she planned to claim as expenses, and a couple of rather squashed and dusty Tampax. No article. She'd been so busy putting together her presentation that she must have left it by the computer. First nothing to wear, now this. It was going to be one of those days.

"Just get it in for copyediting before your meeting," said Jean, striding off with an efficient click of her court shoes.

Chloë looked helplessly at Patsy.

"You've not done it?"

"I was up till midnight finishing it off—that's what makes it worse. I've left it at home. Shit and double shit. She'll be furious! I'll have to do it again. Ah Rob," she remembered. "If I phone now I'll catch him. He can read me the corrections." Hurriedly she dialed the number. Four rings, then the answering machine clicked on. "Rob! Are you there? Answer me, please!"

She was halfway through rewriting the whole thing when he called back. "Sorry. I was in the shower. What's the problem?"

By the time she'd explained and Rob had read the changes with the slowness of one who not only couldn't decipher her writing but also didn't understand what he was doing, it would have been quicker to do it from scratch. However he meant well so she could hardly be cross. She got the article to the chief copy editor with moments to spare. Still pumping with adrenaline, she ran back to her desk to collect her makeup bag and charged through reception to the ladies' room.

Whack! Straight into the arms of a rather attractive man.

"Whoa! Slow up."

"Sorry, " gasped Chloë. "Desperate for a pee."

Oh, no, she cringed, seconds later, sitting on the loo. I just told a complete stranger I was desperate for a pee! Chloë, Chloë, Chloë, what *are* you like?

By now she was so flustered she couldn't pee anyway, so she abandoned the attempt and opted for a rapid repair to her lipstick, a quick spray of perfume, and a halfhearted washing of her hands, followed by an ineffective blast under the ancient dryer. No matter how much profit UK Magazines made, it seemed they were not prepared to shell out on new infrastructure.

"Ah, Chloë," said the receptionist when she emerged. "This is James Slater."

Triple shit, thought Chloë, as she put out her palm.

"Hello," he said, taking her hand and shaking it firmly.

"Nice to meet you. Sorry, I think my hands are still wet."

"Good to know you always wash them after peeing anyway." He grinned.

2

Upon waking in the morning, before talking, eating, drinking, smoking, or getting out of bed, take your temperature, leaving the thermometer in place for at least five minutes.

Easier said than done, when you had a husband and small child to contend with. Maggie yawned and reached over to the bedside table. It was five fifty. She hit the *Snooze* button for Jamie's benefit, put the thermometer in her mouth, and counted to three hundred. She wondered what would happen if she bit the thermometer. Presumably she'd end up with a mouthful of broken glass and mercury poisoning, and all her efforts at consuming a relatively toxin-free diet would be wasted. Time's up. By now she knew the instructions by heart.

Record your temperature by making a dot on the chart. As soon as there is more than one dot, join them together with a straight line in order to bring the record up to date.

Well, well. Her temperature was down. She was ovulating. Lucky old Jamie. She hit the *Radio On* button. It was so early that *Farming Today* was on—hardly a seductive choice of program, but she hadn't the energy to retune it.

"Darling . . ." Maggie snuggled up to him.

"What?" He groaned.

"'Now Humphrey Henderson brings news from Bonn, where farmers are carrying out trials on a new kind of sheep dip suitable for organic herds,'" said the gravelly voiced presenter.

Maggie gave Jamie's shoulders little kisses.

"Jamie. . . ."

"Jesus!" He sat up with a start. "What's the time?"

"Six o'clock. Relax."

"Got to get up." He threw off the duvet and leaped out of bed. "I've a string of meetings today. Back-to-back. Haven't prepared at all."

"Oh," said Maggie, deflated. Maybe it could wait till the evening, although these days Jamie was better at making love in the mornings. Last month they'd missed their chance because Nathan had been up three nights in a row with a virus—something always seemed to be conspiring against them.

Sighing, she got up and followed Jamie into the bathroom where he was already running water for a shave. She switched on the shower and stepped in.

"So, who are your meetings with?" She raised her voice so he could hear.

"Nine o'clock I'm seeing Peter Blandford about a fitness supplement for *Men*. Ten thirty some woman from *Babe* wants to talk about a new idea. Then a lunchtime meeting to go through next year's figures with Susie Davis and Mark Pickles, and a three o'clock at the printer's to discuss whether we can bring our on-sale dates forward to be more competitive."

"It sounds all go."

"Blast!" said Jamie, his face now lathered. "Is my razor in there?"

"Oh—yes." Maggie guiltily passed it to him.

"I thought you had your own. You know how much that bugs me."

His very dark hair meant a daily shave was vital, otherwise he looked stubbly by early evening, and though Maggie secretly preferred him that way, he insisted it wasn't appropriate for an executive in his position.

"Nathan pulled it apart and broke the catch. I haven't had a moment to buy another."

"You let Nathan play with razors!"

"Yes—before I slip cyanide into his breakfast cereal. Look, he's six years old. I can't watch him every second—you know that only too well."

"I suppose so," admitted Jamie. Just last week Nathan, worryingly accident prone, had tripped down the stairs while Jamie had been minding him. For a few days they thought he'd broken his nose, and Jamie had felt particularly guilty.

At six forty-five Maggie went in to wake Nathan. He was sound asleep, fair hair tumbled across the pillow, last night's bedtime reading still open by his side. She shook him tenderly.

"Grab me by my wings!" he said.

What magical world was she wrecking to bring him down to earth? Was he an angel, perhaps? She doubted it. Far more likely he was an insect in midflight. Maggie smiled. "Nathan," she called softly.

"Grab me by my wings!" he said again, insistently, and reached out his arms.

"Here." She hugged him. "I've got you."

"Woah!"

"What were you dreaming?"

"Not sure," said Nathan, puzzled.

Next the ritual fifteen-minute battle to get him ready for the day. Without Maggie's watchful eye, teeth cleaning would be a feeble ten-second encounter with a toothbrush, face washing would leave a grimy neck or snotty nose, and hair brushing would mean missing the back of his head completely. School uniform simplified matters, but there were clean shirts and matching socks to find, and the inevitable loss of a trainer he'd only been wearing the night before.

With so much time devoted to getting her son presentable, Maggie couldn't spend as long on her own appearance as she had in the past. She'd always been reasonably comfortable with her looks and still took care about what she put into her body—indeed, she had long been renowned among her peers for her healthy eating habits and unique dress sense. But these days she often felt drab. A quick dab of mascara had to suffice before she flung on her clothes—something comfortable that she could spill food down was vital in her line of work.

Presently, Jamie left for the office. His publishing house was in the West End of London and he had to drive to Guildford and catch the train. At eight thirty another local mum came to collect Nathan—they took turns walking the children to the village school.

"Bye, love." Maggie kissed him and handed him his packed lunch.

"Bye. Look after Monday." Monday was his gerbil.

"Of course," said Maggie, knowing full well she would ignore the animal. He had been a gift from her friend Jean, who—to Maggie's frustration—indulged Nathan as she had no children of her own. Personally, Maggie found Monday a bit too ratlike for comfort, but because Nathan loved him, didn't have the heart to say so.

Back in the house, she leaned against the kitchen door frame, closed her eyes, and listened. There was the low hum of the refrigerator, the regular *shum, shum* of the washing machine. Otherwise it was silent. It was at moments like these that she persuaded herself she was glad they'd moved out of London. Here in Surrey it was much quieter, and though her social circle was tamer, she loved being closer to nature, noticing what season it was, waking to the sound of birds rather than traffic. Shere, the village where they lived, was exceptionally pretty.

Time to get cracking. Literally.

Today she was testing recipes for "Pulling Dishes," an article for *Men* suggesting meals to help a man to score with a prospective girlfriend. Hardly a credible concept—it would take more than a well-cooked meal to lure me into bed, thought Maggie—but it was more fun than the dreary suggestions many magazine editors went for. It was only a way of dressing up old favorites—soufflé, goat cheese salad, tagliatelli. In an ideal world she'd rather have written something more controversial that drew on her expertise in nutrition and interest in subjects like GM-free crops and organic farming. Yet somehow she'd slipped into producing more traditional pieces because it was easy, the money was good, and Jamie had lots of contacts in the magazine world.

She opened the refrigerator and got out eggs, butter, cheese.

Damn, she thought. I forgot to order more milk. How could I have made such a basic mistake? I'll have to nip out to the shop. As she reached for her bag, she sighed to herself; it's obviously going to be one of those days.

A couple of hours later and she had one recipe almost complete.

Artichoke Soufflé with Three Cheeses

There's nothing more likely to whet a woman's sexual appetite than a well-risen soufflé. But if you want to impress her, don't be fooled into thinking bigger is better. In fact, a small dish with a collar tied around is rather more tempting. Then you can pile the mixture up high and when it's cooked remove the collar to reveal something quite spectacular.

She laughed at the thought of being seduced by a soufflé. She had a vision of being cajoled into the bedroom for some "intercourse" and being surprised by the sight of a man, his penis happily erect and tied with a red ribbon.

I guess the first test of good copy is that it should do something for the writer herself, she thought.

Better focus, make a drink. Maggie had been an early convert to proper coffee. Even as a student, when her fellow undergraduates had been content with the filthiest instant made with—horror of horrors—*powdered* milk, she had had a percolator in her room. In the run-down Victorian terraces of Manchester this had been unusual, but now in their immaculate, well-equipped kitchen her perfectionism seemed less misplaced. These days she had one of those espresso makers that went directly on the gas burner—something about the ritual of using a more basic implement appealed to her sense of authenticity.

Around the house were various tributes to Maggie's ongoing campaign to get things aesthetically right. She would prefer to slave stripping layers of paint off a cornice herself than hire someone else to do it, lest they chip a vital plaster detail. Equally, she was happier to have no paintings rather than twee prints that anyone could have; unlike some of the other stockbroker-belt women locally, Maggie wasn't one for off-the-shelf style. When she and Jamie had lived in London, their friends had admired her individualism and confidence in her own vision—their home had even been featured in a couple of magazines. Here Maggie felt her insistence on using pure pigment paints and real candles on the Christmas tree was probably seen as arty-farty and pretentious. Yet while she wasn't prepared to compromise to keep others happy and seem less threatening—that would have meant denying herself pleasure—sometimes she felt lonely, cut off from kindred spirits and those with more eclectic tastes.

Perhaps that's why I want a second child, she thought. Or maybe it's because as a toddler Nathan seemed happy to be endlessly cuddled, whereas now he's inclined to push me away and say I'm being soppy.

Whatever the reason, over the last few months Maggie had been broody—and with it came a desire to make love so strong that at times it seemed overwhelming, despite the passion-killing thermometers. But Jamie had not been in the mood for sex of late. Maggie knew it was a tough time for him professionally and was loath to seem too pushy.

The coffee failed to do the trick, and no amount of aphrodisiac recipe-testing was going to alleviate her sexual frustration. There was only one solution. Retail therapy.

It's ages since I've treated myself to a spree purely for my own pleasure, she reasoned.

But first, damn it, she would take a little time getting ready. Experience had taught her that shopping in one's grottiest clothes was a mistake—lines failed to flatter, and even her favorite colors made her appear washed out. Thanks to good skin, naturally fair hair, and a leggy physique, Maggie scrubbed up both well and quickly, and within minutes the tired tracksuit had been replaced by a honey-colored silk shirtdress that helped her feel less suburban mum and more city chic. Settled behind the wheel of her car, she pumped the volume up on the CD player *much* louder than usual, blasting an old favorite from her student days into the countryside.

Forty minutes later she was in Kingston. She swept into the mall, got out of the car, scooped up her bag, and flicked on the alarm. First stop, John Lewis. She took the escalators to the second floor, turned left, and breathed a sigh of relief.

There they were. Hanger upon hanger. Push-up bras and basques, F-cups and G-strings, French knickers and frilly panties.

She prowled around like a lion assessing its prey. Yes! That one. And that. And those . . .

There are blessings to being a 34B, she thought. I might not have the bosom to make a man stop dead in the street, but it's relatively easy to find something that fits. And it was well worth driving a bit farther for all this choice.

Within minutes Maggie's arms were full of lilac silk, black lycra, pink cotton, and white lace. Then, on an uncharacteristic whim, she picked up a red-and-black basque with suspenders and headed for the fitting room.

The assistant counted the number of hangers and agreed to hand her the surplus items through the curtain. The good thing about the changing room was that it was private, well-lit, and spacious. The bad thing was it had three angled mirrors so she could see every imperfection.

Still, she reasoned, determined to see the bright side, it means that whatever I choose will look good when I get home. Unlike those mirrors designed to make me appear three inches taller and twenty pounds lighter than I really am.

Although over the years people had told Maggie she had a nice figure, she'd always considered herself rather androgynous. She hankered for a more voluptuous shape, a defined waist, and breasts that hadn't lost their pertness after childbirth. Sometimes she had a vague suspicion Jamie liked women who were more generously endowed . . .

As she tried on the different items, Maggie was amazed how each of the various styles seemed to give her an entirely new persona: white broderie anglaise, and she was pretty, young, and innocent; grey marl, she was doubtless more interested in comfort than sex; in a black lycra G-string and seamless bra, there were several more notches on her bedpost. In the past, she would have opted for the latter—the combination was simple and sporty, not too sexually overt.

Maybe I should be more daring, she urged herself, as she slipped on the black-and-red basque.

She adjusted the straps and swiveled around. Without stockings it was hard to gauge the full effect, but she had a good imagination. Her nipples were clearly visible through the sheer black lace.

Is that truly *me* reflected in the glass? she thought. It seems the kind of thing other women wear—women I usually reproach for their lack of discretion. Yet maybe I should admire their audacity. . . . It's a far cry from my usual purchases and hardly in keeping with my understated style, but there's something about its sensuality—the red ribbon trim, the black boning, its sheer impracticality . . .

She stood back for a proper look. There was no doubt that it pushed her up and pulled her in to great effect.

Damn the cost, damn my usual taste, damn perceiving it as tarty, damn the fact that over the last few years shopping has come to mean Waitrose and things for Nathan or for the house, thought Maggie. Why *should* I be so restrained?

And to her surprise, as she handed her debit card to the matronly woman behind the till, she felt wonderfully empowered.

If that didn't do the trick tonight, nothing would.

3

The meeting room was large for just two people, with empty chairs arranged neatly around a clear glass table. With the air-conditioning on full blast it was cold. Chloë flicked off the fan and laid several magazines in front of her.

"Would you like some coffee?"

"Please. That would be great." James clicked open his briefcase, got out his iPad, and pushed up the sleeves of his jacket in a way that asserted he meant business.

Chloë made a mental note: good hands, attractive wrists, not-too-showy watch. She and Rob often discussed the various components that gave male forearms their unique appeal. She picked up the phone and called Patsy. "Could we have coffee for two, please? We're in the meeting room."

"So," said James, "you wanted to discuss a new magazine idea."

"I have a proposal."

"Oh?"

"I believe there is a gap in the market for a new women's monthly."

"Does your editor know about this?"

Was it Chloë's imagination, or did he sound a little worried about meeting behind Jean's back? Jean had implied that they knew each other socially as well as through work, after all. Chloë endeavored to put him at ease. "I didn't feel she had to yet. What I'm talking about is not a direct competitor to *Babe*." She took a deep breath and started her Powerpoint presentation.

"I realize there are many magazines, and in some ways the market is overcrowded," she continued, expanding on the bullet points highlighted on the screen in front of them. "It's certainly jam-packed in the teen area, right up to women in their late twenties. *Babe* is one of those, as you know, and of course it does very well, with its niche firmly established. And there is ample reading matter for those over forty. But I believe there is a gap for women between those ages, say between twenty-eight and forty."

"You don't think this gap's already been filled?"

"I don't." Chloë moved on to the next slide, titled *The Competition*. "Your reader of these magazines"—she gesticulated to the array before them— "is perceived as pretty traditional. The expectation is that she is married, with children, or certainly in a relationship. She is into clothes, not high fashion. She is into dinner parties, recipes, and gardening. Which is all very well, but I've undertaken research that shows there is another kind of woman, and she's interested in a lot more than this."

"Research?" James sounded impressed.

"Yes." Chloë handed him a copy of her proposal document. "You'll find full details in here, but I'll run you through the basics." She clicked the mouse. "I held a number of discussion groups, selecting ABC1 women I know or friends of friends who work in a cross-section of industries, some with, some without children. All of them, without exception, felt there was no magazine that catered exactly to their tastes."

"Where did you do this research?"

"At my home. I found it worked well if the group could relax over a glass of wine, away from the office and family. I provided samples of all these magazines and asked what they liked and didn't like about them, what sorts of interests they had, what they wanted to see, what they hated, what they loved. And I discovered my initial hunch was right. There *is* a gap in the market."

At that point there was a knock and Patsy came in with a tray. With her hair gelled into spikes and dressed in a miniskirt and clumpy platforms, she could have made an impression, yet she was so busy ogling James that Chloë feared she might drop everything.

"Thank you," he said.

"My pleasure." Patsy grinned like a teenager. James seemed oblivious, but it did allow Chloë several seconds to assess him further. He was well-spoken, she'd already noted, and she guessed he was mid to late thirties. Hmm, she thought. He's not really that handsome, certainly no Ryan Gosling or Brad Pitt—his features aren't regular and his hair needs a trim. He could do with losing a few pounds too. Yet he's one of those men who seems very, well, *male*, I suppose, and that's undeniably attractive . . .

"I see," said James, after Patsy had reluctantly left. "So have you some idea of what this magazine might be like?"

"I do. I'll give you a taste—you'll find more in my proposal. It will have more of an edge. It will be for women who like fast cars, high fashion, and occasionally getting drunk. It will be for women who work, but also for those bringing up children—neither will be the sole focus. It will debate politics and social issues—stirring up our readers' passions. And when we feature food and recipes, we'll offer practical advice, featuring something creative to do when you arrive home and there's nothing but a can of tuna and baked beans in your cupboard, say, rather than meals that take an entire week to prepare. It won't have endless features on how to get your man, or how to lose five pounds in a week—the other magazines already do that. Though it will talk about sex—gay sex, straight sex, dangerous sex, impotence, the lot."

She paused. "Above all, it will be exciting, vibrant, and bold. It will be up-front, plain-speaking, but fun. That, in my opinion, is where these magazines have got it wrong." She picked one up. "Look at the layout and the typography! Dull, dull, dull! The photography? It's *so* five years ago.

"Now," she said, handing him the latest copy of a magazine from

Japan. "This is more like it. The typography, the color, the shots—groundbreaking!"

"I agree." James seemed infected by her enthusiasm. "Graphics is an area where the Far East is often one step ahead."

"Exactly!"

"So your target woman, tell me more—what's she like?"

"Me, I suppose."

"Somehow I thought so." He grinned, and added, almost as an afterthought, "Sounds appealing."

"Well." Chloë blushed a little. "I realize that seems a bit egocentric, what I mean is; I've been working in this business for eight years now, and I still don't think there's a magazine that's exactly me. Anyway," she focused again, "I don't want to lose the thread of my presentation." She reached once more for the mouse.

"It's okay," James interrupted. "I'm interested by all I've heard so far, but I'm rather pushed for time. I'll take this home and read it. Meanwhile, what, precisely, would you like from me?"

"Gosh." Chloë was taken aback by his immediate validation of her hard work. This was something she felt so vehement about; it had been whizzing around in her head for months. But this was the first time she'd talked to anyone who could help make her vision a reality. She'd bounced ideas off Rob, she'd had her discussion groups, but chiefly this was *her* baby.

"I'd appreciate the opportunity to explore it further, but I think I've taken it about as far as I can on my own time. Now I'd like UK Magazines' backing."

"Such as?"

Chloë was impressed he'd gotten to the point so fast. "I was hoping I could be seconded to special projects to develop the idea."

"Mm. I'll need to think about that. I presume you'd want to be the acting editor."

"Yes." Chloë was flattered he thought her fit for such a key role, though it was the very post she hoped for. "So I'd rather you didn't tell Jean quite yet."

"You're taking a risk, aren't you, telling me? And at *Babe*'s offices."

"I am, but I really believe in this." A story came to Chloë's mind and she smiled. "Recently my uncle bought a sports car, after driving around in sensible little hatchbacks for years. He's seventy-three. 'Life is not a rehearsal, Chloë,' he said. 'Don't wait until you're retired to start realizing your ambitions.' It might be clichéd, but I could see his point. That evening I started to draft a proposal for this magazine."

James appeared touched. "I like your thinking. So, tell me, what position are you in here at *Babe*?"

"Features editor."

"I'm sure they'd hate to lose you. *Babe* is doing well. Yet I daresay they can hire a replacement, and a visionary editor to launch a new project is harder to find. I do warn you, though, we're not talking about a permanent post initially. Until you've put together a sample issue of the magazine, gone through more formal research, and tested with potential advertisers, any move would be only temporary."

"Of course."

"And I will have to talk to some others about it. I'll get back to you."

"Fine." Chloë was loath to leave the ball in his court. "Perhaps we could meet for lunch next week?"

"Good idea. I'll call you." James shuffled his papers and the proposal into his case. "I'm sorry to cut this so short, but I'm booked solid with meetings today and there is one I haven't prepared for yet."

Briefly Chloë caught a glimpse of a more boyish nervousness behind the capable businessman. She smiled sympathetically. "Not at all. I appreciate you taking the time to see me."

"Don't forget these," he said, handing her the magazines.

"God, no. Thanks." Though when he passed them to her, a couple slipped out of her hands and onto the floor. Chloë had to bend down to pick them up. As she did so he did the same, and their heads bumped.

"Sorry," she said.

"Oh, don't worry, I'm fine." He rubbed his forehead, then laughed. "That's our second collision today!"

"I'm so clumsy."

"It was my fault."

"No, it was mine," she insisted, opening the meeting-room door and leading him back to reception.

"By the way I like the dress." He shook her hand again. "It shows a certain individual style." He smiled broadly.

She beamed, unable to contain her pleasure. "Thank you."

"I look forward to seeing your fashion spreads," he said, his voice so low the receptionist couldn't hear.

Was there a slight innuendo in his tone? Surely not, she thought, as she sat back down at her desk. But later, she was certain about one thing. The madness of the morning had left her somewhat light-headed.

4

That Jamie wasn't back in time to help put Nathan to bed was not unusual, yet tonight it was particularly annoying.

"Right," Maggie said, focusing on her son. "Supper's ready."

She'd made a second soufflé, chiefly to verify the recipe but with the faint hope of casting an aphrodisiac spell on Jamie.

Quite what it will do to a six-year-old boy, Lord knows, she thought.

Nathan, oblivious to the X-rated world he was about to taste, was playing with Monday. The gerbil's nose twitched as he investigated the myriad smells of the table.

"Monday's going to have to move so you can eat your supper. He shouldn't be there as it is," said Maggie.

"But he's exploring!"

"He can explore all he likes once you've eaten. Take him back to your room."

"Okay." Nathan scurried upstairs to put Monday into his cage. When he was sitting down again, Maggie handed him a plate with a little soufflé and lots of baked beans. He looked askance at his portion. "Can I have some more?"

"Eat what you're given first."

Nathan dug in with relish, yet a few minutes later he began to slow down, until he stopped completely, leaving a soggy pink mess of soufflé and beans.

Maggie raised her eyebrows at him.

Nathan raised his own back, and sped up again, slurping loudly. Then he picked up his plate and licked it.

"Nathan!"

Nathan smiled. "Finished."

That child has me wound around his little finger, thought Maggie.

Once her son was tucked up in bed, she ran a bath. She lit some scented candles, poured herself a glass of red wine, and stepped in. Slowly, she lay back, bubbles floating around her. If she sucked in her tummy, the only part of her body that remained out of the water was her breasts. If she pushed her belly out, she almost looked pregnant. She lifted her feet and rested them against the overflow. They were slim and straight and a pleasing pale brown thanks to a recent week that she, Jamie, and Nathan had spent in a Tuscan villa.

She recollected a trip to New York she'd made with Jamie several years ago: they'd been staying with friends and she had borrowed a gym pass. As she was dressing after her workout, a beautiful fitness instructor had come into the changing room and started telling her pupils about another woman. "Her feet are so pretty!" she'd enthused. "They're kinda delicate, elegant—like hands, you know? Her toes, gee, they're so long and straight, not like most toes at all. She wears those crisscross sandals with little knots in them that accentuate just how pretty they are. And men love her—I've seen it, sat next to her in cafés. They stare at her, transfixed, but not by her face, which is cute, or her figure, which is divine. They stare at her feet! It's quite something."

Maggie had never forgotten this woman's way with words and

enthusiasm for life's minutiae. And she'd resolved right then and there: she would never compromise her aesthetic standards, even over trivial matters, and she would always, always look after her feet.

She took a sip of wine. It was not a particularly expensive bottle (it would have seemed extravagant to uncork one just for herself) but it was a good Burgundy, bought via mail order. She let it roll over her tongue. Moments like these were rare, and a new baby would make them rarer. Still, she thought, reaching guiltily for Jamie's razor, she'd never imagined having only one child, and if she and Jamie didn't get a move on, Nathan would be too old to play with a younger sibling.

After bathing, she moisturized all over and wandered around the bedroom letting the lotion sink into her skin. She phoned her sister, Fran, for a brief chat, then reached for the shopping bag and tipped its contents onto the bed. In the glow of the bedside lamps the basque was even more seductive.

Maggie rummaged in her drawer for some knickers. She knew which ones would be right—a satin-and-lace pair she'd purchased with Fran, who had persuaded her to buy them, but which she'd never worn. She put them on, fastened herself (with extensive swiveling) into the basque, and unwrapped a pair of sheer stockings. Carefully she eased one up over each newly shaved leg, clipped on the suspenders, and stood up. Finally, shoes. The stilettos bought for a Christmas party a few years ago when she'd wanted to impress Jamie's colleagues were perfect. The effect was astonishing—a whole new Maggie.

At that moment she heard a key in the front door and the familiar rustle of Jamie throwing his coat over the bottom banister. Quickly she pulled on a floor-length wrap and ran out to the landing. "Hi, darling." She spoke in a hushed voice so as not to wake Nathan.

"Hi," said Jamie. He sounded tired.

"We saved you some soufflé." She led him into the kitchen. "Though I'm afraid it'll be past its best."

Jamie poured himself a glass of wine and leaned back against the counter. "Phew. That was quite a day."

"Poor lamb." Maggie brushed away a stray strand of his hair.

"You smell nice," said Jamie, inhaling. He looked down.

The shoes.

"Ah, yes." Maggie let the gown fall open. "I went shopping today."

"So I see . . ." Jamie paused and took it all in. "Wow."

They made love in the kitchen—for the first time in ages. And he hadn't had so much as a bit of soufflé, smiled Maggie later as she drifted off to sleep.

5

Patsy pressed the mute button. "It's James Slater. Are you in?"

"Oh, er, yes," said Chloë.

A week had passed since their meeting, and she had begun to wonder if it would be inappropriate to call him. She picked up the receiver. "Hello."

"Hi. Can you talk?"

"Mm, a little." Chloë was in the midst of debriefing her assistant on some facts that needed checking in an article and was aware Patsy was earwigging every word.

"I'll keep it brief. I'm afraid I'm having a frantic week and lunch is going to be difficult." Chloë's heart sank. Why did men always turn out to be so flaky where she was concerned? Yet James continued, "I know it's short notice, but I usually play squash on Thursday nights with a friend up here in the West End, and he's just canceled. So I *could* do tomorrow, although it would have to be dinner. Can you make it?"

Could she make it? Of course she bloody could! She stopped herself from blurting an enthusiastic "Yes" in the nick of time. She recalled all those books that banged on about the importance of playing hard to get. Maybe it applied in business too. And then she remembered her mother's slightly cruel (but accurate) observation that sometimes her natural exuberance could be misinterpreted as "lacking mystery."

"I'll just check my diary." She counted to five. "My week's looking pretty hectic. Tomorrow, you said . . . Er, what time?"

"I should be through around seven. What about you?"

"I think I can make that." Chloë rummaged through her in-tray in the hopes she sounded busy.

"There's a charming little restaurant on Lexington Street," he continued. "It's called Louisa's, and it's unusual in that you can bring your own wine, which means we can enjoy something particularly good. How about if I pick up a couple of bottles and meet you there?"

"Sounds great." Excellent! Nice and near the office—and two bottles of vino. She hated people who scrimped—but then, he could probably charge it. It sounded like he knew a bit about wine too. How sophisticated. "I'll see you there."

"Looking forward to it."

She put the phone down, and immediately had to get up and walk around to calm herself.

"So?" asked Patsy, when she sat down again. "When are you meeting Prince Charming?"

"Tomorrow. Though he's not Prince Charming—it's business."

"Then why are you blushing?"

"I am not!" cried Chloë, going ever redder. She didn't want Patsy knowing she was meeting James outside office hours. "It's work," she reiterated, hoping her assistant wouldn't pry further.

"If you say so."

"He's married!" Chloë tried to laugh it off.

"So was Prince Charles," quipped Patsy. "Didn't stop him and Camilla."

"Chloë," said Rob, with the air of one with insight into such matters, "you're telling me that this man cancels lunch, rearranges it for dinner, says he's going to buy two bottles of wine, and that he's looking forward to seeing you, and you reckon he doesn't fancy you? Dear girl, at times I may find the male psyche hard to fathom, nonetheless this seems a classic case of get-this-woman-intoxicated-on-the-pretext-of-a-business-liaison-so-I-can-try-to-get-into-her-knickers."

"But he's married!"

"So are half the men I sleep with, darling." They were watching television but the ads were on, allowing two minutes for a chat.

"That's different," said Chloë.

"How, exactly?"

"The men you sleep with obviously want something they can't get from their wives."

Rob raised an eyebrow.

"Anyway, it doesn't really matter what his motives are—though I think you're wrong. Mine are quite pure."

"So why ask me what to wear?" asked Rob, who at times seemed to know Chloë better than she knew herself. "I'm sure nuns don't give a fig for such worldly matters."

"Because it's vital I create the right impression." Chloë was firm. "This man could help me get my magazine off the ground."

"Well, be careful. If your motives are so pure, wear your Whistles suit. That'll show him you mean business."

This was not what Chloë had been planning on; she'd in mind something rather less formal. "Mm," she muttered, aware she'd be gone before Rob got up.

"I just don't want you falling for another inappropriate male."

"I won't!"

"OK. Only don't make the mistake of being one of those women who uses flirtation to get what she wants professionally, then gets in a muddle because she's not been clear about the distinction between business and pleasure. Now shush."

The ad break was over.

Perhaps it was a sign of growing maturity that Chloë was finally learning not to be early for dates. (Though this wasn't a date but a business meeting, of course.) Restless by nature, she'd discovered the best tactic was to keep herself occupied till the last minute. So she remained in the office and rattled off a couple of e-mails—including a long one to Sam—and before she knew it, it was six fifty-five.

Quick trip to the ladies' room, third (but most thorough) repair of the day to her makeup, and she was off. Fortunately it was only a few minutes from Covent Garden to Lexington Street and she knew which backstreets to cut through.

If she checked her appearance in one window she must have checked it in twenty, and by the time she arrived she was convinced she looked a right state. But at least James was there before her. As she walked into the restaurant she could see him through the back window. He was sitting outside, reading at a small round table in the patio garden, having grabbed a prime spot in the last of the evening sun.

"Ah." He smiled and stood as she joined him.

From the documents before him, she gleaned he'd been working. He bent to put them in his briefcase, and as he sat back up he ran his hands through his hair to sweep it away from his face. Seeing him out of the office, in the sunshine, in this enchanting restaurant, made Chloë view him differently. God, he *was* attractive! She was punched in the stomach by a whoosh of desire. Still, she reminded herself, he's married.

"How are you?" he asked.

"Oh, I'm well." As if she was going to admit she was all of a jitter! "And you?"

"I'm fine. Would you like a glass?" He pulled a bottle of white wine, dripping, from an ice bucket. It appeared invitingly cool, the perfect antidote to her nerves.

"That looks lovely." Chloë watched as he poured the pale golden liquid into her glass with a satisfying *glug*. She took a sip.

"Rather good, isn't it?"

"Yes," Chloë agreed, thinking that anything other than Liebfraumilch would have done at this precise moment.

"So," said James. "Busy day?"

"The usual." She was relieved to focus on work. "We've just gone to press so it's not too bad. Today has been fun—brainstorming ideas with my assistant. How was yours?"

"OK, actually. I had a meeting I was dreading at our printing house. I'd expected it to be a nasty confrontation, but in fact it went well. And," he paused, "I spoke to Vanessa Davenport, the special projects manager.'

"Yes?" said Chloë. She'd seen this thin-faced, imposing woman gliding around UK Magazines. Her reputation for making or breaking a project—and a career—was legendary.

"We had lunch yesterday, so I brought up your idea, and she'd like to meet you with a view to taking it further."

Chloë could barely restrain herself from clapping her hands.

"One thing she did insist on, though, was that you make up some kind of dummy."

Chloë reached for her bag. It was all so exciting! "This may sound presumptuous . . . but here's one I prepared earlier." She pulled out a mocked-up magazine and laid it on the table. "The reason I didn't do this before is most dummies tend to be made up of cuttings from other magazines and what I have in mind is so different I wanted you to consider the concept in theory before seeing something definite."

As James flipped through the dummy, Chloë sipped her wine. It rapidly imparted a warm glow.

Eventually he looked up, beaming. "This is great—not the usual approach at all! I think Vanessa would love it. You two should hook up as soon as possible."

Chloë's confidence grew. "You'll see"—she leaned over the table enthusiastically—"that because I believe no magazines here get it completely right that I've hardly used any examples from British women's monthlies. Instead I've taken cuttings from a range of publications—such as this US magazine, and run-outs from the Internet, club flyers, even book jackets and CD covers. What you've got here is more of an indication of layout—the kind of photography and typography I have in mind. I've provided a collection of article ideas separately." She handed him a second document.

James paused at a spread in the dummy. "I like this."

"It's from a U.S. website. Wicked cartoons, don't you think?"

"Yeah. Why is it British women's magazines are so humorless?"

"God knows!" said Chloë, relaxing. "If I want a laugh, I'd rather read some of the men's. Maybe people think women are right miseries."

"Well, not *all* people. *You* don't seem a misery to me. Though I do agree the magazine industry could be accused of such."

"Oh, I can be miserable, believe me," confessed Chloë, "though I reckon there's a time and a place for looking at serious issues—in fact I think that's extremely important. Still, to me life's not worth living if you can't have fun, at least *occasionally.*"

"Hmm . . ." James said, and looked at her. Their eyes locked for just a bit too long. His were the most amazing deep hazel. He glanced away. "It's strange," he muttered, then added, frankly: "You remind me of someone."

"Really?" Chloë was surprised. The conversation appeared to have taken a personal turn. "I thought I was unique."

"Well, I'm sure you are." James laughed, and looked at her again for a bit too long. God! Did he know what that did to a woman? Chloë's stomach lurched. "But you *do* remind me of someone."

He must be referring to his spouse, Chloë told herself firmly. "Don't tell me," she said. "I remind you of your wife."

"Who told you I was married?" James sounded disarmed. Clearly he wasn't aware she knew.

"Jean, I think. I gather she and your wife are friends."

"Ah, yes, Maggie and Jean go back a long way. Though no, you're nothing like Maggie."

Chloë didn't know how to take this, but curiosity got the better of her. "Who, then?"

"A girl I once knew."

"Oh." Chloë was fazed.

"Broke my heart, though I didn't admit it to her or anyone else at the time. But enough—you're not here to hear about my problems . . . Anyway, it was years ago. More wine?"

"Yes, please." What kind of problems? He seemed the picture of a man who had it all. But Chloë wasn't a journalist for nothing. She wanted the whole story. Especially because the longer she sat there, the more appealing she found him . . .

Still, the indirect approach was probably the way to get him to reveal more about himself, so she shifted the conversation in a different direction. She could lead him back to this later.

"Let's order," she prompted. "I'm starving."

Over the starter they talked further about the magazine. James explained that although he was happy to give it his blessing, she would have to get first Vanessa then the board to back her. And while Chloë knew she had a lot further to go, she couldn't help but feel a burst of pleasure, boosted by his support. By the time they'd finished the first course, she felt on a real high. She was flushed and needed a breather.

"Just going to powder my nose," she said. "Back in a minute."

As she got up, James's mobile rang. He fished it out of his briefcase and looked at the number calling. Over his shoulder Chloë glimpsed it too.

Maggie, it said.

6

Damn Jamie and his sports equipment! Why couldn't he ever tidy it up instead of throwing it in the hall cupboard after using it? It meant that Maggie, who was searching for her trainers, could never find anything.

Ah, there they were.

It was over a week since her shopping spree, and Maggie was pretty sure she wasn't pregnant. She had all the signs of a pending period, so she had decided to adopt an additional strategy to occupy her till she ovulated again: get fit. She'd considered joining a health club, but communal classes weren't her scene. No, she'd rather be able to decide when and where she would exercise. It was simply a question of disciplining herself. She pulled on the trainers and lifted first one foot then the other onto the towel rail of the stove to stretch her hamstrings. Leaning forward, she was glad to discover she was still quite flexible.

Outside on the gravel drive she jogged up and down, inhaling and exhaling to get used to the rhythm, and set off down the lane. She decided to follow her old route, thinking she would only manage one circuit.

Ah, the blue, blue sky, the fresh air pumping in and out of her lungs, the sound of her feet on the tarmac—*this* was why she loved running. She flew past neighboring cottages with their lovingly tended gardens—little surprise that Shere had won several "Best Kept Village" awards—pounded up and over the wooden footbridge by the ford, alongside the vegetable patches by the river, and as she raced on through the main street, past the antiques shop, museum, post office, and out on to the country roads, Maggie surprised herself.

Maybe I'm not *that* unfit, she thought, and it's so rejuvenating being among growing things! There's something about going to a gym that's so phony—all that rowing and running and stepping on equipment made specially, surrounded by MTV and metallic décor and people puffing and panting. Why would anyone want to use those silly machines, when they can have contact with the outdoors, the feeling of being part of the bigger scheme of things? Surely exercise should be enjoyed in its natural setting: on rivers, in lanes, up hills, come rain or shine.

Spurred on by this appreciation of her surroundings, Maggie ran up the hill, with fields of ripening corn on either side of her. Then through the woods and past the farm, with its comforting whiff of cow dung and hay. This was where she bought her free-range eggs direct from the farmer's wife every week.

I must get a commission for that piece I want to do on supermarkets' continued selling of factory-farmed products, she berated herself. Instead she was writing an uninspiring feature on Christmas cakes aimed at women who planned menus months ahead of the festive season. Yet Jamie's always on about how we need the money, she thought. If I have to compromise, it's partly his fault. Perhaps we should never have taken on such a big mortgage.

Energized by frustration, she headed back into Shere at an impressive speed. She had plenty of stamina, and before she knew it, she'd done two circuits. As she rounded the corner into the village for a second time, a car passed her, and the woman driving gave her a friendly toot of encouragement. Maggie waved appreciatively.

Panting, she ran up the drive, and slowed to a walk. Well, she concluded, pushing damp hair off her forehead, maybe it wouldn't take ages to get back to the level of fitness she'd previously enjoyed. Before Nathan was born, she'd even run the London Marathon once.

Later that afternoon Maggie had to go in to Guildford to pick up a book she'd ordered to help with the cake article.

"I think I saw you earlier," said the woman in Waterstones as she checked the computer screen.

"Oh?"

"Running, in Shere. I honked at you."

"Oh, yes. That was me."

"You were running very fast." Maggie was flattered. "Made me feel quite guilty—but I'm such a lazy cow, I drive everywhere."

Maggie smiled. The woman was about her own age, with an open face and messy chestnut hair. She exuded warmth and friendliness.

"Do you live in Shere?" asked the woman. "I've just moved there myself."

"I do," said Maggie, thinking perhaps at last there might be a kindred spirit in the village. "In the big white house, on the corner."

"That gorgeous Georgian one?"

Maggie was even more pleased. "You must come over."

"I'd love to. I don't know a soul nearby." She put out her hand. "My name's Georgie."

Maggie introduced herself, shaking Georgie's hand. "In fact, what are you doing on Saturday night?"

That evening, Thursday, was traditionally Jamie's squash night. Maggie was more than happy for him to meet up in town with his old friend Pete once a week.

Letting him vent his work frustrations on a tiny ball within the confines of a squash court saves me a lot of aggro, she thought.

Tonight she decided to use the opportunity to visit her sister in Leatherhead.

Maggie and Fran were close, but their relationship was marked by a healthy sibling rivalry. Maggie was older by a year, and in a pale-skinned English way they looked alike, although Maggie was prettier. Both had married successful men within a couple of years of each other; it was partly when Fran saw Maggie being the focus of everyone's attention at her wedding to Jamie that she'd decided Geoff was the man for her. Then Maggie had Nathan, and six months later Fran's son, Dan, was born.

Luckily Dan and Nathan got on well and as they thudded about in Dan's bedroom overhead, Maggie and Fran settled down for a chat in the kitchen.

"So." Fran stretched out her legs and propped her boot-shod feet on another chair. "How's your week been?"

"Okay," answered Maggie. Realizing this sounded rather downbeat, she went on more positively, "Actually, rather productive. I had a fun piece on aphrodisiac recipes to do for *Men*, and Jamie and I have been getting on a bit better."

"Good. I told you, he's just working too hard. Any sign of it letting up?"

"Oh, a leopard and his spots, you know. Though at least he's been slightly more communicative recently."

"Excellent!" Fran, who was a part-time teacher, sometimes sounded like she was giving Maggie's life grades. "So does this mean you've been having more sex?"

Maggie smiled at the memory of their kitchen exploits. "Yes, as a matter of fact, we have." She always felt slightly embarrassed talking about sex with her sister, who seemed to show no such reserve. Fran appeared to relish telling Maggie how well she and Geoff got on "in the sack." It made Maggie feel inadequate.

"Mum." Nathan came in and interrupted. "I want to watch *Ben 10* and Dan won't let me."

"Oh, darling, I don't know if we've got time," said Maggie.

Fran checked the clock. "It's only half past six. Dan! Come here!"

Dan came into the kitchen, sheepishly.

"How often do I have to tell you that when someone comes to our house you must be nice to them because they're the guest?"

"Nathan's not always nice to me when I go to his house," Dan retorted. "Last time he said I had to watch what he wanted because it was his DVD."

"Oh, for goodness' sake, boys!" said Fran. "I don't care what Nathan does in his house, but when he's here you play by my rules, and I say you've got to be nice to your guest. Now, scoot!"

The boys left the room, Dan stomping, Nathan grinning.

"Ooh," exclaimed Maggie, "I forgot. I brought some food. It's in the car. I thought we could have it for supper. I'll go and get it."

She returned with a big saucepan clutched to her breast and a couple of packs of fresh pasta balanced precariously on top. "It's tagliatelli al amore," she explained, putting down the pan.

Fran lifted the lid. "Mm, smells delicious!"

"Seafood sauce with oysters. Designed to woo a woman virtually all on its own."

"So this is one of your aphrodisiac recipes?"

"Indeed, it is—the second batch, to test I've got it right."

"I'll put some on aside for Geoff. Can't have him slacking!"

"Of course not," said Maggie, as an unwelcome image of Geoff and Fran popped into her head. She wondered if they had sex every night. It sounded like it, but surely not. "Anyway, these things are best eaten fresh. Shall we heat it up now?"

"Let's have a glass of wine first," said Fran. "The boys can have their fish fingers in front of the television."

A couple of hours later they were still in the kitchen. Fran picked up the bottle. "One more?"

"Better not—I'm driving."

At that moment Nathan and Dan burst in.

"Mum . . ." said Nathan, kissing her.

Given Nathan rarely kissed her these days, Maggie knew he was after something. "What?"

"Can I stay the night?"

"I thought you two were at each other's throats."

"Oh, no," said Dan sweetly. "Nathan wants to share a bath so we can have a go with my special intergalactic bubble wash."

"We ought to get back for Daddy."

"He'll be all right," encouraged Fran. "Why don't you both stay over?"

"Go on, Mum, *please*," whined Nathan.

"Go on, Auntie Maggie."

"You could have some more wine then."

Maggie looked at the bottle. It was rare these days that she ever had more than a couple of glasses, and she and Fran were having a satisfying rant about Tory sleaze. "Oh, okay," she conceded. "Though no mucking around in the morning, Nathan. We'll have to hurry to get you to school in time."

"You're a lovely mummy," said Nathan, and thundered upstairs again.

"Start running the bath!" yelled Fran after them.

"Obviously the oyster feel-good factor." Maggie reached for her bag and rummaged for her mobile. "I'd better tell Jamie we won't be home." She dialed his number. "Hi, it's me—I'm still at Fran's." She could hear the sound of people laughing and chatting in the background. "Where are you?"

7

By the time they'd finished their main course, Chloë was feeling mellow, woozy, and well fed. Not being one to hold back, particularly after several glasses, she had given James the lowdown on her life. She'd started with her career and progressed to where she lived and her relationship with Rob, explaining they'd been roommates for years.

"Sometimes I think I'm closer to him than some of my straight friends are to their partners, but maybe that's because there's nothing sexual between us," she said. She wound up with her current single status, though she was careful to make it sound very short-term.

It grew dark and the waitress came out and lit small candles on the tables. James shifted his chair nearer, and as the atmosphere became more intimate, Chloë led him to reveal he'd grown up in Sussex, that he had a sister, and had been to the university in Bristol. Silently congratulating herself on her discoveries, she brought him back to the subject that had intrigued her earlier.

"So." She reached to pour them each a final glass. "Tell me about this ex. Why do I remind you of her?"

"I'm not sure." He frowned.

Chloë waited.

"You do look a bit similar."

Chloë blushed. "Really? What was she like?"

"Oh, you know, smallish, about so high . . ." He gesticulated. "Curvy, sort of voluptuous."

"You mean she was fat?"

"No, not at all. Just very, um, hourglass. What I think of as a real woman." He twisted his glass. "Not conventionally pretty, but kind of sexy. At least, I thought so. And dark—like you. Though what really reminds me of Beth is your energy, your vibrancy. You're a bit like her—sort of feline . . . and you have a similar spark." He looked directly into her eyes. "It's quite something."

Chloë was speechless. Help, she thought, fascinated, flattered, and frightened all at once. Clearly Rob *has* hit the nail on the head. She needed a few minutes to ground herself—she hadn't expected him to reveal so much, so fast. She switched to the other subject she wanted to find out about.

"So what's your wife like, then?" Perhaps he'd gush about her. If he was clearly unobtainable, she could prevent herself rushing in headlong.

"Maggie? She's, um, very different."

"What, physically?"

"Yes. She's quite tall. Blond. Leggy. Sort of naturally athletic."

"Sounds lovely," said Chloë, genuinely. It was the way she'd always hankered to be.

"And she's more reserved, I suppose. Not introverted exactly . . . just contained. Sometimes I'm not sure what's going on with her."

"Oh." Chloë was confused, but curiosity had her on the edge of her seat. "What made you go for two such different women? Beth, I mean, and her?"

"In all honesty I don't know. I guess I may have been a bit on the rebound from Beth when we met, though I certainly didn't realize it at the time. I'd finished with Beth, after all."

"Why?"

James hesitated. "I guess I got scared. Found her too much in some ways. Then, when I met Maggie, she seemed less of a handful, less up-front, more manageable. Oh, she had her passionate beliefs—animal welfare, her vegetarianism, and so on—and I loved that. Still, emotionally she was a lot less demanding—more English, if you know what I mean. We started seeing each other and one thing led to another, and here I am." He stopped again. "Actually, that's not quite true. One thing did lead to another, but not in the way I'd planned. Maggie got pregnant, you see."

"Oh? Before you got married?"

"Well, not exactly. We got married when we found out she was pregnant."

"But wouldn't you have gotten married anyway?" Chloë was agog.

"I'm not sure," admitted James. "It's not as if I didn't love her—I did. I still do. We'd been living together for a couple of years, all her friends and her sister were settling down, and then, wham! She gets pregnant."

"So how old were you both, if you don't mind me asking?"

"I was thirty-one, she was thirty-two. It was nearly seven years ago."

"I see."

"What?"

Chloë stopped herself—to say what she really thought wasn't appropriate, either personally or professionally.

"Go on," urged James. "I'm interested."

Oh, to hell with it. "It's just it never ceases to amaze me," Chloë burst out, "how many women seem to get *accidentally* pregnant in their thirties. Until that point they can find their way to a packet of condoms or the pill with their eyes shut, then, 'Abracadabra!' They forget completely about them."

"That's rather unsympathetic of you." James seemed taken aback.

Chloë flushed, guilty she'd been so outspoken. "Hmm . . . Actually I do understand. I've been feeling a bit like that myself. There we all go, trundle, trundle, through our twenties, having one relationship after another, focusing on work, no huge pressure to settle down . . . then oops! Before we know it, time is running out. But only for us women; men are happy to carry on for as long as they feel like it. Enjoying relationships, yes, yet unwilling to commit to anything more. So is it any surprise some women resort to that time-honored tactic—the 'accidental' pregnancy?" She indicated quote marks in the air. "They may not acknowledge it even to themselves, nonetheless their motives are sometimes more complex than they seem."

James shifted in his chair. Oh dear, I've overstepped the mark, thought Chloë. He appears uncomfortable. Then he said, "You have a point. I suppose I've wondered . . . Though Maggie had very strong principles about certain things, and when we found out, she said there was no way she wasn't having it."

"Anyway," said Chloë brightly, conscious she'd best backpedal some more. "I'm sure you're glad it happened now, aren't you?"

"Ye-es . . . I mean, I don't regret having Nathan, not at all. I love him to death. And Maggie's a fantastic mum. It's just . . . sometimes I think about it."

"Think about what?"

"What might have happened if Beth and I hadn't split up."

"You'll probably never know." Chloë felt sympathy for this woman apparently so like her. "You can't turn back time. Where is she now?"

"She returned to New York years ago. She's married with two children."

At that moment the waitress stopped at their table. "Dessert?"

"I'd like a coffee," Chloë stated, without waiting for James to contemplate whether he wanted any pudding. I'd better sober up, pronto, she thought. She was quite tipsy. Or was it all the emotional honesty and sexual tension in the air?

"Me too," said James, and the waitress left.

"You'd better be getting back soon. What time's your last train?" Her conscience was niggling. She shouldn't have brought all this up.

James looked at his watch. "Oh, I've ages yet."

"Won't Maggie be expecting you?"

"No. She called to say she's staying at her sister's tonight with Nathan." Chloë's heart missed a beat. Lord, she *was* in deep.

––––––––

Two coffees each later, they tumbled out onto the pavement. The August night was still warm, and Soho was buzzing. The theaters were emptying, and the excited exchanges of tourists mingled with the more cynical critiques of locals. The lights of Piccadilly, the smell of the city, the energy of the crowds—it was intoxicating.

"What now?" asked James and, to Chloë's horror and delight, he grabbed her hand.

Chloë tried to be firm. "I think this is when I should go home."

"So should I." James's expression said the opposite. "But I haven't been out late for ages. Shall I tell you what I'd really like to do?"

"What?" She was afraid she knew the answer.

"Go to a bar."

Chloë, who was already drunk though by no means out of control, realized she should accept the compliment of James's obvious attraction to her and run.

But he's so sexy, her alter ego argued. Surely one more drink won't hurt?

She sensed his hand in hers—it was as if an electric current was shooting up her arm. It fuzzed her brain and sent rationality running for the hills.

"Okay."

James led the way to a late-night club on Broadwick Street that barely advertised its existence outside. Down a flight of stairs and in a cellar, the atmosphere was sultry; dim red lighting made everyone appear their most beautiful, and seduction hung in the air. Clearly it was designed for an elite who knew precisely where to go when the night was yet full of possibilities.

"What'll it be?" he asked, leaning against the counter. Chloë squeezed in next to him, acutely aware of his presence by her side.

"A margarita." Nothing beat tequila when she was in a reckless mood. "No salt."

"I'll join you," said James and, with the assurance of a man who could get the attention of anyone he chose, signaled to the girl behind the bar. "Make them large ones, in a tall glass."

"Cheers," he said, when the drinks arrived.

"Cheers." Chloë clinked his glass and looked him in the eye. For a second she thought he was going to kiss her right then.

" 'Scuse me." A drunken young man in a suit pushed her out of the way in his keenness to get served, nearly knocking her drink flying.

"Shall we go and sit down?" asked James, and they headed for a table surrounded by low sofas.

Chloë took a seat. She noted that although he could easily have sat on his own sofa, James sat next to her. Again, she was conscious of his physicality, the crisp white of his shirt, the crumpled linen of his trousers, the polished leather of his shoes. By contrast her own outfit seemed frivolous and girlie, but she liked that.

I wonder how he looks in out-of-work clothes, she thought. Suits make it hard to place a man. Although somehow she knew that whatever his taste, she was bound to approve.

James picked up on her thoughts. "Great shoes."

"Thanks." Chloë held her feet up so they could both admire her sandals' offbeat shape. As she swung her legs down, she maneuvered slightly closer to him. "Is that all that's great?"

"I think you know the answer to that." James began to stroke her arm, with tiny movements of his fingers at first and then, as Chloë didn't rebuff him, with more assured motions of his whole hand.

He edged closer to her. And, almost before she knew it, they were kissing. Softly at first, then more intensely, and finally with full, caution-to-the-wind passion. The couple sitting opposite, the people at the next table, the woman whose elbow Chloë accidentally bumped off the back of the sofa behind her, none of it mattered. It was sensual, magical, heavenly. Wives, work, principles, conscience, even tomorrow—none of it had any relevance. There were only the two of them, here, now.

And now she *did* want to go home—though not alone. She pulled away from him, just enough to speak. "Mmm," she murmured, in a way that unashamedly expressed her appreciation.

She reached forward for her cocktail, and as she did so, he ran his hand up her back, then inside her top. Fuck! When was she going to outgrow this sort of behavior? He smelled gorgeous—*irresistible*—and she kissed him again. Desire overwhelmed her. "We could leave," she said moments later.

"We could." James took a large gulp of his margarita. "C'mon." He pulled her to her feet. "Let's go."

Chloë drained her drink and, as they left, slung the glass on the bar. Her apartment was on his way home, and things got even more heated in the taxi. Inevitably, he invited himself in "for coffee"—the very thing she wanted too. Fumbling, she dropped her keys in the porch, and as she bent to pick them up, level with his crotch, she thought she could see his hard-on.

Inside the apartment, he pushed her up against the wall in the hall and kissed her again, more intensely still, urgently.

"Shh! We'll wake Rob," she whispered, taking his hand and leading him into her bedroom.

Immediately they fell onto the bed and within seconds he'd removed her top, her skirt, her shoes. She undid his belt, his trousers—yes, he did have a hard-on—and they kissed all the while. They shouldn't be doing this—but hell! She'd left resistance somewhere in Soho.

He slid his hand into her knickers—wow—he certainly knew where everything was—and then, because what he was doing was *so* good, *so* delicious, she let him peel off her underwear and kiss her there too. He seemed content to do it for ages—bliss—knowing when to be gentle, when not to be . . . and not to stop too soon, but to carry on . . . and on . . . She was going to come any minute—any second—now, NOW! (Oops! The noise—Rob!) Then she wanted it all, inside, and there was no point in stopping and, anyway, she didn't want to.

At four in the morning she woke, after about an hour's sleep, parched. James was asleep beside her, his arm flung over her shoulder. Gently she lifted it off and slid out of bed, hoping she hadn't disturbed him. When she returned, he was awake and half sitting up. The room stank of sex. Lord, she could scarcely walk!

"You are one of the horniest, sexiest, most gorgeous women I have ever met," he said, grabbing her and pulling her back into bed.

"Thank you." At that moment Chloë felt all of those things, head to toe. "You're okay, too." And to show she meant it, she slid slowly under the covers and licked down his chest—that oh-so-male broadness—down his belly. Down. Down.

Later, much later, she called another taxi so he could go home and change. And, later still, she bade him farewell on the doorstep, hastily slung-on silk petticoat exposed to the early morning light of Battersea Rise.

8

It hurt. Really hurt. With every pulse, the back of her head throbbed. She could feel the blood pumping around. White wine, red wine, tequila. Ouch. It was seven forty-five in the morning. Friday . . . Fuck.

Even Radio Four seemed loud.

Ibuprofen.

If Chloë took painkillers on top of that lot, it would be a drug too far. She had one rule about drugs: wait for the last ones to wear off before taking more. Except tea. That didn't count.

She tiptoed into the kitchen. Such a mess! She was glad James hadn't seen it. As she stood waiting for the kettle to boil, she cast her mind back to the night before. What had she done? What *hadn't* she done? She'd had sex. Sex with a married man. Not just had sex with a married man, but one who, while he wasn't her boss, could play a vital role in getting her ambitions off the ground.

Lots of people have to approve my magazine concept aside from him, she tried to reason. And I didn't sleep with him because of that.

Yet she could hear a voice—partly her mother's, partly her own: *"Now you're one of those women."* What women? *"One of those women who sleeps with men to get what she wants."*

Chloë poured the water into the mug. God, she felt awful. She opened the fridge, sniffed the milk—still OK—poured it into the tea, and returned to her room trying desperately to get her act together.

It had been great sex, though.

Even through her hangover, she felt a warm, sensual rush as she recalled it. Her fingers still smelled of him, them.

Fuck!

Why was it so . . . so *good* with some people? It wasn't that it wasn't good with others—Chloë tended to enjoy sex with most of the men she slept with, especially now that she was older and more confident about saying what she liked—but there were a few with whom it was . . . well . . . better. More . . . fun? Yes. Passionate? Yes. Daring? Yes, that too. Or was it that she'd believed he was safe—because he was married—she was less guarded, more at ease? She remembered his touch. Stroking her right from her feet, slowly up her thighs, over her hips, in at the waist, up to her breasts, circling there, teasing—oops, she was getting turned on all over again— stroking her neck, then her hair . . . his mouth, kissing . . .

That was why I did it, she recalled. The kissing was the point of no return. Then there was the tequila, of course. And before that, the things he'd said about Beth, his ex. He seemed to really like me, fancy me. And, damn it, I really liked him . . . It was a lovely—no, *unforgettable* night. We got on so well—he was so open and easy to talk to. So interesting, so interested in me, so charming, so sexy . . .

Better have a shower. Go to work. I *have* to go to work, she told herself. Shit! Will I see him? Will everyone be able to tell?

Round and round, the thoughts went. Bong, bong, went her head. It was a weird combination—the bus to work (normal), the hangover (not unheard-of), the lack of sleep on a weekday (unusual but something she had done before), the *I-went-out-for-dinner-with-the-publisher-of-UK-Magazines- who's-married-with-a-child-to-discuss-my-idea-which-he-likes-and-we-slept-together-*

and-it-was-great (a totally new scenario). It was all so recent, so complicated, so awful, so fantastic. It was beyond her comprehension.

"Bloody hell!" said Patsy, as Chloë plonked her bag on her desk. "What happened to you?"

"Nothing."

"You look like shit."

"Thanks."

"Bacon sarnie?"

Chloë thought for a moment. "Good idea." She fumbled for her purse.

"It's on me," said Patsy, and she bounced out of the office appearing sickeningly healthy. A little later she returned with a white paper bag, grease seeping through already.

"You're a doll," said Chloë, peering into the bag. It looked foul. Would it help? She took a bite. Delicious. Brown sauce squidged onto the article she was trying to read.

"So," chivvied Patsy. "Tell all."

Ten minutes had given Chloë time to fabricate a tale. "Rob. His birthday. You know. His crowd—they love to party. We hit Soho."

"You're such a fag hag!" laughed Patsy. "And I thought you'd had sex."

"Ha!" feigned Chloë. "Not bloody likely. Well . . ." She rummaged in her in-tray for authenticity. "What's on today?"

She got through the day with the help of several cans of Red Bull and Patsy, who fended off callers with a heroism that would have made Robert the Bruce proud. At lunchtime they resorted to their favorite hangover cure—heading to the Top Shop superstore on Oxford Street, and Chloë, who didn't really have the energy to remove her clothes again, waited patiently outside the changing room while Patsy tried on endless outfits.

There was one call that afternoon, however, Chloë did take—it came through internally on her direct line so she didn't have much choice.

"Chloë?" It was a woman's voice that Chloë didn't immediately recognize.

"Yes?"

"It's Vanessa Davenport here. Is now a good time?"

"Er, um, ish." Chloë glanced over at Patsy, who was busy typing but whose gossip radar was legendary.

"I've just had a word with James Slater."

Chloë's heart lurched.

"He showed me your proposal and says you've made up a dummy. I thought we ought to meet for a chat."

"That would be great."

"Obviously James can recommend ideas," Vanessa explained, "though it's me you'd be working with, should we decide to take on the project." Chloë understood the subtext: *You might be in with James, but you'll have to win me over too.* It was Vanessa's job to handle the day-to-day business of launching new titles. "How about lunch next week, say, Tuesday?"

"Lovely."

"I'll call you that morning and we'll arrange somewhere then."

When Vanessa had hung up, Chloë couldn't help but wonder what James had said about her. Presumably it was good or Vanessa wouldn't have phoned. And she must have been on his mind for him to contact Vanessa in the first place.

Is he as hungover as I am? she wondered. Will he ever call me again? I doubt it—surely he'll only be able to get away like that for one night. So I presume our relationship will be purely business from now on. Will having had sex affect his professional dealings with me? I hope not . . . Will he tell his wife? Chloë felt a pang of remorse at the prospect. Of course he won't, she told herself. Though she might find out anyway. Some women just *know.* Horrors—what if she comes by and confronts me? Worse, if she confronts me at the office, in front of Patsy, Vanessa, Jean, and everyone! Imagine if James is so bowled over he decides to leave Maggie at once—and turns up on my doorstep later tonight with a suitcase and hangdog expression . . .

Chloë's mind was in overdrive. She wanted to call him, but what would she say? And with Patsy tip-tapping away right by her—not to mention all the other complications—she knew that it would be foolish in the extreme. For once she must curb her inclinations to talk about anything, although she was itching to confide in someone. It would have to wait until she got home. There she knew she could offload it all on Rob. So, once she'd clarified that he was going to be in, she put her whirling thoughts on hold and busied herself sorting through her pending tray.

Back at the apartment, Rob and Chloë curled up on the sofa with the cat snuggled in a half-moon in his favorite spot between them, and waited for the delivery of a fifteen-inch extra crunchy supreme pizza.

"Well," said Rob, "was that you I heard crashing around the hall in the small hours? Either you were so pissed you were making enough noise for two or you had a man with you. Please tell me it was the former."

Chloë jerked her head toward the TV. "I think we'd better record this program."

"Oh, my God! That means trouble! You did, didn't you? You brought him back here! Oh, Lord! You actually slept with him?"

"Yes," admitted Chloë.

"So . . ." Rob leaned forward. "Was it good?"

It was one thing she loved about Rob—he was very nonjudgmental. Perhaps it was because his own behavior was pretty reprehensible at times that his moral code was so flexible.

"The best," sighed Chloë.

"OOOH!" shrieked Rob. "This warrants a glass of wine." He virtually skipped into the kitchen. Sex, scandalous sex, forbidden sex—he was in his element. "Want one?"

"I couldn't." Chloë shook her head. "But you go ahead."

Once Rob had settled back down with his glass and Chloë had set the recorder, she began. "So we met at this little restaurant on Lexington Street—"

"Stop, stop!" Rob held up his hand. "I want to know what you were wearing!"

"Ah, yes," said Chloë, conscious it hadn't been the Whistles suit. "That, um, crisscross turquoise top, black lace skirt, and my Miu Miu sandals?"

"The crisscross top that makes your boobs appear the best in Christendom?"

"The very same."

"Shit. You're *irresistible* in that. Almost enough to turn me straight. Jesus, woman, you are so naughty! I warned you, dress like you mean business!"

"Anyway," Chloë ignored this, "I arrive at this restaurant—Louisa's, do you know it?"

"Indeed I do. Great menu and fab décor. Hangout of the discreet media in-crowd. Good choice—his?"

Chloë was proud to be mixing with someone who knew such prestigious venues. "Yes."

"And what was he wearing?"

"A suit."

"I want more! Be precise girl."

"Okay, okay. A navy linen suit—I didn't see the label, but it looked expensive—only he wasn't wearing the jacket, he'd taken that off when I arrived—and a white cotton shirt. He had his sleeves rolled up."

"Could you see his forearms?" gasped Rob.

"They're to die for."

"Oh, stop! I'm horny already."

"So he pulls this bottle of wine from the bucket, dripping—"

"How erotic!"

"—and offers me a glass."

"Which you guzzle 'cause you're nervous and you always knock back the first drink rather quickly."

"Exactly! And then we discuss the magazine."

"Oh." Rob looked deflated. "Cut that out. We'll come back to that. I want the sex, now!"

"Okay." Having been restraining herself all day, Chloë was glad to cut to the chase. "So then, he starts to look at me strangely, you know, a bit too long, and begins confessing about this ex-girlfriend of his in New York, Beth, her name was, and says how I remind him of her, how I've got the same spark, and that he, well she broke his heart, though he left her and . . . to be honest, Rob, it sounded like he was still in love with her and not really in love with his wife at all!"

"No!"

"Well, that's what he said . . . Though I suppose he could have just been saying that."

"Mm," Rob mused, a cynical tone creeping into his voice. "It's amazing what some men come up with to get their end away. But we'll analyze later. I want gore! So tell me—did he have a big willy?"

"Of course."

"Thick?"

"Very." Chloë grinned.

"I am so jealous!"

"Don't you want to know what he did with it?"

"Oooh, no, all that heterosexual stuff. Makes me feel a bit squeamish. I suppose you could tell me about giving head though. I can cope with that. So, did you?"

"I did."

"Before, or after, he did it to you?"

"How do you know he did it to me?"

" 'Cause you'll never let a man get away without doing it, you love it so much."

"True, though I hardly had to ask. Anyway, I like to make sure a man has earned it."

"How many shags?"

"Two," said Chloë. "But they lasted for hours. Or, at least, a long time. The first was all, you know, heated, the second more slow and sensual."

"Did he take you from behind?"

"Rob!"

"Well, did he?"

"Yes, actually, he did—at some point during the first time. But the second time he didn't—we just, well, looked into each other's eyes."

"Boring soppy stuff," said Rob. "I suppose you came together too!" Chloë's expression obviously said they had. Rob stopped and looked at her seriously. "Oh dear."

"What?"

"You're not hoping this is more than a one-night stand, are you?"

"Of course not!" Chloë lied.

"Good." Rob slumped, relieved. "Because what with his being married, your publisher, and all, it would be a disaster to take this any further."

Chloë knew that was true. But when she recalled the sensation of him deep inside her, she couldn't bear for it never to happen again.

9

"Who did you say was coming tonight?" asked Jamie. He was sorting their silver cutlery, a wedding present from Maggie's parents, which they used on special occasions.

"I've told you." Maggie was concentrating on the chocolate mousse—it was not a good moment to interrupt a perfectionist.

"Tell me again."

Why couldn't he listen the first time? "Jean and Simon, William and Liz, Alex and Georgie."

"Alex your ex-boyfriend?" asked Jamie. "I thought his wife was called Stella."

"She is. Or rather was. They're divorcing."

"Really? Why?"

"Don't know the full story." The mixture was ready. Skilfully Maggie poured it into eight glass bowls. "Perhaps we'll find out more later. Never liked her much, anyway. Thought she wasn't right for him—too out for herself."

"You were always so nice to her."

"I know. I didn't want her to be threatened by me."

"Was she? She didn't seem the insecure type."

"I don't know. Alex said she was."

"Oh?" Jamie sounded miffed—the response Maggie had hoped to provoke. He'd been rather preoccupied the last couple of days, and had shown little interest in the dinner party she was looking forward to enormously. "He's still got a bit of a thing for you, hasn't he?"

Maggie felt guilty for winding him up. "Not really. Anyway, I met this very nice woman the other day. She's just moved in around the corner so I thought I'd ask her to even up the numbers. You never know, they might take to each other."

"And she's called Georgie. So, why's she moved here? Not much of a place for a single woman."

"Maybe she likes the country." Maggie resented the implication the area was only suited to the dull and married. "I gather her job has just been transferred to Guildford. She runs Waterstones there."

"Hmph. A bookworm. Sounds right up Alex's alley."

Maggie carefully placed the bowls in the fridge. "Why are you so foul about him?" Yet she knew very well. Alex had been the major relationship of her student years and they'd long had a soft spot for each other. Then, years later, only weeks before her wedding, Alex, who had no idea she was pregnant, had asked Maggie to get back together with him. She'd never told Jamie, but he seemed to have picked up that Alex had carried a torch for her until the last minute.

"Actually," she said pointedly, "Georgie seems good fun." She checked her watch. "They'll be here in half an hour. Have you finished?" Jamie grunted. "Then you'd best put Nathan to bed while I get changed."

Fifteen minutes later she was showered and sitting wrapped in a towel at the dressing table, feeling better now everything was under control.

"There." Jamie patted his face dry as he emerged from the shower. As

Maggie put the final touches to her makeup, she watched his reflection as he got ready.

The ritual was virtually the same as it was each morning. First, he dried himself thoroughly—the bathroom was too steamy, he maintained. Then he dropped the towel on the floor.

"Please hang it up, darling."

He did as he was told, and rummaged in a drawer for a clean pair of underpants. As he pulled on the fitted boxers she smiled: they're the black ones I gave him for Christmas, she noted. Next he selected an almost new pair of trousers, and a shirt. He pulled on the trousers, zipped the fly, and with a *swoosh!* removed the belt from his work suit, and threaded it through the loops. He's doing it up on the final hole, she thought. Is he getting tubby? No, even though he had put on a couple of pounds in the last year or two—no doubt thanks to her cooking and an increasing number of business lunches—he was broad shouldered enough to retain the pleasing *V* shape that made his outline so different from hers. Yes, she concluded, he's still a very attractive man.

"Inside or out?" he asked about the shirt, tucking and untucking it.

She realized with a jolt he was dressed and ready before she was. "Out."

He headed downstairs, while she selected her clothes.

The navy shift dress, she decided. And the new basque.

The doorbell rang—it was Jean and Simon, as usual meeting a deadline with time to spare. Jean looked chic in black chiffon; Simon—bless him—had made the effort and put on a suit. Fifteen minutes later William and Liz arrived, equally smart, then Georgie—I like her dress, thought Maggie—and, finally, Alex. Typically, he was half an hour late, and hadn't dressed up at all. Yet he grinned at Maggie winningly, said "you look ravishing" and handed over not just wine but her favorite dark Belgian chocolates, so she decided to let him off.

With the guests gathered, drinks in hand, and introductions over, Maggie began to relax. She turned to Jean. "How's work?"

"Exhausting!"

Maggie smiled to herself. She knew that Jean really loved being editorial queen; long sufferance was just a role she played.

"You know how it is. And I must say, though I have a good team, at times I *despair* of some of my junior copy editors. Call me old-fashioned, but it does seem education isn't what it used to be. I'm constantly picking out grammatical errors at the eleventh hour! And the spelling! I was thinking on the drive down here, *please* make sure Nathan goes to a decent secondary school, won't you? Only last week I picked up a classic error in an article about agoraphobia. We'd split 'therapist' over two lines into 'the' and 'rapist'—changed the meaning completely. Had to get my features editor to go through it with a fine-tooth comb. Actually—" she turned to Jamie "—didn't you come in and see her the other day? What was that about?"

"Eh?" Jamie, who'd been gazing absentmindedly out of the window, was forced to jump to attention.

"Chloë Appleton. Didn't you come in to see her last week?"

"Oh, er, yes. I thought it'd be a good idea to introduce myself to the senior members of staff at UK Magazines. I'm eventually hoping to get around everyone. Information gathering, you know."

"Well, how *thorough!*" said Jean. "Sounds a bit over-keen to me. Rather like when you've got a new car. For the first few weeks you're out there cleaning and polishing every Sunday but sooner or later you're back to your old ways. I'm sure that once you've talked to a couple, you'll feel you've talked to them all."

"Maybe. Though so far I've found it most enlightening. Well," Jamie turned to Georgie, "all this magazine chat must be rather dull for you. How's life in the fast lane at Waterstones?"

Maggie winced; she could recognize Jamie's sarcasm. She hoped it would pass Georgie by.

"You'd be surprised." Georgie grinned. "It's one earth-shattering crisis after another. 'Are the stocks on *Roget's* running low?' 'Have we got that order in for Mrs. Bradshaw yet? She's called twice already today.' 'Is it worth persuading that local author to do an evening signing, or will the sales not warrant paying staff to stay late?' "

Maggie warmed to Georgie even more. She liked a woman who didn't take herself that seriously. She glanced at Alex. From the way he was leaning forward, it seemed he might like her too.

"How did you get into the book world?" asked Jamie.

"Oh, it wasn't some major career plan. It was just the first job I got after college."

"Know the feeling. But you must be pretty good at it. Maggie said you're in charge of the one in Guildford. It's one of their biggest branches, isn't it?" Clearly he was prepared to be more charming now Georgie had revealed she could hold her own.

"It is. I like working out which books might sell and helping give them a push. But what I most enjoy is the people; managing my staff and meeting customers."

Maggie could see she'd be good at that.

"Well, you're obviously getting something right," continued Jamie. "I gather Waterstones is doing better these days. I must admit, I'd hate to lose the chain—I've always liked it."

"I'm glad you think so." Georgie relaxed visibly at his compliment.

Maggie listened while Jamie drew Georgie out, helping put her at ease among strangers. He can be such good company when he wants to be, she thought proudly. It was one of the things that had first attracted her to him.

"Anyway, everyone," interrupted William, "we've got an announcement to make."

"Ooh, goodie!" Jean clapped her hands. "I love announcements."

"We're having another baby!" Liz beamed.

Maggie felt a jolt of both pleasure and envy. "Congratulations! When's it due?"

"I'm four months." Liz smoothed down her flowing top to reveal a small bump. "So, just before Christmas."

"How *wonderful*," said Jean. She was always far too much in demand to spare time for a child so had never wanted her own. Still, at least she was honest about it, she was invariably happy for others, and Simon didn't seem to mind.

"Well," said Liz, turning to Jamie and Maggie, "when are you two going to have another?"

"Actually we're trying now," said Maggie. Such an intimate revelation was unusual for her, but these were her dearest friends.

"Oh, how exciting," said Liz.

"That's half the fun, isn't it, darling?" William kissed his wife.

"So, Jamie, looking forward to being a father again?"

"Um," said Jamie. "All those late nights. Can't wait."

"But it'll be worth it," Liz prompted.

"I suppose so."

Maggie glanced at her husband. Was he sounding detached; not as happy at the prospect as she was? She took a sip of wine and galvanized herself. Somehow, being surrounded by her friends gave her the courage to say what she might otherwise have avoided. "I think I'm keener on the idea than Jamie," she said, hoping he would contradict her. When he didn't, an awkward silence filled the room. It seemed endless. Maggie was too upset to speak.

Eventually Simon came to her rescue. "Oh, Jamie, I'm sure you'll come around when it's born."

"Remember how much pleasure Nathan gave you when he was tiny," said Jean. "I've never seen a father more in love."

"True," admitted Jamie. "I guess I'm a bit fraught at having to deal with it all and a new job. I worry about the money, too. This place cost us an arm and a leg as it is."

"Oh, goodness!" cried Jean. "Look at you both! Huge house in the country, both of you working—surely you can afford it. Women in council flats have dozens of children on a tenth of your income."

"And they're pretty miserable," said Jamie.

"I'd better get on with the dinner." Maggie got up, thankful to leave the room.

"Can I lend a hand?" asked Alex.

"Yes."

In the kitchen Alex held out the tureen while Maggie sloshed in the soup.

"Don't worry," he said. He knew her so well she didn't have to explain how bruised she was feeling. "You always said Jamie's lousy at stress. He'll be all right once he's settled into his new job."

"Yes, of course he will," Maggie replied quietly, trying to convince herself. But laying bare her soul was not her way. She changed the subject. "Anyway, what do you think of Georgie?"

10

As Maggie drifted in and out of sleep that night, a faint sadness tinged her dreams. And when she woke fully, the feeling grew heavier, so that a movement to brush away silent tears was her first conscious action of the day. It took a few seconds for her to remember why.

Jamie.

The dinner party had been a great success. She was proud of how the food had turned out, and her guests seemed to get on very well. Jean had drunk too much—nothing new there. The relief of not having to be a dynamic editor on a Saturday night meant she had knocked back a couple of glasses too many and had released her tension in a series of outbursts on unrelated subjects, most of which she knew little about, although she had a strong opinion on them all. Finally she'd fallen asleep on the sofa, court shoes off, normally neat bob splayed on the cushions, snoring while everyone else continued chatting around her.

William had diplomatically dropped the subject of Liz's pregnancy, using her instead as a foil for amusing tales of their university days with Maggie and Alex.

"Remember that row about M&S food?" he'd reminded Maggie. "How I sent you the container and highlighted the ingredients to prove their meals weren't full of additives?"

"I do. But I seem to recall what really got me riled was the way you were prepared to spend half your grant on preprepared food—"

"—when half the world was starving," William had finished for her. "You were quite the activist in those days."

The real hit, however, had been Alex and Georgie, who had bonded noticeably over a mutual loathing of Martin Amis's writing, and finally Alex had offered to give Georgie a lift home.

Maggie knew it was churlish, yet she couldn't help feeling upset when she recalled their chemistry. She'd done a marvelous job of disguising her own feelings and acted the charming host all evening, but underneath she was smarting from Jamie's remarks. Watching her old boyfriend flirt with another woman had only made her feel worse.

Not that Alex hadn't been nice to her—he'd taken several opportunities to check she was okay, jumping up from the table before anyone else had the chance to carry out the dirty dishes to grab a moment alone with her in the kitchen. But Maggie was too keen to ensure everyone had a good time to be drawn into discussion, so had deflected his inquiries with a repeated "I'm fine." Instead she'd numbed the hurt with a couple of extra brandies, which doubtless now had deepened her post-party blues.

Seeking solace from the person who had caused her pain, she reached over to touch Jamie's hair.

It's beginning to curl around the nape of his neck, she noticed, and could do with a trim.

He was still asleep, tucked under the crisp white cotton sheets, his back to her, a familiar pose. They both found sleeping too close stifling and claustrophobic; he'd always said it made him hot.

Last night she'd believed that making love might make her feel better, but taking the initiative was not something Maggie felt confident in doing. So she'd said nothing, and now the new basque lay neatly draped over the dressing-table chair—a sad contrast to the way it had been flung on the floor so passionately ten days previously. Over it lay her stockings, still showing traces of the three-dimensional shape they'd borne the night before.

Maybe erotic underwear isn't my scene after all, she thought.

Eventually, Jamie rolled over and opened his eyes. For a moment he looked mystified, then he seemed to realize she was crying. "I'm sorry," he said, stroking away her tears. It sounded heartfelt—as if he was upset to have made her so miserable.

"Shall I make us a cup of tea?" he asked, clearly uncertain how to re- pair things. This was hardly the closeness Maggie craved, but it was a start.

Later that morning Jamie took Nathan to play soccer.

Perhaps a run might make me feel better, thought Maggie. I fancy a change, and if I run around the edge of the field, I can watch them play.

So she followed Nathan and Jamie to the recreation ground.

"Mum!" shouted Nathan, on seeing her. "Look at me!" He focused on the space between the two jumpers that had been laid out as the goal and kicked with all his might. Jamie obviously sensed it was important for Nathan to score in front of his mother so he dived dramatically the wrong way. The ball rolled past his feet—not fast, but it was a goal all the same.

"Hurray!" whooped Nathan. "Silly billy, Daddy."

"Ouch," said Jamie, getting up and rubbing his knees. These days he wasn't really fit enough to land with the aplomb with which he'd dived.

"Well done!" called Maggie, stopping to jog on the spot and clap. "Silly Daddy."

Jamie threw the ball down to the far end of the field. Nathan ran after it, and began dribbling back to the goal. "Lampard . . . neatly picks the ball up from defense," roused Jamie.

Maggie recognized his mockney as an impression of a passionate com- mentator from Five Live. "Still Lampard . . . he feints past Arteta, now shrugs off Diaby. It's still Lampard. Oh . . . this is impressive stuff from the

man. He's passed Gibbs, it's only the keeper to beat now, Lampard . . .
Agggh!" Nathan kicked and missed. "Obviously today he's on somewhat
erratic form."

Maggie laughed. She loved watching Jamie and Nathan being boys
together. As she continued running, her spirits began to lift. She noticed
Jamie always allowed Nathan to remain a couple of goals ahead and when
Nathan was goal-keeping, Jamie encouraged him to move the jumpers
closer together so it was easier for him to save.

Given Jamie's so competitive, that's quite a sacrifice, thought Maggie.
Nathan is the only person he'll happily allow to humiliate him.

After six circuits she was ready to return home, but she'd an urge to
go back via Georgie's to see if Alex might have stayed. She ran up to the
cottage by the church and a quick scan of the street revealed no sign of his
car. So he either made an early morning exit or didn't stay, she thought.

Georgie was in the garden, bent over pulling up weeds.

"Hiya!" said Maggie, reaching the gate.

"Oh, hi." Georgie straightened and attempted to scoop her defiant hair
back into its clip. "I just phoned you but no one was there."

"I was out running," Maggie puffed, "and Jamie and Nathan are playing soccer."

"Gosh, you are good, going for a run after all that booze! How do you
do it?"

"I enjoy it," explained Maggie truthfully.

"Yes, but being so fit and such a wonderful cook! It's impressive. Not
only are you talented and gorgeous—you've a beautiful home and boy
too. I'm quite jealous."

Well I never, thought Maggie. If only Georgie knew how miserable I
was earlier.

"Anyway, I was calling to thank you. It was a terrific party."

"My pleasure. You seemed to get on especially well with Alex."

"I thought he was lovely," Georgie gushed. "Nice looking too, in a cheeky
sort of way, don't you think? And, ooh, that voice!"

Perhaps I underestimate his appeal, thought Maggie. "Now you come
to mention it, I suppose it is rather nice and deep."

"I'll say. In fact, I know I shouldn't have, but when he dropped me off I asked if I could see him again."

"Really?" said Maggie, uncharitably pleased that the pass had come from Georgie rather than the other way around. "What did he say?"

"He seemed pretty keen. We're supposed to be going to see something at the National Film Theatre next week. I said I'd give him a call."

"That's great!" Maggie would never have dared to be so bold.

"Yes, isn't it? He seems a very nice guy."

"He is. What you see is what you get with Alex. I expect you'll have a great time. I'd better get back—got to put the lunch on. Let me know all about it."

"I will." Georgie grinned. "And thanks again," she called after her.

When Maggie got home there were three messages on the answering machine, from Georgie, then Fran—apparently she was planning on doing some basic cooking with her class at school and was after some recipes for children—and finally Alex, to thank her for a lovely evening. First Maggie spoke to Fran, then phoned Alex.

"Did you have a nice time, then?" she asked, hoping he would spill the beans.

"*Super*," he said, then obviously remembered that maybe she hadn't. "Did you?"

"Yeah, yeah." Maggie brushed his concern aside. "I've just been for a run. Feel much better."

"Really?" Alex sounded sceptical. "I must say you looked as delicious as ever"—Maggie couldn't help laughing—"and as for the food, you surpassed yourself. *Fantastic* starter, that oyster soup."

How ironic, she thought. Maybe the aphrodisiac worked on him and Georgie.

After lunch Fran arrived. "Are you okay?" she asked, the moment Maggie opened the front door.

Heavens, thought Maggie, do I look that bad? "Yes. Why?"

"You sounded a bit upset on the phone."

"Oh, well, I feel better now."

"Now you do. So you didn't earlier?"

"It's probably nothing," said Maggie, leading her into the kitchen. Jamie and Nathan were in earshot, watching television in the living room. Then the pressure of keeping things to herself got too much. "Jamie doesn't want another child—he said so at the dinner party last night. In front of everyone—it was awful. Then, when we went to bed, I asked him again, and he said it's not that he doesn't want one ever, it's just he'd rather wait a bit. But, Fran, I'm thirty-nine next month. If we wait much longer—Nathan's seven in October and, well, I don't know if I can."

"Hmm." Fran filled the kettle as if this were her own home. "It's the other way around with me and Geoff. He wants one now, I want to wait."

"Yes, but you're younger."

"Not much. Still, isn't it funny? Even when you've got one, it's not that easy deciding when or if to have a second. All the way through life, it seems everything comes down to timing. And I thought it only affected whether or not you could persuade a chap to settle down. How wrong I was."

Maggie sighed. "Sometimes I feel as if Jamie and I are a year or two out of sync."

Fran tried to make light of it. "Perhaps it's because he's the same age as me."

"Maybe."

"I tell you what you need . . ."

"What?"

"A little extracurricular. That would take your mind off it."

"Fran! You can't be serious."

"I'm not, entirely. But I think you're suffering from a severe case of being taken for granted. What you need is attention from another admirer. A bit of flirtation."

"I couldn't. Jamie would be so hurt."

"I'm not suggesting you tell him!" protested Fran. "And I'm not meaning you should even *do* much, just enjoy being fancied by someone else. Here you are, stuck in this house all day on your own while Jamie's up in town. He probably gets to flirt with hundreds of girls at the office."

"I'm sure he doesn't." Maggie couldn't imagine it. Or could she?

"I promise if he does it's harmless. But I bet he does. Even Geoff admitted it once. Not that he'd do anything either, of course, but he said good old-fashioned sexual chemistry can get clients to spend a little more . . . you know the kind of thing." She noticed Maggie's worried expression. "Anyhow, we're not talking about our husbands, we're talking about you. And you need something to distract you. When Jamie sees you're a bit less focused on him, believe you me, he'll come running back. Next thing, wham, bang! You'll be pregnant, he'll be delighted, and everything will be tickety-boo."

"Gosh." Maggie was taken aback her sister should be so matter-of-fact. Even if she was only talking about flirtation, wasn't mental infidelity just as bad? Nonetheless, she was intrigued. "How am I supposed to meet this man? The village is hardly chock-full of bachelors beating a path to my door."

Fran paused to consider while Maggie got to her feet and reached up to the top shelf of the dresser for the teapot. "Now there you have a problem. Let me think what I did."

"*What you did?*" Maggie was amazed. Her sister was surprising her at every turn.

"Oh, yes, I had an affair. Didn't you know?"

"*Fran! You didn't!*" Maggie nearly overfilled the teapot.

"I thought you knew," said Fran, knowing full well that Maggie did not. It was her way of having the upper hand in their relationship, keeping a few trump cards close to her chest, ready to be revealed when they'd have the most impact. "It was nothing major, you understand. At least, I realize it wasn't now, although I didn't see things that way at the time."

Maggie carried two mugs to the table and suppressed a smile. Fran even seemed to need to get one up on *herself* just as she did everyone else. Hence the older, wiser Fran always knew more than the younger, naive Fran.

"So who was he?" she asked, getting the milk jug out of the fridge. "When did it happen? Why didn't you tell me?"

"You never tell me anything."

"There's nothing much to tell. Anyway, tell me now."

"Promise not to laugh."

"I won't."

"He was the postman."

Maggie hooted.

"I knew you'd think it was funny. But he was really attractive. A six-foot-two young Robbie Williams type."

"Not your average Postman Pat."

"If you're going to take the piss, I won't tell you," Fran huffed. They were nine and ten years old, once again.

"Aw, go on, I want to know, honest. After all, even Shere has a postman. Maybe you can help me seduce him." Maggie knew Fran would like being cast as the expert, albeit in adultery.

"*He* seduced *me*," she continued buoyantly. "We first met when I walked Dan to school. Tim, his name was. He was always very friendly, and we were headed the same way, him with his trolley. He'd let Dan push it, then give him letters, and show him where to post them. Dan loved it, loved him. You know what it's like—someone's nice to your child, it makes you warm to them."

"I suppose so." But surely there's warming to someone and having the hots, thought Maggie. The two are quite distinct. I hardly succumb to every man who's nice to Nathan—I'm married, as is Fran. And what about Geoff? Are things stickier than they seem? I guess you never know what goes on behind closed doors.

"I always had the impression you and Geoff got on so well. When was all this?"

"About two years ago." Fran lowered her voice. She looked uncharacteristically embarrassed. "We'd stopped sleeping together."

"No! I thought you two . . ." Golly, thought Maggie, is all Fran's swanking mere bravado?

"Well, we do *now*, but for a while, when Dan was younger, it tapered off a bit."

"Why? There must have been a reason."

"Do you think there's a reason that things have slowed down between you and Jamie?"

The idea made Maggie uncomfortable. Might Jamie's lack of libido relate to some deeper issue? "Our sex life hasn't died. It's only not as frequent as it used to be. After so many years together that's quite common, isn't it?"

"Yeah, it is. Though things with Geoff and me had got worse than that. I think it started because he was having a dreadful time at work. It was when his firm merged with that other one—remember?"

Maggie did. Geoff had been nervous that he might be made redundant; she had felt sorry for him.

"After a while he got anxious about sex too. Pretty soon it became a vicious circle. I felt he wasn't communicating so I wanted affection, he felt I was demanding, emotionally and physically, and he couldn't answer my demands. So he worried and I got more demanding."

Maggie could just imagine how Fran's impatience might make a man—especially one as sensitive as Geoff—insecure. Poor chap. Yet surely the solution was not to sleep with someone else?

"Anyway." Fran, breezily recalling the excitement of her liaison, was oblivious to her sister's concern. "In the end Tim the toy boy satisfied my desires, or at least for a while."

"How old was he?"

"Twenty-four," said Fran proudly. "Showed me a thing or two, I must say."

"So you slept with him?" Maggie was horrified.

"Of course. I said I had an affair—it's hardly an affair if there's no sex."

"I suppose not." Maggie felt distinctly unworldly. Just how did one end up sleeping with a postman? "What happened?"

"I'm not going to tell you *everything*," said Fran, relishing withholding the very information she'd promised, "but I will say one day he had to get me to sign for something—a registered letter, I think it was. I'd already taken Dan to school, and he invited himself in, and we knew each other quite well by then and one thing led to another, well, almost before I could stop myself—he was so attractive—we were shagging in the hall. I think he had a bit of a thing for older women," she added, as if this explained the entire episode.

"Good God!" Fran "shagging" the postman! The phrase that made her squirm—it seemed so mechanical. In fact, it sounded like the kind of thing men said to impress their mates in the pub. Not something her slightly too tall and skinny younger sister would confide in her, seated at her very own kitchen table.

Fran got up and opened the cupboard where she knew her sister kept the biscuits. She rummaged around in the tin and took the last of the Bath Olivers.

"The reason I'm sharing this," she said with her mouth full, "is because it helped my relationship with Geoff no end."

"It did?"

"Yup." She swallowed. "Because I stopped wanting to sleep with him so desperately. I don't know if it was 'cause he sensed something was wrong, and it made him appreciate me more, or whether the pressure being off meant things got better between us. We started making love again, and gradually I even introduced some more adventurous things into our sex life—positions I'd learned with Tim—a little mild S and M using silk scarves, stuff like that. Then, finally, I didn't need Tim anymore so I finished with him, and now everything's just great. *That's* why you should have a fling."

"And Geoff never found out?" Maggie was agog. Fran was attractive, but outlandish positions? Mild S and M? With silk scarves? Her primary-schoolteacher sister!

"Of course not."

Somehow Maggie couldn't help sympathizing with the men in this scenario: the Robbie lookalike who'd been dumped the moment Fran's marriage got back on an even keel, and her brother-in-law, whom she'd known for ten years and was fond of.

Dear Geoff, thought Maggie. He puts up with Fran's incessant one-upmanship and bossiness. No one deserves to be treated like that, least of all such a kind, if occasionally bumbling, man like my brother-in-law. For what sounds like months he was unaware that my sister was satisfying her lust elsewhere. On the hall carpet . . . Maybe they even tied each other to the marital headboard! Surely he must have had some idea. I would,

I'm certain of it. And what about Dan? Cavorting with the postman is hardly the behavior of a responsible mum. What if my nephew picked up on something while they were supposedly innocently posting letters? I know from Nathan it's uncanny what small boys understand.

Maggie shuddered. Infidelity—what a horrible, *horrible* idea. She'd never let things between her and Jamie get that bad.

No, she thought firmly. A flirtation elsewhere is not the solution, not for me. Not ever.

11

By Tuesday morning Chloë had convinced herself she wouldn't hear from James again, not in that way, at least. Anyway, today she was meeting Vanessa Davenport for lunch, and she had more important things to think about. Or so she'd persuaded herself until she pushed open the rotating doors to UK Magazines' Covent Garden offices. There he was, in the foyer, waiting with a couple of members of staff for the elevator.

True to form, Chloë went pink immediately. James, on the other hand, with his jacket thrown over his briefcase—it was hot outside—appeared incredibly cool. She was struck again by how effortlessly well-dressed he was. In some ways men have it easy, she thought.

"Hello," he said, on seeing her.

"Hi."

"How are you?"

"Oh, I'm okay." Should she ask how he was? No—far too familiar. Silence.

A bell signaled the arrival of the elevator. The doors opened and all four of them got in. James took control of pressing the buttons.

"Which floor?" he asked the others.

"Two," said a man in a pinstripe suit.

"Three," said a middle-aged woman.

He didn't bother to ask Chloë, just pressed the button for her floor regardless. Then he stepped back. Did that mean he was getting out with her? Or at the second or third? Chloë's heart raced. If they were both headed for the fifth, they'd have a few seconds alone. Help!

They all stood pressed against the walls, looking everywhere rather than at each other. What was it about elevators that made chatting with people—even those one normally got on with easily—so impossible?

Ping! At the second floor, the man in pinstripes got out. He probably worked in accounts. More silence. *Ping!* At the third, the middle-aged lady disappeared.

James and Chloë were alone.

"I'm meeting Vanessa Davenport today," said Chloë, thankful to have thought of something to say.

"I heard. She told me."

This threw Chloë again—he'd been talking about her. But before she had time to consider every possible reason why, James said: "I couldn't stop thinking about you all weekend."

She looked him in the eye, trying to be stern. But . . . POW! There it was again. Chemistry so intense Chloë could imagine it causing the elevator to explode out of the top of the building.

"Me neither," she said.

"I'd like to see you again," said James. He seemed a little nervous.

Chloë virtually came on the spot. "Er . . ."

"Thursday night?" asked James, as the elevator arrived at the fifth floor. The doors opened.

To hell with her diary—she'd cancel anything she had arranged. "Yes," she said quickly.

He followed her into reception. "I've a meeting with your editor," he explained. "Good luck with Vanessa," he added, giving her a broad grin.

"Thanks," said Chloë, wondering what it would be like to kiss him right then. There were several people she didn't recognize sitting waiting on the sofas and the receptionist's face was raised in anticipation, ready to greet James politely, so a hushed "see you" was the most Chloë could manage before heading to her desk.

Three hours later she was sitting across from Vanessa Davenport in the Soho restaurant Petit France. Vanessa looked good in a ghoulish way, with her rather sharp, beaky nose and gaunt cheeks. She was elegantly dressed in black Gucci (UK Magazines must rate her for her to afford that lot, thought Chloë), and they were surrounded by a precarious mêlée of papers, side salads, and glasses. It was a challenge for Chloë to eat pasta and present her documents while maintaining a semblance of decorum.

Vanessa was guardedly positive in her responses to the idea, and Chloë tended to feel most at ease with people who were more intuitive in their reactions. As a result, she had a wicked urge to say casually, "Did you know that after discussing this last Thursday, James Slater spent the night with me and I discovered he has a *huge* willy." I'd like to see whether Vanessa could be so disconcertingly formal about *that*, she thought.

All morning Chloë had been trying to fathom what that second date meant. The more she analyzed it, the more sure she was: he was keen. One encounter and she could have put James's behavior down to the heat of the moment, but two after-work meetings—with him suggesting both—that was a different thing altogether. *"It's very dangerous,"* she could hear Rob warn her, but she'd never had such an attractive and successful man interested in her before and she was flattered and thrilled.

Lit up by the knowledge that James liked her, Chloë glowed throughout the meeting, despite her distracted mind and Vanessa's daunting reputation.

Vanessa must have picked up on her confidence, because at the end of their lunch she agreed tentatively to take Chloë's idea to the board. "But it does need a title," she said crisply, as Chloë got up. "As you doubtless know from working on *Babe*, that's not easy. Try and come up with something, if only to work with for the time being. It's important if people are going to take this seriously higher up the company. I'd like your thoughts by early next week and eventually you'll need to find something really memorable."

"Okay." Chloë shook Vanessa's hand. Her long slim fingers were laden with silver jewelry and her nails were immaculately French-manicured: the weapons of a woman who knew how to intimidate another. Yet Chloë could stand up to her—especially today—and said with genuine self-assurance: "I'll come up with some ideas. And thank you for lunch and for seeing me."

"My pleasure. I look forward to working with you." Then suddenly Vanessa smiled. "James was right. It's a great idea, and your enthusiasm is infectious."

"Thanks again," said Chloë. Everything seemed to be going her way, and leaving the restaurant, bouncing on her lucky sandals, she felt as if she was walking on air.

Back at her desk, Chloë was checking a proof when the phone rang.

"Hello, Chloë?" It was Craig Spencer, one of her favorite freelance journalists. A warm, likeable man with a background in counseling, he wrote regular pieces for *Babe* and promised to be a pleasant antidote to the brittle Vanessa.

"I've got an idea for an article. Thought you might like it."

"Hang on a tick." Chloë folded the artwork and reached for a pen and notebook. "Right, go ahead."

"Well, I'm a stepfather, if you weren't aware, and for a long time I've been thinking about children after their parents' divorce. Don't get me wrong," Craig must have detected Chloë's scepticism down the line, "I'm not talking about focusing on young kids—I appreciate that's been done before. I'm thinking of interviewing children who are now grown-up, asking them to consider in retrospect how the experience of their parents' rows, affairs, separation, and so on has affected their adult relationships. I could talk to a range of people, maybe one who's several times divorced, one who's managed to maintain a happy marriage of their own despite a traumatic childhood, and one who's perennially single, that kind of thing."

"You could interview me, then," said Chloë, not entirely joking.

Craig grabbed the opportunity to convey the pertinence of the idea. "Pity I can't, but it shows it's got universal relevance."

"Hmm . . . It just doesn't sound very *Babe* . . ."

"I'm convinced it could be, if we get the right sort of interviewees and tone."

"That might be a shame. I'd hate to see you not do it justice because you were forced to make it too upbeat and simplistic."

Craig obviously thought this was a polite way of giving him the brush-off. "If that's how you feel."

Just then Chloë had a brainstorm. She checked over her shoulder— Patsy was away from her desk. "Actually, I'm working on another project at the moment, but I'm afraid I'm not in a position to give you any details quite yet. This article could be suitable for that. Yes." She grew more certain. "I think it's the kind of subject we could put a spin on and make work."

"Oh?"

"Do me a favor, Craig. Don't tell anyone else about this idea. Don't offer it to any other editors. Give me a week, and I'll get back to you."

"I'm on tenterhooks. So I'll wait to hear from you?"

"Yes, do. And thanks for calling." Chloë put the phone down. She could see it now. Engaging and emotionally provocative, touching rather than titillating, and written by a psychiatric professional with personal insight. It was exactly what she wanted for her new magazine.

That night Chloë decided to catch up on a few ongoing features she was editing for *Babe*. When she finally left the office it was past eight o'clock, but at least that meant the number nineteen would be quicker getting home. Propped up against the bus stop on Charing Cross Road, Chloë felt the high that had buoyed her all day ebb away, leaving her strangely deflated.

Shortly her bus arrived. Chloë mounted the steep spiral stairs to the upper deck, where she was pleased to find that the seat with a prime view at the front was free. It was muggy, so as the double-decker lurched around Trafalgar Square, she wound down the window, hoping the air might help clear her thoughts.

She flashed back to her conversation with Craig—momentarily this had brought up uncomfortable memories. Yet paradoxically this was what attracted her to the article—she knew it could push other people's buttons, if it did hers.

Chloë had been an adolescent when her parents began not to get on, and as the eldest she'd taken it hard. Again she could hear Rob's voice appraising: *"We're two of a kind,"* he'd say, and it was true, they were both afraid of commitment—he thought it was because she'd spent years caught between an arguing couple. *"You're always picking unsuitable partners,"* he'd observed only this last weekend. *"Your boyfriends are never good enough for you—either you go for men you can walk all over, or else you go for the challenge, hoping to win them over, and then you end up hurt. And I worry this James is another one. I know, I know"*—he'd held up his hand as she opened her mouth to protest—*"I'm a fine one to talk. Though I'm just saying to you what you'd say to me."*

It was true Chloë's longest relationship had lasted only a year—and very off-and-on it had been too.

As the bus stop-started down Piccadilly, rounded Hyde Park Corner, and headed down Sloane Street, Chloë gnawed at her lip, thinking of her mum and dad. Before they'd retired, they'd both been actors and prone to bouts of melodrama; their relationship gave credence to the cliché: can't live with each other; can't live without each other.

God, I was relieved when Dad announced he was leaving mum for another woman, thought Chloë. It had been a mess for far too long.

Even now she didn't feel warm toward the memory of her father's girlfriend, Julia, a TV producer many years his junior. Still, Julia can't be held responsible for the breakdown of their marriage, she thought. His meeting her merely precipitated some long-overdue decisions. Mum and Dad are so much happier these days, both settled with new partners—Julia probably did us all a favor.

She was forced to acknowledge, however, that Julia hadn't come out of it well. *"Pah! I knew it was a transitional relationship. It was never going to last,"* Chloë's mother had said after her father had dumped Julia because he needed time alone "to think."

Chloë sighed. One never knows how things will turn out, she thought. Nevertheless, life seems to be going pretty well. Yes, she reminded herself as the bus picked up speed over Battersea Bridge and she rose to her feet ready for her stop, I've heaps to look forward to. Not least that on Thursday I'm seeing James again.

She recalled their intimate conversation, their steamy sex, his gentleness, the way he'd made her feel so wanted and wonderful.

I shall live for the moment, she vowed, and pushed her negative thoughts aside.

12

Chloë was filling the kettle when Rob staggered, bleary-eyed, into the kitchen.

"You're up early," she said.

"Tell me about it." Rob scowled. "Seems the world and his wife are desperate to lose a few pounds before their bloody holidays so they're all wanting extra personal training sessions. I've got the world's longest day."

"So, you'll be out tonight?" Chloë acted disinterested as she reached for the coffee.

"Yes, blast it. It's late opening at the gym—my last appointment's not until nine."

"You poor thing," said Chloë, secretly thinking, Ooh goody! He won't be back till after eleven.

"You look posh," said Rob, his eyes now sufficiently open to take in her carefully assembled outfit—a flimsy skirt and a satin shirt she'd picked up on Portobello Road, both in shades of green, which she hoped offset her dark coloring rather well.

"Posh?" Chloë was disappointed. Ravishing was more what she'd had in mind.

"Yeah. But you look nice."

"Good." Chloë poured milk into her coffee. Rob was usually a fine judge.

He stood back for a full assessment. "Surprisingly sophisticated."

"Not sexy?" asked Chloë hopefully.

He eyed her suspiciously. "Why is it so important to appear sexy on a Thursday?"

"Oh, no reason." Chloë grabbed her mug and made a hasty exit.

"I hope you're not seeing that man again today!" he called after her. "You know I think he's bad news."

When James phoned, Chloë suggested they meet for a drink in Clapham Junction.

"Good idea," he said. "It's easy for me to get the last train home from there."

It sounds as if he's planning on being out as late as possible, so maybe I can lure him back to mine, thought Chloë, living for the moment just as she'd vowed. It's coming together nicely.

But when she arrived at the Slug and Lettuce, it was heaving. She bought herself a glass of red wine and tried to find a table. There wasn't one. The music was blaring—they wouldn't be able to hear themselves think. Perhaps it hadn't been such a great choice of venue.

"Hi," said James, coming up behind her and surprising her. He grabbed her around the waist and *smack!* gave her a firm kiss on the cheek. He was close enough for her to get a waft of his scent. That, and the sheer confidence of the gesture, brought heady recollections flooding back. "Can I buy you a drink?"

Chloë shook her head. "I've got one."

She watched him make his way to the bar. He was undoubtedly a little older than most of the clientele, but had the kind of effortless ease that meant he seemed at home wherever he was. It's odd, isn't it, she contemplated, that some people get more attractive the better one knows them, while others become more ordinary? Mm, she concluded, in a well-fed-Heathcliff-meets-curvaceous-Cathy kind of way, perhaps we complement each other. I wonder if anyone else has noticed we make rather a good couple . . .

They soon agreed that it was too noisy and hot inside, so opted instead to join the crowd spilling onto the pavement, although the busy main road was far from the most romantic location.

"Did you get home all right last week?" asked Chloë, keen to avoid any pretense that nothing had happened.

"Yeah. A cab's amazingly fast at five in the morning, and my wife and son were out for the night, so I was able to grab an hour's nap before schlepping back into town."

My wife. Chloë flushed. She'd been avoiding contemplating the fact that he was married. Yet his choice of words also seemed a bit distant—made Chloë think of the kind of girl who referred to "my boyfriend" rather than calling him by his name, as if he was more important as an accessory than anything else. But she wasn't in a position to comment, so she let it go.

That Chloë allowed more than a split second's silence while she contemplated this was unusual, which obviously worried James.

"Chloë?" he said.

"Um?"

"I hope you don't think I make a habit of this kind of thing." A particularly loud truck thundered past, billowing exhaust and James coughed, whether from awkwardness or the fumes, Chloë wasn't sure.

I don't know what to think," said Chloë truthfully. She could swear James was trying to assess her feelings.

His hazel eyes looked anxious. "I've never had an affair before." God! He'd called it an affair. Already! "You haven't?" Chloë was surprised, even doubtful. She found him so irresistible that she couldn't imagine other women didn't—she knew Patsy did. Though of course fidelity isn't just a matter of being desired by others; it means reciprocating that desire and acting on it, she reminded herself.

"No, not really." James appeared keen to explain himself. "To be honest, I haven't been so attracted to anyone this much before. Not for years."

Bullshit! Chloë could hear Rob's voice. I bet he says that to all the girls. But instinctively she believed him. She said encouragingly, "You don't need to justify yourself to me."

"I don't?"

"No."

"Why's that?"

"Because—um . . ." Chloë paused. Should she risk being so open? She'd nothing to lose. "I've never done anything like this before either."

"So you're not like the woman who wrote that book in the papers?" James appeared relieved.

"The serial mistress? Never goes out with anyone other than married men?"

"Yes, her."

"Hardly!" Chloë laughed. "I read about her too—I thought she seemed vile. Totally without scruples. And you'd never have known she was such a goer, would you? She looked so prim."

"Not my type, certainly. Though I guess you know that."

"In what way?" How she loved fishing for compliments from him. He always seemed to come up trumps.

"Well, *you're* much more my cup of tea."

"Cup of tea? How tame!"

"You'd prefer to be my margarita?" He laughed. "God! I had a dreadful hangover last Friday."

"Me too." Chloë shuddered at the memory.

"Took the whole weekend to get over it. I'm not as young as I was."

"We didn't drink that much."

"No, but we didn't have much sleep either."

Chloë noted the reference to sex. It made her feel intimate with him, and excited at the thought of doing it again. "I slept in on Saturday," she said.

"Not an option in my case. Nathan wakes up at eight. Bounce! Bounce! 'Daddy's day to get breakfast!' "

"Ah." Chloë didn't know what to say. For a moment she felt truly terrible. What was she doing fooling around with a married man who had a child?

Belatedly, James seemed to realize the tactlessness of talking about his family, and to make up for it said, "I love your outfit." Chloë beamed. "You wear such great clothes. They really accentuate your figure." He was blatantly gazing at her breasts.

"Thanks," said Chloë, not minding.

He adjusted his focus to her face. "So, how was the meeting with Vanessa?"

"Weird." Chloë was glad to have the conversation on more secure ground. "I think she liked the magazine concept, but she's a strange woman." Oops! She was talking about a close colleague of his. "I mean—she's, um, a bit difficult to make out."

"You didn't like her?"

"No, no, it's not that," said Chloë hurriedly. That was a bit strong—Vanessa had given her the go-ahead, after all.

"Well, she told me she liked it," James reassured her. "She even said she liked you."

"Really?" Chloë was surprised and pleased. Recklessly she added, "Blimey, if that's how she behaves when she likes someone, I'd hate to see when she doesn't!"

"A total bitch, believe me." James grinned.

Now a bus stopped at the lights, engine spluttering loudly.

"It's horrid here," said Chloë. "I tell you what—I presume you've got to be home later?"

James stared at the pavement. "The last train's at eleven fifteen."

"Well"—she raised her eyes—"we *could* always go back to mine now . . ."

"What about your roommate?"

"He's out this evening."

"Okay, then, let's."

As they strolled up the hill, she said, "If you don't mind me asking, where did you say you were going tonight?"

"I said I was playing squash. I play every Thursday." He appeared uncomfortable.

"Till midnight?"

"Lame, I know. Though I told you, this is kind of new to me."

"So you've never been unfaithful before? Not once?"

James took her hand. "Do you want me to be honest?" Blimey, thought Chloë. What's he going to say? That I've swept him off his feet? But he said, "I have been, yes." Her heart sank. He was a philanderer, after all. "Once, at a company do, in Paris."

This didn't sound so bad. "It was a one-night stand?"

"Barely that. We didn't even spend the night together. We were drunk. She dragged me back to her room—she was a Spanish ad exec, very attractive, from what I recall. Must be a couple of years ago. We had sex once, then I left. It was no big romance."

Chloë was thankful. It was one thing having an affair with someone she was beginning to like a lot and who seemed to think she was special, quite another to be one of a series of lovers.

By now they were back at her apartment. Thank goodness she'd spent fifteen minutes tidying up before work. It was far from pristine, but at least the washing-up was done and her dirty clothes were in the laundry bin. They went into the kitchen.

"Hey, this is nice," said James.

"You think so?" Chloë was amazed—its haphazard style was hardly in keeping with his designer suits.

"Yeah." He sauntered around, casually taking stock, peering at the fridge smothered in photos of Chloë with her friends, examining the quirky knickknacks on the windowsill, chortling at Rob's camp fifties B-movie posters.

He wandered through the double doors into the living room.

It's less tidy in there, Chloë worried. There were magazines everywhere and stacks of CDs that had been separated from their covers from last Sunday's gathering with her girlfriends.

"Ah!" James kicked off his shoes. "Sorry, old fella, my turn." He shoved the cat off the settee so he could stretch out on it lengthways. "This is just my kind of place, you know," he called through to Chloë. "Reminds me of where I lived when I first got to London." She came to the door. With his feet propped up on one of the sofa arms, he looked as if there was nowhere else he'd rather be.

"Do you want some more wine?" she asked. Living hand to mouth as she and Rob tended to, they had far from a cellarful, but they always had a couple of cheapish bottles in stock for emergencies. "I'm afraid it's nothing spectacular."

"Please."

Chloë grabbed the red, two glasses, and the corkscrew and followed him into the sitting room. "Budge up."

He lifted his legs so she could join him, then promptly put them on her lap. And yes, there it was again—that whoosh of sheer, unstoppable desire. Chloë found it hard to concentrate on the corkscrew.

"Let me." James reached for it. He opened the wine easily, poured them each a glass, and placed the bottle on the coffee table. "Come here." He reached for her.

Chloë shifted so she was half lying on him, their faces level. With some men she worried at moments like this that she was ungraceful in the way she moved and too heavy, but not here, with James.

"What time's your roommate back?"

"Not till eleven." Chloë could feel his breath.

He stroked her cheek. "You're lovely," he said, and kissed her. Ooh—it was even better than before! Maybe it was because she was sober, or more relaxed. Maybe it was because she was now pretty sure he liked her—a lot. Maybe . . . Chloë's energies shifted out of her head, her brain went mushy, and . . . mmm . . . she could sense the bristles from his five o'clock shadow . . . She was being taken over by a divine sensation lower down. He undid the buttons of her blouse without a hitch—she'd known it was a good choice for that reason—and slid his hands into her bra. Yes, *please* . . . She was feeling very horny; certainly not like plump, clumsy Chloë now. With her satin shirt slipping off her shoulders, his own half undone— she'd forgotten how sexy his chest was—she felt wonderfully wanton.

She knelt up and looked at him.

"Take off your skirt," he directed.

There was no way to achieve this and remain close to him other than for Chloë to stand on the sofa astride him, balanced on wobbly cushions. Nevertheless she managed to accomplish the task by standing momentarily on one leg. More incredibly, because she was being watched by a thoroughly appreciative man, she did it with real grace.

"There!" she said, still standing. Thank God for her best bra and knickers. He ran his hands up her legs. And thank God she'd shaved.

She looked down at James, enjoying watching him taking her all in and relishing the sight of him, still in his trousers, his eyes full of lust.

"Jeez," he said, spellbound. "You look amazing. You are all woman."

"This is where I like my publishers to be." She laughed, and knelt down, still astride him, the flatness of her crotch directly above the bump of his erection. She gently rubbed herself against it, knowing full well the effect it would have.

"Chloë," he groaned.

Slowly she undid the remaining buttons of his shirt.

"Thank God all features editors aren't like you," he muttered, unzipping his fly. "There wouldn't"—he slid down his trousers—"be a hope in hell"—he pushed her knickers to one side—"of me being remotely able to keep my professional"—he began to thrust—"distance."

13

"Open the door," Jamie said to Nathan. They were home from playing soccer again, all tired and sweaty.

Nathan opened the hall closet and stood back, ready for the ritual.

"He shoots, he scores!" Jamie whacked the ball through the door, knocking a couple of coats off their hooks.

Nathan squealed, delighted.

"I wish you wouldn't do that." Maggie sighed.

"Oh." Jamie sounded deflated.

"That closet's enough of a mess as it is."

"Gee, I'm sorry," said Jamie sarcastically, and he winked at Nathan in camaraderie.

"Boring Mummy," said Nathan, which only made Maggie more irritable. She was tired and sweaty too, but not from having fun: she'd been vacuuming and scrubbing all afternoon. Plus it was the second day of her period—always the worst.

"Actually," she said, "I would appreciate it a lot if you could tidy it up

in there. It's full of junk. I don't know how you can ever find anything—
the other day it took me ages to unearth my trainers. I felt like I'd worked
out before I even started running."

"Ooh, *dear*," said Jamie, "what's got into Mummy today? It's probably
that time of the month."

That he was right and addressed this remark to Nathan was the last
straw. "In fact, I'd like you to do it now."

"What—*now*?"

"You might as well. Before you shower."

"But the results are on in a minute! We've come back specially."

"Nathan can tell you them." In need of no further excuse to escape,
Nathan scarpered into the sitting room and switched on the television.

"Why do I have to do it this second? Why not tomorrow?"

He's just like a child, thought Maggie. "Because you *won't* do it tomorrow."

"I will."

"No, you won't. And, anyway, I want it done now. Then I can relax."

"You can't relax when there's mess in the hall closet?" He seemed determined to provoke her.

"No, I bloody well can't!" Maggie raised her voice.

"Jesus, Maggie. Sometimes I worry about you. You're obsessed with
everything being so goddamn tidy!" It was incredible how he managed to
turn his own messiness into a failing of hers.

"I am *not* obsessed. Anyway, if I am, it's because someone's got to be
around here."

"Why? It's hardly as if the world would stop turning if I didn't tidy up
your precious closet."

"Because if I left it up to you the whole house would be a fucking pig-
sty." This was not a word Maggie used readily, and she checked Nathan
was out of earshot.

"Why don't you just let it be for once? Then maybe *I* could relax."

"That's rich. You know damn well you'd hate to live like that."

"That's where you're wrong, Maggie." The use of her name, pointedly.

"Tell me, how *would* you like to live?"

"I wouldn't have everything so anally goddamn perfect. It's bad enough having my dinner plate washed up before I've even finished my pudding, but all our CDs arranged alphabetically! All my bloody underpants rolled in my drawers. My socks in color-coordinated rows. I don't mind when you do it to your stuff, but I *hate* it when you do it to mine. Come to that," he was so angry his cheeks were flushed, "if you *really* want to know how I'd like to live, I wouldn't choose to live here at all."

"Oh?"

"You're the one who wanted some beautiful sodding period home out here in the middle of nowhere. I'd much rather still be up in town. All this commuting, it's wearing me out. If I don't have any energy for housework, that's damn well why!"

Maggie was shaking. "You've got the energy for soccer."

"It's not the same and you know it! Look, we've got this huge bloody house with a huge bloody mortgage. I take care of the mortgage—"

"So the least I can do is take care of the house?" Maggie couldn't believe what she was hearing.

"Yes."

"You do *not* take care of the fucking mortgage!" She was close to screaming now. "We both do!"

"Yeah right," said Jamie. "And I've told you before, if you need some help, get a cleaner."

"I can't *find* a cleaner!"

"If you weren't so snotty to them maybe they'd stay."

He'd struck a nerve. Maggie acknowledged she could be a tough taskmaster. "I never knew you felt that way about the house," she said more soberly.

"Well you do now," muttered Jamie, calming down too.

"You should have told me before." She was close to tears.

"I didn't know what it would be like until we moved here."

"No, nor did I," said Maggie regretfully. She missed her London friends—especially at times like this. Here she had so few people to confide in.

"And I wanted to make you happy," added Jamie. By now Maggie was crying and Jamie looked as if he really hated himself. "Though I don't seem to be very good at that."

"Oh, it's not *you*," said Maggie, despising herself for being so foul to him.

They both paused.

"I'm sorry," he said eventually.

"Me too," she said, and stepped forward as he reached to fold her in his arms.

14

As she lay in bed on Sunday morning, Chloë dozily replayed Thursday night, carefully selecting the memories that made her feel good and skipping over the issues—James's family—that made her feel bad. She allowed herself to linger extra long on the compliments James had paid her, which made her feel all warm inside. He'd said she was "lovely," "amazing," that he loved her breasts (she quite liked them too—they were her favorite part of her body) and even (madman) her curvy hips, her belly. What was that phrase he'd used? "All woman." She liked that . . .

Ooh! She was suddenly fully awake. All things to all women . . . every aspect of an individual woman . . . something for every kind of woman . . . the whole truth about women . . . It certainly had several meanings. It even sounded a bit risqué, but that was no bad thing . . . Yes. *All Woman* would be a good title for her magazine.

———

A week later she got a call.

"I've got you the go-ahead," said Vanessa, not bothering with small talk. "And the board likes the name. You've three months seconded to this department initially, working with me and another assistant."

"That's *fantastic!*"

"It should prove interesting." Vanessa sounded a few degrees above freezing. "I'd like to start at the beginning of October, as I'm going away for a couple of weeks next Monday. It would also help if you took any vacation time owed to you before we begin. That way we can get our teeth into it." She probably sucked blood with hers, thought Chloë. "So you'd better tell your editor, sharpish."

Yes, thought Chloë. Not a task she relished. "Leave it to me." She tried to sound capable. "I'll let you know when I've spoken to her."

Well, no time like the present. Chloë pushed back her chair and marched purposefully to Jean's office. The door was open—it was one of Jean's I'm-one-of-the-girls practices (though as the boss there was heaps of gossip from which she was excluded). Chloë stood on the threshold and tapped lightly.

Jean looked up and smiled. "Ah, Chloë," she said. While she bore a resemblance to a more well-rounded Coco Chanel, beneath her polished and classically suited exterior, Jean was not a cold woman. And Chloë was aware that while her unconventional approach sometimes frustrated her boss, Jean had a soft spot for her. She'd nurtured Chloë's career from editorial assistant onward and upward.

She's going to be pissed off no matter what, thought Chloë, but I owe her a lot, and I don't want to ruin any future chances I might have with her. Diplomacy is key.

"Ahem." She cleared her throat, unusually nervous. "I don't know where to start."

"Sounds ominous," said Jean. "Have a seat."

"You know how much I love working here at *Babe*."

"Ye-es." Jean was on her guard already.

"And you know how much I appreciate all you've done for me——"

"You're leaving."

"Not exactly . . . I've been invited to work in special projects for three months."

"You have? They asked you? Just out of the blue?" Jean knew full well that this would not have been the case, but Chloë wasn't surprised an immediate sense of betrayal made her snappy.

"No, I approached them," she admitted.

"I see. And why was that, if you're so happy here?"

There was nothing else for it; she would have to be honest. "I've been developing another magazine concept."

"A women's magazine?"

Chloë knew exactly what Jean was driving at. "Yes, but it's not a competitor to *Babe*, Jean, honestly."

"If you say so," said Jean, sitting back. "I overheard Vanessa talking about it and I expected as much. I presume you kept it from me until it was definite. I want the whole story, beginning to end. And quit buttering me up."

Lord—as if Chloë was going to tell Jean everything! She related a highly censored version, emphasizing her work had all been out-of-office hours, and playing up Vanessa's role. (Vanessa would like that, so no harm there.)

When she'd finished Jean said, "It sounds very exciting. Though you know a lot of these projects come to nothing, don't you?"

"Oh, yes."

"I suppose I'll have to keep your job open for you." Jean did not even try to disguise how much this put her out.

"That would be great."

"Not for me it won't be. But it's UK Magazines' policy, so I've no choice."

"I'm sorry," she ventured.

"No, you're not!" retorted Jean, spot on as usual. "Though I do understand. It's because you're good that I don't want to see you go. So, from a selfish point of view, I hope you fall flat on your face and have to come back to me. But for yours, I wish you luck. I can't begrudge you your ambition, given mine's got me where I am today. Now off you go, before I throttle you!"

———————

Another fortnight, and a couple of snatched clandestine meetings later, Chloë was longing for the opportunity to spend more than a few hours at a time with James. Especially as she was taking the next week off to use up her leave before starting work with Vanessa. She wanted to get to know him better, to discover if the connection that promised so much ran any deeper. In spite of her best efforts not to think of him too seriously, she was beginning to hope and believe that it did. As they lay curled up together at her place one Wednesday evening—this time James had used the hackneyed working-late excuse, believing he genuinely ought to play squash with his friend the next day—he said, "I'm afraid I'm not going to be able to manage this next week."

Chloë could scarcely conceal her disappointment. She'd hoped to persuade him to take an afternoon off with her. "Why not?"

"I'm going away."

"Oh." I suppose he's going on vacation with his wife, she thought. It's only to be expected. Still, the idea made her feel left out and rejected. It was a familiar emotion—she'd experienced it watching her parents bickering, too preoccupied to be aware of the impact on her; and with men she'd been involved with in the past, as well. Because she didn't expect her feelings to matter to James either, she said nothing.

"Aren't you going to ask me where I'm off to?" he asked, idly stroking her arm.

"Mm," she said quietly.

"New York. For a week."

She couldn't help it. She was so jealous—it was somewhere she'd always wanted to go. "You lucky thing," she said, trying not to sound envious and turning her arm so he could stroke it from a new angle. "Where are you both staying? Do you know people out there?" Yes, of course he did—Beth. She didn't suppose they'd be staying with her. Though one never knew—perhaps enough time had passed that she and Maggie were friends by now.

"Both? Ah!" He laughed, realizing her mistake. "I'm not going with Maggie."

"You're not?"

"I'm going on business, and Maggie's got to stay here and look after Nathan."

"Of course," she said, feeling stupid for not thinking of this.

"I'm going to visit US Magazines. It's the annual conference."

It was obvious he'd be attending. UK Magazines sent their key people to the parent company event every year.

"I'll miss you," she said.

"And me you."

"It's a shame, actually."

"Why?"

" 'Cause I'm off work next week."

"You are?"

"I have to use up my vacation days before shifting departments. I'd kind of hoped . . . you might have taken a day off to spend with me or something."

"That would have been nice." James sounded regretful.

"Oh, never mind." Chloë changed the subject, unwilling to seem overly keen. "Better make the most of this, then." She kissed him persuasively. "Fancy giving me a massage?"

The next day Chloë was at her desk when an e-mail popped up from James. She read it at once.

Have you opened your internal mail yet?

She hadn't bothered with any of her mail. With only forty-eight hours on the magazine to go, she hadn't been able to get excited about anything to do with *Babe* that day. She riffled through the pile until she located the thick brown manila envelope tied with string those at UK Publishing still found occasional use for. Her name was scrawled at No. 15, the last on the list. It contained another smaller envelope labeled *Chloë Appleton* and underlined *Private and Confidential*. She tore it open and caught her breath.

Inside was a plane ticket. To New York. Leaving the following evening (Shit! She'd have to leave work early on her last day at *Babe*—Jean would be even more cross) and returning a week—a whole week—later.

She screamed in excitement.

"What?" asked Patsy.

"Oh, er, nothing," said Chloë.

Patsy clearly didn't believe her. "What *nothing*? You're just screaming out of the blue?"

"I'm afraid I can't tell you." Chloë knew this would drive Patsy nuts.

"Tell me, tell me, tell me."

"I'm sorry. It's confidential." Chloë thought quickly. "To do with this new magazine. Vanessa would kill me if I disclosed it."

"Oh." Patsy pouted.

"When I can say, I promise you'll be the first to know." Chloë simultaneously clicked *Reply* on her e-mail.

WOW!

she typed in 72 point font, and then smaller

That is the best surprise I have ever had!

And before Patsy saw what she was doing, she pressed *Send*.

15

That evening Jamie got home from squash earlier than he had recently, yet he bolted his supper without asking Maggie how her day had been. Mindful of their argument, she waited until he had finished both courses before clearing his dishes, but he didn't notice, simply racing upstairs to pack, leaving Maggie standing in the kitchen, reeling.

What is going on? she thought. Is something up—something serious? It's not just a question of day-to-day niggles—after nearly ten years, I suppose they're only to be expected. It's more than that, though I can't put my finger on it.

She cast her mind back to the incident with the hall closet. At times Jamie can be downright immature, she thought, although maybe he has a point. People do say I can be a bit serious sometimes, and we are very different . . . I'm nowhere near as gregarious—Jamie seems socially at ease almost anywhere. And I've always been more radical politically, more passionate about aesthetics, but aren't those differences what make our relationship work? We complement one another, surely.

Certainly the idea of being with someone who was exactly like her didn't appeal to Maggie—Alex had also been different from her in many ways. As for the prospect of two people together like Jamie . . . She shuddered. What an overwhelming duo they would be!

Nonetheless, *we aren't spending enough time together; Jamie seems to be working harder than ever*—and though that's to be expected with this new role, *recently he's been very quick to criticize me.* She frowned, assessing; *yes, he seems most critical of those things where my behavior differs most sharply from his own. It's not just my tidiness that seems to irk him, it's the way I treat Nathan. What was it he said a few days ago? "You're so damn traditional—can't you be a bit spontaneous for once?"* Only this morning he said, *"Why don't you branch out and do something more exciting? You've been doing the same sort of articles for years,"* when he'd been getting dressed. *"Thanks for the insight,"* she'd replied, cross because she was depressed by the style of features she wrote already. No wonder it had provoked another argument. *Jamie was even critical of my clothes,* she remembered, *and on a day when I thought I looked particularly nice!* Again, he suggested Maggie try something new and bold, "sexier" was how he put it. Yet when she'd tried dressing up in that way on the night of the dinner party, he didn't even realize she'd had the basque on.

And now he's going away on business for a week, she thought. *Being thousands of miles apart is the last thing we need.*

However desperately she wanted to go with him, Maggie couldn't: she had to stay and take Nathan to school. *I wouldn't want him to feel that his mum and dad would rather be off gallivanting together than with him, would I?* she reminded herself.

She leaned against the kitchen sink, gazing out of the window into the dusk, recalling the visions she'd once had of her future. *I used to think I'd be running a chain of health-food shops by now,* she thought. *Alex used to joke I'd be "the queen of green cuisine," with a string of eco-friendly cookbooks to my name. I'm not even a proper vegetarian anymore*—these days I eat fish and chicken, albeit free-range. *Worst of all, I seem to have ended up a walking cliché—a bored, sexually frustrated housewife in Surrey. How has that happened? Who is to blame?*

Tears pricked behind her eyes; she blinked them away and mounted the stairs after her husband. Jamie had just finished packing when she entered the room.

"I'm whacked," he said. "I should go to bed—I've a long day ahead in the morning."

"Yes." Maggie was able to read the signs all too clearly. "We'd better go straight to sleep, hadn't we?"

16

"Oh my good God! He's taking you to *New York*?"

"Yes." Chloë was frantically emptying the contents of her wardrobe onto the bed while Rob stood by.

"For how long?"

"Just over a week."

"A week! A whole *week*? Why isn't his wife going?"

"She has to stay and look after his son."

"Poor cow," said Rob.

Chloë felt a sharp stab of guilt.

"Did it occur to you to say no?"

"Are you mad? Turn down an invitation to the place I've wanted to visit my entire adult life?"

"You're right. You absolutely have to go. It's a one in a million chance. So I take it this is a business trip. All expenses paid?"

"Yeah," said Chloë. "He's going to the annual conference at US Magazines. We'll be back next weekend."

"He needs to be there over a week? And has to go on a Friday?"

"It runs Monday to Thursday, but, hey, I'm hardly going to argue, am I?"

"I guess not. Still, if I was his wife, I'd be a mite suspicious."

"He said he hated being jet-lagged for meetings so he likes to arrive a day or two early to recover."

"And shag you."

"If you must put it like that, yes. Though he was going anyway—I'm just coming along for the ride."

"Some ride!" Rob laughed. "Well, firstly, I'm jealous as hell—'cause you know I love, love, love that city, and September's a fabulous time to go. Secondly, let me help you decide what to take 'cause I know the scene and you obviously haven't a clue, and thirdly, allow me to give you one piece of advice."

"What's that?" Chloë was sure she wasn't going to like it.

"Don't, whatever you do, ask him if he is going to leave his wife."

"What makes you think I would?" Chloë had studiously avoided anything too heavy so far.

"Because I know you, Chloë. You've been seeing each other—what? Once a week for a month, roughly? So far, it's been great fun. But it's been mainly about sex—"

"It hasn't!"

"Aw, c'mon, hon—have you ever seen him without shagging?"

"No . . ."

"Right. Which means it's still at that rampant stage, but when you go away, you'll be entering a different phase. You'll talk more, do things together, just the two of you . . . You'll develop your own set of romantic memories . . . You'll get closer . . . Then, wham! You'll fall in love with him."

"How can you be so sure?" asked Chloë, but she knew she was already more involved than she was prepared to acknowledge.

"Because all the ingredients are there. Only remember what your dear friend Rob said to you: you're a long way from home, you're also a long way from reality. Back here, this man has a wife and kid. Whatever you feel while you're out there, this is where you live, where your work is, where your friends are but, more important, it's where *his* commitments are."

"Yeah, yeah," said Chloë, feeling distinctly uncomfortable.

"And remember, if it goes hideously wrong, I'm on the end of a phone for you."

I wish he hadn't said that, she thought. It's not going to go wrong. There's nothing to go wrong. It will be fine. Nonetheless she said, "I'll remember," just the same.

"Now, lecture over." Rob's tone brightened. "Let's decide what the girl's to wear! You'll need this." He reached for the Spunky dress. "Perfect for when you want to hang out in those SoHo coffee bars. You'd better take this," he picked out the Whistles suit, "because you never know when you might have to attend some smart business lunch, though I rather doubt he's gonna be parading you in front of his colleagues. Come to that, are you planning on doing some networking of your own while you're there?"

"I hadn't thought of that—it's a good idea. You never know who I might meet."

"And you'll need this, this, this, and this," Rob continued, rapidly selecting two floaty dresses, a knee-length lace skirt, a short suede mini, some faded jeans, half a dozen tops, and a couple of scarves, including her favorite black-and-red satin one. Finally, he darted off to his room, and returned, proudly brandishing a feather boa. "From day . . ." he said, campily wrapping it around his neck, " to evening!"

Chloë laughed.

"I'll leave you to sort out the most important thing in private." He turned to go.

"What's that?"

"Your underwear," he replied, and shut the door.

They had little chance to speak until they met at the airport, and they weren't able to chat much on the plane either, because James was traveling business class, which, when he came to book Chloë's ticket, was full. It was economy or nothing—naturally he'd opted for economy, but he'd said he was worried she'd think he was mean. Chloë couldn't care less: she was far too excited to have a single negative thought. And while it meant no canoodling during the flight, at least they could both get a little sleep.

"Chloë?"

She woke with a start. James had to stand in the aisle and lean over two other passengers to talk to her. "Ye-es," she said, gradually coming to.

"We're nearly there. The plane's in a holding pattern. Look."

Out of the window, she could see it.

Manhattan.

Teeny weenie from their height, nevertheless enormous compared to the panoramic urban sprawl and dense highways that surrounded it. There was the Empire State, the Chrysler Building, and now she could see Ellis Island, the Statue of Liberty . . . Configured from a thousand movies and TV shows, symbol of her passions and dreams, it was a familiar silhouette— Chloë's Oz. Yet even though the baby-pink clouds of sunset made it look more fairy tale than ever, it was somehow different from what she'd expected.

She prodded herself. Yes, that was why: because this *wasn't* a movie or a dream, it was real. Finally, at twenty-nine years of age, she was arriving in New York. Or rather, and better still, she was being taken to New York by a man who she fancied and liked more by the minute. She was so overwhelmed she thought she would burst.

No picture can do it justice, she observed, as the plane continued to descend. The reduced scale can't convey the magnitude of the place in 3-D. And that Manhattan is an island is somehow unexpected too. It seems larger as we're getting closer—and if the buildings seem big from this height, they must be *huge*! Coming into Heathrow compared to this, I mean *puh-lease*.

For a second, carried away by the view through the window, Chloë forgot James was still standing in the aisle. Yet she wanted to share how she was feeling, so struggled to put it into words. "It makes London look so wimpy," was all she could manage.

"Excuse me, sir," said the steward, tapping him on the shoulder, "could you return to your seat and fasten your seat belt for landing?"

What might have been the drag of immigration and customs was fun because at last they could be together. Then there was more mythology made real—the exhilaration of Chloë's first New York taxi ride.

"Can you open the trunk?" he asked the driver, immediately adapting his vocabulary to the environment. How worldly, thought Chloë. "Here's where we're going." He handed the driver the address, who nodded in response. From the outset James had refused to tell Chloë where they were staying. "I want to surprise you," he'd said.

Inside, an unsmiling passport-sized photograph of the driver, accompanied by his ID number, was taped crudely on the dirty glass partition in front of them; the seating was functional plastic. It was a far cry from the spacious luxury of a London cab, but Chloë loved that; it had the echo of De Niro danger that a black taxi never could.

As they sped along the freeway through suburban New Jersey, Chloë was struck by the sheer *otherness* of it all. Not only were they on the wrong side of the road surrounded by cars much wider and more angular than their rounded European counterparts, but the hoardings were bigger, brighter, brasher too. NEED THERAPY? screamed one in thirty-foot scarlet letters followed by a 1–800 number. Only in America, thought Chloë. Though the way I'm living at the moment, Rob would say I should give them a call.

They'd missed rush hour, so although the roads were busy with people coming into the city for the evening, they made it through the Lincoln Tunnel and up into Manhattan in little over half an hour.

James tapped the partition. "Could we make a detour via Sixth Avenue, please?" He turned to Chloë. "Then we can see a bit more before we get there."

"So where are we?" she asked, gazing in awe up, up at the buildings.

"Midtown. This is Forty-Second Street."

We're not *watching* a movie, thought Chloë, we're *in* a musical.

"Previously I've tended to stay downtown," James explained. "It's where Beth used to live so I know it better. It's more our scene really." *Our* scene. He'd said "our scene"! Linking them together, as an item, an "us" . . . "But I wanted to be well away from the rest of the UK Magazines crowd—far as I'm aware, they're all staying in SoHo. I've somewhere very special booked for us, plus it's nearer the conference venue, so we can spend more time just me and you."

She glanced over at him. Already he appears more relaxed, far freer than he is in London, she thought. Seeing him like this, I can picture him as a small boy—so eager and enthusiastic.

She pushed the down arrow to open the window. The warm wind in her hair was exhilarating and Chloë felt high.

The city even smells different from home, she realized. The combination of steam from the subway, the plethora of restaurants, and so many people tightly wedged together makes it sweeter, more intense. And the crossings really do have signs that say WALK/DON'T WALK, every building really does have a fire escape on the outside, vendors really do sell anything and everything on every corner, sirens really do scream all the time . . .

At that moment—oh wow! A razzle-dazzle of pulsating neon lights.

"Times Square!" Chloë grabbed James's arm as if he'd never seen it before.

He grinned, clearly enjoying her reaction.

Presently the taxi pulled up on Forty-sixth Street.

"We're here," he said and handed the driver his fare as Chloë got out.

On the sidewalk, Chloë scanned for a hotel sign, but there was nothing to indicate where they were; only a smart coffee shop to their right and a dark bar filled with hip-looking people sipping cocktails to their left.

Surely if we were somewhere that legendary it would be advertising its presence in giant letters and bright lights? she thought, deflated.

Yet James picked up both suitcases and swept through the doors with confidence. Chloë followed him.

"Oh," she said, once inside—she was so gobsmacked, it was all she could manage.

As a magazine journalist, Chloë had been to almost every landmark hotel London had to offer—launch party at the Dorchester, tea at the Ritz, drinks at Claridge's, and more—but this lobby was like nothing she'd seen before.

An architectural showpiece with the ambience of a nightclub, she needed several moments for her eyes to adjust to the dim lighting so she could take everything in. The checkered carpet resembled a giant chessboard on which a bizarre collection of seating had been assembled by a playful curator. Chairs upholstered in mixed materials and jewel colors jostled alongside rotund ethnic stools and comfortable colonial-style sofas, even a chaise longue. A stone staircase swept in a crescent down into the atrium; in the candlelight it appeared suspended in midair.

"Welcome to the Paramount," said James.

"Ah, of course." Chloë loved it: how could she ever have doubted him?

They lugged their cases over to reception, and James gave all his details to the nice-looking man behind the marble-topped counter. Then they took the elevator up to the fourth floor and made their way along the corridor, checking for their room number. Finally, James inserted the card into the lock and opened the door.

"Phew," he said, dropping the suitcases. "At bloody last."

The room was not huge—this is New York after all, thought Chloë, space is at a premium—but it was decorated in white throughout, which ensured the few features created real impact. There was an asymmetrically designed marble-topped desk and a huge double bed, and where one would expect the headboard to be, Vermeer's *The Lacemaker* stared knowingly out of the corner of her eye onto the covers, as if defying Chloë and James to shock her with their antics. The bathroom was similarly compact, but on the cone-shaped chrome sink with its swordlike point was a single bloodred rose, creating a distinct S & M air.

"Aaah!" said Chloë, flinging herself onto the bed. "Do you know what? My senses have gone into utter overload. For once, I'm not sure I'm up to a shag."

"Thank God for that." James laughed. "Because I'm not up for anything until I've had a nap."

"Hey, James," whispered Chloë the next morning, kissing the dip between his shoulder-blades. "This is your rude awakening . . ."

He rolled over to face her. For a moment he looked confused, then he seemed to realize where he was, and—unless she was mistaken—who *she* was.

"Hi." He smiled. They'd been curled up together throughout the night, although James had said that he wasn't normally comfortable sleeping spoons-style. But they had both been out for the count for hours, so Chloë concluded that he didn't seem to have a problem with this kind of closeness where she was concerned.

Nor did he seem to have a problem getting aroused, and they made love slowly and sensually, enjoying the luxury of it being their first morning together and not having to rush.

"That was lovely," sighed Chloë, when they'd finished. Maybe it's because I'm still getting to know him, she thought, but, I feel incredibly liberated sexually with James—and this is just the start of our stay.

As she got up he gave her bottom a mischievous smack. "Let's go paint this town red."

They made their way down for breakfast. Tables in alcoves overlooking the lobby allowed Chloë and James to watch as other guests headed off to work while they ate. Nonetheless the dimly lit dining area was disconcerting first thing in the morning, and tucking into coffee and croissants in a Gothic setting left Chloë even more confused about the time difference than she already was. The choice of food was lavish—everything was topped with a single strawberry: the yogurts, the fruit cocktails, the grapefruit halves, the pastries . . . It was such a heady concoction that Chloë felt quite intoxicated before they'd even left the building.

First stop was the pier at West Forty-second Street to catch a boat tour around Manhattan.

"The Circle Line is the one touristy thing we're going to do," said James. "It will help you get your bearings, so when you're on your own in the city you'll know where you are."

It was a warm, crisp day with clear blue skies and a light breeze. Inevitably, the boat was full of tourists, but to Chloë's surprise, many New Yorkers too. They sat out on the deck as the boat circumnavigated the island, down the Hudson River, past the West Village and Tribeca to the Financial District. They passed Ground Zero and the constructions being erected where the World Trade once was, and Chloe sensed a shiver go up her spine. They went around the Statue of Liberty and back to Battery Park City, then up the East River and under the bridges—Brooklyn, Manhattan, and Williamsburg. Chloë took photos of them all. They glimpsed millionaires' mansions with vast gardens leading down to the water and poor tenement blocks; the dominating presence of the United Nations alongside the Chrysler building glinting in the sun; even a prison and a monastery, and throughout were kept amused by the anecdotes of a very ironic guide.

"So that's why the natives do it," she said to James when the boat docked three hours later. "It was the best touristy thing I've ever done. Though I'd like to persuade you to make one more exception to your rule—it's only a few blocks from our hotel according to this map . . ."

And so they went up the Empire State. At 102 floors up, Manhattan stretched out on all sides below; now Chloë could see the rectangle of Central Park, the gridded regularity of the streets, the varying heights, shapes, and architectural styles of the buildings. Momentarily she felt as if she could reach for the skies, achieve anything, be anyone she wanted to be.

But back at the hotel the receptionist brought them down to earth with a bump. "You had a message while you were out," he said, handing over a slip of paper.

James unfolded it and paled. "Shit! Maggie!" he said. "I never phoned her to say I'd arrived safely." He glanced nervously at Chloë. The receptionist looked away—doubtless he'd seen worse indiscretions.

"Why don't I stay down here and you give her a call from the room?" she offered.

"Thanks," said James. He charged off in the direction of the elevator, leaving Chloë unsure what to do with herself. In the end she made her way up the floating staircase to the bar and ordered a double espresso. Then she took a seat overlooking reception as they had at breakfast, and tried not to think about James sitting on their bed talking to his wife, and to focus instead on the people coming and going below.

Exotic beauties with pierced and bejeweled rock-star boyfriends, businessmen who could be Mafiosi, two apparently gay men with a newborn baby—what an unlikely mix they were! Yet try as she might, Chloë couldn't help wondering what James was saying to Maggie on the phone upstairs.

The fact he's too wrapped up in being here to have remembered to call is a reflection of the amazing trip we're having, she decided, pleased to have made such an impact. Yet at the same time her heart went out to Maggie. I bet she was worried, she thought. I'm sure I would have been. And all the while her husband is not only safe and well, he's having a ball with me. If he'd promised to phone at the first opportunity, he should have done so before we went out this morning. Then again, she reasoned, he's very successful; Maggie must be used to him spending time away from home. Didn't James say she was capable and efficient? Doubtless she's good at dealing with his foibles and takes it all in her stride.

Chloë was torn by conflicting emotions. And as she finished her coffee and got to her feet, a voice inside her cried out in frustration, "Oh, why, in God's name, does he have to be married?"

17

Maggie edged her way in through the kitchen door laden with four Waitrose carrier bags, followed by Nathan, dutifully carrying the fifth. She looked over to the answering machine and frowned; the light wasn't flashing. She dumped the bags on the table, picked up the phone, and dialled 1471. The computerized voice gave Fran's number from earlier that day. Maggie checked her watch. It would be past midday in New York.

Even allowing for jet lag, I'd have expected Jamie to have called by now, she thought. I told him not to bother when he arrived as I'd be fast asleep, but to call when he woke up instead. Maybe he's having a lie-in. We so rarely get one. She resolved to ring him later and began to unpack the food.

"Can I have one?" asked Nathan, grabbing a packet of Wagon Wheels Maggie had bought him in a moment of weakness.

"Yes, but first help me put everything away."

By seven thirty Jamie still hadn't been in touch. Once she'd put

Nathan to bed, Maggie rang his mobile. It went straight to voice mail, so she tried the hotel.

"I'll try the room for you, ma'am," said the switchboard operator.

Maggie listened to the extension ring and ring.

"I'm afraid there's no reply, ma'am," said the operator eventually. "Would you like me to pass on a message?"

"Yes, please. Could you tell Mr. Slater that his wife, Maggie, called?"

Maggie was curled up on the sofa watching TV when the phone's ringing made her jump.

"Hi, Maggie."

"Jamie!"

"I'm sorry I didn't phone you earlier."

"I was so worried. I know it's silly, but you'd promised to call."

"I know, I know, I'm really sorry. I guess I completely forgot, what with jet lag and stuff."

Maggie was hurt, but didn't want to nag. "How was your flight?"

"Oh, fine," he said. He sounded very far away. "The usual, you know. All that drag of getting through customs and immigration—it seems to take longer each time. I didn't get in till very late."

"Mm," said Maggie. Before Nathan had been born she and Jamie had been to New York together. He'd said he loved it, and although initially she had been uncomfortable because she associated it with an ex of his who lived there, the more time she'd spent in the city the more it appealed—the amazing art galleries, the unparalleled choice of restaurants, the value-for-money designer clothes. Back then there had been an antiestablishment vibe to the Village around NYU and Christopher Street which struck a chord with her, reminding her of the way she'd been as a student.

Nevertheless, she thought, if I'd gone this time with Jamie I wouldn't have had much chance to explore. Doubtless I'd have been roped into socializing as "the wife of the publisher." She shuddered; it was her idea of hell. No, best leave Jamie to it, she concluded, he's much better at schmoozing than I am. And Nathan needs me here, after all.

"What have you done today?" she asked, tucking her feet under a cushion on the settee in readiness for a chat. She was so glad to hear from him that their recent argument seemed light years ago.

"Oh, nothing much." A pause.

"You must have done *something*—you were out of your room all afternoon."

"I, er, went to Bloomingdale's."

Great! thought Maggie. Perhaps he's bought me a present. "Did you get anything?"

"Um, yes." He sounded evasive. Maybe he had! "Something for Nathan."

"What?"

"Wait and see. It'll be a surprise."

"You don't need to surprise me if it's for Nathan. Tell me, what is it?"

"It's hard to explain. It's the latest American gadget. You'll have to see for yourself."

"I'm fascinated." What could it be? "Did you get anything for me?"

"Yeah, a little something. That will have to be a surprise too."

"How exciting!" exclaimed Maggie. "You are a lovely man!"

"Thanks." Jamie sounded ill at ease. Then again, thought Maggie, he's always been bad at receiving compliments.

18

Chloë listened at the door. It seemed as if James had finished on the phone. She knocked lightly and went in. He was sitting on the bed, his head in his hands.

"James?" she said softly.

He glanced up. She could swear he had tears in his eyes.

"Are you okay?"

"Mm." He didn't sound it.

She sat down next to him on the white bedspread. The weight of the two of them propelled her closer. She took his hand.

James sighed unsteadily. "I feel like such a prick," he whispered.

It was a tone she'd not heard before. Oh dear, she worried, here we go. He's going to get cold feet. Regret the whole thing. Finish with me. And we've only been in New York a day! The prospect of rejection was more than she could bear.

He looked at her. "I'm sorry," he said. She'd never seen him so sad.

They were silent.

After a while she said, "It's Maggie?" trying to control her voice.
James nodded. "Kind of."

"Tell me." Chloë wasn't sure she wanted to know, but they were in too deep now.

"And Nathan . . ." James put his hand to his mouth as if he could hardly bear to say what he was saying. "Oh, Chloë!" He gasped. Then he squeezed her hand hard, as if to establish that she was definitely there.

Chloë was caught in a maelstrom of emotions. Part of her wanted to end this conversation right now, to move on to something lighter, less serious. They'd been having such fun, and she didn't want it to end. Part of her wanted to make him feel better, to take his pain away, no matter what it cost her. And part of her wanted to run as fast as she could back to England, to Rob, her apartment, her friends, Patsy, her job, before she also got hurt.

Instead she sat there, saying nothing, paralyzed.

"I don't know what to do," he said, after a while.

Chloë stroked his hand. "You don't have to do anything."

"Honestly?" He stared up and into her eyes. He appeared lost, vulnerable, like a small boy.

Lord, thought Chloë, feelings veering wildly. I don't want to lose him, or to curtail the time we're sharing. Perhaps I am falling for him, after all. "No." She wanted to reassure him. "You don't."

James sighed again, but this time he sounded a little relieved.

"You're quite a woman." He smiled in acknowledgement.

"Thank you." Chloë smiled wanly. "I try." She had a mad, impulsive desire to tell him she loved him.

"I don't want you to get hurt."

She pushed away the thought of potential pain. "I won't."

He started fidgeting with the bedcovers, pulling at a loose thread. Then he took a deep breath, "It's just . . . I have a son . . ."

"I know," said Chloë, the full force of his words hitting her like a truck at ninety miles per hour. "I'm not asking you to leave him."

"I know . . . I know . . ."

Chloë's thoughts rushed back to that conversation she'd had with Craig, the journalist, a few weeks ago about the damaging effects of divorce. She felt a sudden jolt of identification with Nathan, remembering how she had once been helpless in the face of her parents' preoccupation with their own affairs. Incapable of making her mum and dad behave any differently, incapable of understanding them.

"I don't expect you to leave them," she murmured. She sensed her eyes fill with tears. Before she could stop them, they were coursing down her cheeks.

"Oh, Chloë," he said again, and kissed her.

It was the only thing that could possibly, possibly make her feel better, so she kissed him back, blotting out the sorrow and the confusion.

"I'm so sorry," he said, brushing away her fringe so he could look into her face.

"Me too." She sniffed. And they kissed some more, falling backward onto the bed. She giggled through her tears. "I guess we're both just being a bit overemotional . . ."

". . . and jet-lagged . . ."

". . . and jet-lagged . . ."

James began to kiss her again, more passionately, as if he couldn't bear for them to be apart. Then Chloë was swept up, up, and once more the future and the past didn't matter—neither did she, Nathan, Maggie, or anything, other than being on the bed, in the Paramount, in New York, at that moment. And as they made love she thought of the view from the Empire State of the huge, huge city and the tiny, tiny people, all in their apartments, with their own lives to live and their own paths to tread. And she thought that she and James were just two ants in the whole scheme of things, and that the world would keep on turning regardless, and that she was powerless to stop herself, and what would be would be. Then, as she felt him move inside her, she started to come, softly, gently at first, then on and on, as if it was never going to end.

19

The next day Maggie dropped off Nathan at Fran's to play with Dan, and caught the train into London to meet Jean at the Tate Gallery. True to form, Jean was already waiting on the steps of the museum overlooking the Thames when Maggie arrived.

"Well." Jean lifted her sunglasses to air-kiss Maggie's cheeks. "How are you?"

"I'm fine," replied Maggie, as they entered the foyer and headed for the ticket counter.

"Are you sure? Jamie was a bit of an arsehole when we all came to supper."

Gosh, Jean doesn't pull her punches, thought Maggie. That was weeks ago. "Oh, we're over that now," she said, joining the line. "I spoke to him last night and he's already bought me a present in New York."

"How sweet. So . . ." Jean nudged her in the ribs. "Been having lots of hanky-panky to conceive a sibling for Nathan, have we? I've noticed Jamie's been looking pretty good recently. Glowing, I'd say. And I thought it was only women who so clearly betrayed when they were getting some action."

"Oh, er, yes." Maggie was too embarrassed to contradict her. *Though Jamie doesn't look any different to me,* she thought. *If anything, he seems more exhausted. Maybe he's putting on a front at work—it being a new job—driving his energy into impressing his colleagues.*

"Ooh, I *shall* enjoy teasing him at the conference later this week," Jean plowed on. "Meanwhile, I await the happy news. Remember, this time *I* want to be godmother!"

"Of course. I wouldn't dream of asking anyone else."

As they wandered around the exhibition, Maggie found herself unexpectedly moved by the paintings. Alex had always said she looked like a fair-haired, prettier version of Virginia Woolf, and there was one striking portrait of her sister, Vanessa Bell, by Duncan Grant where she appeared both stoic and vulnerable. It was accompanied by a quote from Virginia: "A spirit given to contemplation and self control. Decision and composure stamped her."

Jean came up beside her. "Vanessa reminds me of you in that," she said.

Maggie moved on to a series of male nudes by Duncan Grant.

To think he and Vanessa were lovers, she pondered. *Yet the passionate strokes of paint over the muscular forms suggest he was far more interested in men than women. His bisexuality can't have been easy to bear; I get the sense she always seemed to be yearning for him, even when she was married to Clive Bell . . .*

What a weird triangle that must have been to be part of—Vanessa, Duncan, Clive—with Vanessa having children by both of them . . . Apparently Vanessa and Duncan's daughter wasn't told who her real father was until she was eighteen. God, that Bloomsbury bunch got themselves into terrible muddles; their relationships often seemed built on such shaky foundations. They might have produced great art, but at what cost to their children?

Maggie stood in front of a self-portrait of Duncan Grant as a young man and looked deep into his eyes.

The self-love is evident, she observed. What did Vanessa see in him? How on earth did she put up with living in such close proximity to him throughout his various liaisons? Perhaps she excused it as they were with men and she was married. Though it must have hurt all the same . . . And he wasn't even that good-looking, thought Maggie indignantly. If Jamie manages to be faithful, and he's much more attractive—why couldn't Duncan be—if not to Vanessa, then at least to one man?

As she turned to the next series of sketches, Maggie caught her breath. A man was standing with his back to her, examining a landscape. The way he was holding his head, coupled with the line of his shoulders, was Jamie to a T. A woman came up beside him and he placed a hand on her bottom in a manner that was both intimate and confident.

Now *there's* a hot-blooded heterosexual male, she decided. She moved to get a glimpse of his face. He's remarkably handsome. Even if this woman is his wife, lots of other women must throw themselves at him . . .

In a flash, she recalled Jean's words that Jamie had been "glowing." But he's not been sleeping with me, has he? she thought, as a wave of nausea overtook her. And while I'm sure he wouldn't sleep with men . . . Oh, Christ—could Jamie be sleeping with another woman?

Maggie went hot and cold, started to shake. All at once the portraits seemed to be crashing in on her.

She looked around desperately for Jean, who was standing a little way off. She went up and grabbed her friend's arm. "Jean, you don't think Jamie's having an affair, do you?"

"Goodness!" Jean started. "It's powerful stuff—this exhibition's really getting to you, isn't it?"

Perhaps I'm being silly, Maggie told herself. Still, she was too rocked to reply.

"Why on earth would you think that?"

"Oh, I don't know." Maggie couldn't face putting it into words; saying it might make it real.

"Don't be ridiculous!" cried Jean, causing a few people to turn around. Then she added more quietly, "You were only just telling me that things between you are fine. This lot were far more experimental in their sexuality than most, I assure you." She gave her friend's shoulders a comforting squeeze. "Sometimes you worry too much, Maggie darling."

"Mm . . ." Maggie's panic subsided. She was probably imagining things. "Perhaps I spend too much time on my own."

"I'm sure that's what it is. I know Jamie adores you—and Nathan." Jean laughed. "And I'll tell you one thing, if he ever messes around on you he'll have me to answer to!"

Maggie was cheered. If there was one person she could rely on to poke fun at her, it was Jean.

"If it will make you feel better, I'll have a word with him. I'm flying out tomorrow for the editorial presentations, and we'll be in the same venue for much of the week."

Maggie hesitated. Jamie would be furious if he found out they'd been talking about him. "Don't tell him I was worried."

"I won't. I'll simply hint that he's so wrapped up in his work that he might be forgetting to pay you enough attention, that's all."

"OK." Maggie was apprehensive. "Only if it comes up without looking forced. Be subtle, won't you?"

"Leave it to me." Jean winked conspiratorially. "Now then, my dear, I suggest we give this last room a miss. What we need is a cup of tea and a *huge* slice of cake."

20

"I'm going to skip the conference this afternoon," said James as he was getting dressed on Tuesday morning. "I want to go to Bloomingdale's."

"Fab!" Chloë kissed him. "I haven't been yet. Shall I meet you there?"

"If you like." James hesitated. "I was going to get something for Nathan."

"Oh." Not for the first time in the last couple of days, Chloë was unsure what to say. Should I help him choose? she wondered. No, that would be interfering. But I do *so* want to go to Bloomingdale's, I've hardly done any shopping. So she said, "Perhaps we can meet after you've bought something," and they arranged to rendezvous at the MAC beauty counter on the ground floor at three.

Once he'd gone, Chloë had a burst of loneliness. Mention of Nathan concerned her, and she was yearning to speak to Rob, yet calling the UK was exorbitant at this time of day. Instead she would have to make do with instant messenger on her mobile—she could use the wireless connection at the hotel, and had already updated him this way on Saturday.

Cooey Rob! she tapped. You there? No reply. Chloë continued anyway. So, update 2 from the Big A . . . Followed your recommendation on Sunday morning and went for a walk around Central Park. Saw something that would have cracked you up—a mother-and-stroller exercise class.

Just then: I'm here, I'm here! from Rob.

Yay! from Chloë.

Describe!

OK, well, on the edge of the track by the reservoir there were a group of women, complete with pushchairs and offspring, doing a slow stretch-and-tone class.

Ballet with babies?

Sort of. The instructor was fearsome.

Bizarre! Maybe I should add it to my personal training repertoire. So what else have you been up to?

Best be careful how much I reveal about James, thought Chloë. Although she'd have liked some input into how things were evolving, she couldn't face another lecture.

Sunday afternoon, Metropolitan Museum, she tapped. There's something about art galleries on a Sunday that feels so right.

If you say, Rob responded.

I do! tapped Chloë. And it felt especially right with James, she thought, recalling how they'd wandered around together, discussing their likes and dislikes and pointing out their particular favorites. Sometimes they'd agreed, sometimes disagreed vociferously, and it was stimulating arguing with someone whose opinions were as strong as her own. But Rob wasn't into art like she was, so she carried on. In the evening we went to that restaurant you recommended in the meatpacking district. And I saw a transvestite hooker on the corner!

No way, replied Rob.

Chloë went on to describe the meal in detail, omitting how she and James had talked of their pasts—childhood memories, school successes and failings, first relationships, their siblings and parents. They'd spoken about the first time they'd smoked pot, and discovered a shared appetite for champagne and—very occasionally, as a wicked treat—cocaine. And finally, freed by being a long way from anyone who might know them, they'd exchanged saucy tales of their fantasies in hushed whispers.

It was one of the most romantic days of my life, thought Chloë. If James wasn't married, I would have believed I'd died and gone to heaven . . .

Monday, she continued to Rob, James was at the conference, so I went to the Tenement Museum.

Eh?

It's on the Lower East Side—ever so interesting—shows you how tough the living conditions were for immigrant workers.

Bit chastening then?

Yes, though I made up for it by having lunch in Battery Park and eyeing up the wealthy bankers! She joked, not wanting Rob to think she only had eyes for James—although, increasingly, she did. By the end of the day I was in love with New York.

Long as that's all you're in love with, he replied.

It seemed there was no deceiving Rob, however hard Chloë tried.

Two thirty p.m., and after testing a dozen different perfumes and concluding that she didn't like any of them as much as the one she wore, Chloë located the MAC counter. She still had half an hour before she was due to meet James, but luckily the thickly powdered beautician was free to give her a makeover. She stripped Chloë's face of its usual makeup and clipped her hair back in order to transform her attractive yet far from supermodel features.

And that is exactly where Chloë was—one eye half made up, the other bare—when there was a screech from across the counter, a screech that made her blood run cold.

"Chloë! It can't be! *Chloë!* Is that you?" Out of one eye—she couldn't move her face—Chloë verified that the voice matched the person she feared it did.

Jean.

Oh, fuck. Fuck. *Fuck!*

Now Jean was at her shoulder. After years of working together, she'd recognize Chloë anywhere.

"Hi," said Chloë weakly, the powdered beautician still determinedly dabbing at her eyelid.

"Have you come to the conference?" asked Jean.

Chloë had to think at supersonic speed. "Er, no . . ."

"Gosh, really? How strange. Well, what a coincidence!"

"I'm on vacation. If you remember, I had to use it up before starting work with Vanessa." When lying, stick as close to the truth as possible, she'd always been told. And deflect: "How about you?"

"I'm here for the conference, of course. You should know that!"

If she thought about it Chloë did, but she was playing for time.

"So," continued Jean, "where are you staying?"

"With some friends in the Village." Chloe spoke as best she could with her jaw wide open as the beautician lip-lined her mouth. God, being made up by this woman and grilled by her ex-boss—what a torturous combination. "How about you?" Oh, please, please, not the Paramount.

"The Algonquin. I know it's not trendy like some of the others but I love it there. I can kid myself I'm almost literary."

Phew, thought Chloë. Maybe this wasn't so bad. But—oh, heavens— James! James was meeting her here! If she squinted sideways she could just see her watch: 2:55. She had five minutes to get rid of Jean, at most.

Yet Jean seemed to have no desire to go. "So, if you're here anyway," Jean continued, in her most I-mean-business voice, "you should come to the conference, Chloë. Or at least tomorrow. They're talking about special projects, I believe. I'll arrange for you to attend. Call me in the morning at the Algonquin before nine and we can meet up and go together."

Aargh! Worse and worse! "That would be great." Chloë opened her eyes extra wide in horror. The powdered beauty misread the signal, and leaped to attack her with another layer of mascara.

"Afterward, if you like, we could go out for supper."

No, no, no! thought Chloë. James and I have only got a few nights left. "I'm afraid I've arranged to meet my friends," she said. Then, in case

Jean decided to invite herself to join them, added, "They've booked at Nobu for a birthday bash." She plucked a well-known restaurant from the air.

"Really?" Jean was evidently impressed. "I gather you have to reserve a table weeks in advance."

"That's right," said Chloë, thinking, exactly—there's no way you can gate-crash.

"What a hip crowd you must know here."

"Oh, I do," said Chloë. In for a penny. "My friend Matt is a playwright. Lives in the East Village."

"Is that where you're staying?"

"Um, yes."

"Where, exactly?"

Addresses! "It's on Spring Street," she fabricated.

"Gosh, how *trendy*," said Jean. "Though I'd call that SoHo."

"SoHo, East Village, NoHo . . . it's all the same," laughed Chloë, desperately. "Eh?"

"If you say so."

At that moment, just when she thought she was winning, Chloë saw James weaving his way through Lancôme, Chanel, Bobbi Brown . . . And as Jean had her back to him, he was bound not to realize who she was talking to . . .

Drastic action was called for.

There, on the side, was a huge bottle of eye-makeup remover. Hideously oily, but . . . "Oh, my God, *Jean!*" Chloë shrieked theatrically as she sent the bottle flying. The liquid spilled all over Jean's designer suit. Then again, to make doubly sure everyone in the vicinity heard the ruckus, "*Jean!* I am so sorry!"

James was almost upon them, only ten feet away, armed with a Bloomingdale's bag signifying success on the Nathan front. Jean was bent over frantically sponging her jacket with some tissues. The powdered beauty was mopping the counter—it needed one more shriek.

"Oh, JEAN, how can I make it up to you?"

And—thank *God*—all at once James seemed to realize what the commotion was about. Chloë saw him dart behind a pillar, just before Jean stood upright again, and flee as fast as he could (without running), through Christian Dior and Trish McEvoy, past women's belts and gloves, and out of the nearest door onto Lexington Avenue.

Half an hour later Chloë was back at the Paramount. Believing James would have returned immediately too, she was surprised and disappointed not to find him there. She was still shaken, so she sat on the bed and tried to calm down.

That was pretty nifty footwork, she congratulated herself. Nonetheless, she was lumbered with going to the conference—probably not only tomorrow but on Thursday as well. And while Chloë was passionate about magazines and her job, experience of such events had taught her one normally had to sit through hours of mind-numbing facts, figures, and forecasts to obtain a morsel of interesting information.

I'd far rather be exploring New York, she thought huffily. Surely that's a more useful way for an up-and-coming magazine editor to spend her time? And James will be at the conference, so I'll have to fake not knowing him that well, and there's even a possibility Vanessa will be there—how *stupid* of me not to have realized this was where she might be going too—and God knows who else besides . . .

As minutes ticked by and there was still no sign of James, she grew increasingly pissed off. Why hadn't he hurried back at once to sing her praises for being so quick-thinking and avoiding a nightmare situation?

About an hour later, James returned.

"Where have you been? I was worried."

"Sorry. I had some other things to get." He plonked several carrier bags on the bed.

"Wasn't that awful? Imagine if she'd seen you!"

"It doesn't bear thinking about." James shook his head. "And Jean of all people. My God! She's Maggie's best friend!" He looked as traumatized as Chloë felt.

Chloë, though she knew it was unreasonable, was hurt. I suspected it—now I know: James is ashamed of our affair, of me, she concluded. Immediately, she pushed the observation aside. "And I've got to come to the bloody conference—Jean's arranging for me to attend. She'll see me as lacking dedication to my job if I don't go."

"Maybe it'll be useful," he said with equanimity. "You could find out some stuff for your magazine."

"Pah!"

"Well, there are a lot of interesting developments in the American market. It might not be such a bad idea to learn more."

"I suppose." This was not what Chloë wished to hear. She wanted him to be grateful to her, while instead he was coming over pragmatic and professional. "So." She changed the subject—her usual ploy when things got sticky. "What did you get? Anything for me?"

"Er, no," said James. "I had to buy some stuff for Nathan . . ." Then he added, as if being honest would alleviate his guilt, ". . . and I thought I ought to get something for Maggie."

"Oh." This upset Chloë further. Clearly it was Maggie who had been foremost in his thoughts over the last hour, not her. Nonetheless, punishing herself, she had to find out more; she wanted a better idea of the woman. "Can I see?"

James looked surprised. "Suppose so, if you want."

She emptied the bags onto the bed. For Nathan he'd gotten an American football shirt and some computer games, and for Maggie—Chloë unfolded several layers of tissue, shook out the contents, and gasped. He'd bought a beautiful hand-printed silk chiffon scarf. In soft shades of blue and gray and pink, it was very, very elegant, the kind of thing Chloë would never wear. She checked the label. Fendi. It must have cost a bundle. "God. It's lovely." She tried not to sound bothered.

James obviously picked up her vibes. "I was going to get you something," he said, ruffling her hair. Chloë flinched—for a second she imagined him ruffling Maggie's hair in the same way and despised him. "Which I need to meet someone for." He looked at his watch. "In fact, I've got to go to meet them pretty much now."

"Oh. Right." Chloë couldn't keep the sarcasm out of her voice. He's lying, he's trying to dig himself out of a hole, she thought. I can see through it. "I can't believe you're going out again," she said.

James had already risen to his feet and picked up his wallet. "I won't be long," he promised, and left before she could protest, banging the door behind him.

21

While James was gone, Chloë got herself into something of a state.

It was our first row, or nearly, she worried, biting at her nails. Was I too stroppy? Although surely I've some right to be demanding.

She started writing a postcard to Sam to distract herself but gave up after one line. She hadn't even told him she was seeing a married man, let alone in New York. Brotherly concern might lead to disapproval of her behavior, and that was the last thing she wanted. Enough's enough, she decided, I *have* to talk to Rob. At least now it's evening in the UK and he might be home.

"Oh, I'm so glad you're there!" she said, when he picked up.

"What do you want now?" he teased her. "More showing off about what a fantastic trip you're having? I don't know if I want to hear!"

"No. Do you mind calling me back? It'll be cheaper that way. I could do with your take on today." He did as requested, and this time Chloë held back less on her feelings—there seemed little point when Rob could read her regardless—and it was such a relief to talk instead of texting. So she filled him in on the phone call to Maggie and James's upset. Then she told him about the encounter with Jean—which, to her irritation, Rob found funny—and finally details of the near-argument.

"Hmm," said Rob, when she'd finished. "Well, honey, what did you expect?"

"I don't know!" wailed Chloë.

"I did warn you . . ."

"Yes."

"And I could tell you were falling for him, whatever you said. So, let's have a moment's pause here."

"Okay."

"I want you to be honest."

"I will be."

"Question one. Do you love him?"

"I think so."

"Oh dear. I *knew* as much. Question two. Have you told him?"

"No."

"Good. Question three. Has he told you?"

"No."

"Fine. Question four. Have you asked him to leave his wife yet?"

"No."

"I give you till Friday."

"Rob! I won't! You told me not to!"

"Chloë. Darling. When have you ever listened to me?"

"Er . . ." Chloë racked her brain. "I ditched Bob Andrews 'cause you said to."

"I'm flattered you see it that way, but far as I recall, you ditched boring Bob 'cause he wasn't bright enough for you. It's just I was the only one honest enough to tell you so."

"Okay . . . But, anyway, I promise I won't ask him to leave Maggie. He's got a son—I couldn't do that to him."

"Couldn't do it to who? James or his son?"

"His son, Nathan."

"*Now* you say so."

That observation pained her.

"Look," said Rob, "you know what I think."

"What?" Chloë supposed he might as well tell her it like it was. This was why she'd called him, after all.

"I think he sounds great, to be honest," Rob continued, obviously keen to express his take on the matter at last, "absolutely right for you in many, many ways. He's successful, he's bright, he's funny; you like the same kind of things. He says he doesn't make a habit of affairs, which—if you believe it—means he could be serious. And from what I glimpsed of him from behind my net curtains that time—" Rob had sneaked a look a couple of weeks previously when James had been leaving "—I've got to concede he's pretty damn gorgeous. Infinitely shaggable, I'd say."

Chloë purred.

"But," he added, "you silly, silly girl, the man is married!"

"I know," said Chloë, in a small voice. "I couldn't seem to stop myself."

"You're too much of an adrenaline junkie for your own good," said Rob. "And if anyone knows, I should. It's only I don't want you to get hurt."

Ouch. That again.

"And from my experience—which admittedly isn't quite the same—if a man is married, especially if he has a child, the commitment runs much deeper than might seem to be the case."

"I realize that."

"Has he ever, for instance, told you he doesn't love his wife anymore?"

"Um, no, not exactly . . ."

"Well, then, I'm sorry to say that my guess is he does."

"Oh." Chloë hadn't fully faced this idea. James's behavior had seemed to suggest otherwise, yet it was true he'd never said he didn't love Maggie. He might even have said the opposite on that first night in Soho, but Chloë had ignored it.

"Which means one of three things. Either he's going to string you both along until he sorts his head out—in which case he may finally decide to leave her for you but it could take a long time, trust me. Or he's going to leave her eventually, but you'll end up being the relationship that instigates that, not the one he ends up in. Or he'll stay with her because he loves her and because of Nathan."

Chloë felt her hopes being swept away by a hurricane. "So what do you suggest I do?"

"Quite frankly, my dear, I think you should go to the conference, glean all you can about magazines, shag him senseless till Saturday, then quit while you're ahead."

"You mean finish it? I can't do that."

"I know you can't. If it's any consolation, I'm not sure I'd be able to either."

"What then?"

"Prepare to ride it, my girl. Like a wild stallion. See where it takes you. Though you're gonna have to hold on tight. This is by no means the worst it could get. You'll know when you've had enough, I promise."

"Okay . . ." said Chloë, gradually acknowledging this was what she had been unconsciously prepared to do all along.

At that moment there was a soft knock at the door, and James breezed in, looking surprisingly pleased with himself. Chloë pulled herself together and sat up. "Rob," she said quickly, "got to go."

"Is he back?"

"Yes."

"Did he get you a present?"

"I've no idea."

"Ask him—I wanna know!"

"Okay." She put her hand over the receiver and looked up at James. "Did you get me a present?"

"Yes." James grinned. First he handed her an Astor Wines and Spirits carrier bag. Inside was a bottle of Bollinger champagne. "I had to go to the East Village."

"Oooh," she said appreciatively.

Then, from his pocket, he pulled out a tiny, carefully folded packet of paper.

"Oh, my God!" said Chloë. "You didn't!"

"I did."

She opened it. From its glistening white color and lumpiness it appeared to be very high quality.

Cocaine.

Chloë was a hedonist, but nonetheless she and James decided to hold off on doing a line until after dinner—the coke would curb their appetites, and they didn't want to miss the chance to try another New York eatery. James said he'd spotted an interesting place on First Avenue when he'd been in the East Village. "Looked like we could eat upstairs, then dance downstairs later," he said, and Chloë agreed it sounded fun.

The moment they'd finished their main course, she wrinkled her nose excitedly. "Go on, give it to me, then."

Quickly he handed her the packet under the table. Holding it tightly lest anyone see, she got up and made her way to the restroom. She had to wait for two women to go before her (they went in together—a giveaway they were doing drugs) before a cubicle was free. Inside, she double-checked the door was locked properly and opened the wrapper. The coke would need chopping first, but she'd done this before—not often, yet enough to know what she was doing. She took out a credit card, thinking how decadent this all was, shook some of the powder onto the top of the toilet cistern, and broke up the lumps. Then she racked out a line—long, thin, elegant, the promise of pleasure to come. She rolled up a twenty-dollar bill (*dollars*, how wild!) and sniffed half up one nostril, half up the other, flushing the lavatory simultaneously so no one would hear.

Ooh, yum. She could taste it as she swallowed. She licked her index finger and picked up the remainder from the cistern to rub on her teeth, vaguely conscious of the lack of hygiene. No point worrying about that, she decided, soon I'm going to be high on Class As. What are a few germs in comparison?

Back at the table, she handed the packet to James, who left to follow suit.

While he was gone, she appraised the other diners. An offbeat, creative-looking ensemble, were they writers or poets, musicians or painters, she wondered. Presently—whoa! There was a delectable whoosh as the chemical hit her brain. She had the same feeling she'd experienced at the top of the Empire State—an exhilarating combination of powerlessness and omnipotence. It was as if because she was just one small person on a very huge planet she could do anything, behave however the hell she liked.

When James got back, he sat down, looked across at her, and asked, "Don't you sometimes feel that what counts is the good time, the experience, the sensation?"

"Yup, I do."

"You make me feel like that a lot." He grinned.

"It's mutual." She grinned back.

"It's kind of dangerous . . ."

"That too," she nodded, "but so irresistible."

"Totally." He laughed, wickedly. "We're probably very bad for each other."

"Without doubt." The coke gave her the guts to be more provocative. "Do you think I'm worse for you than Maggie?"

"Yeah."

"Really?"

"For sure. She'd never do anything like this. She doesn't even know I still do."

"Do you? How often?"

"Oh, I've only done it a few times since we've been married. But I did it at that conference I told you about."

"The one where you met the Spanish girl?"

"Yes. And at a couple of parties we've been at. Actually," he paused, "I shared a packet with Jean once."

"You didn't!"

"I did, one New Year. It was a little treat I got for us both. Not that you'd know with Jean—she's so hyper she hardly needs it, but she likes it very occasionally."

"I'm surprised." Perhaps there was more to Jean than Chloë realized. And perhaps, given Jean was Maggie's best friend, there was more to Maggie too. "So how come Maggie's not into it?"

"Oh, I don't know, it's not really her scene. She's quite clean-living, really. Likes to look after herself. She eats well, exercises a lot. I guess . . ." He paused, searching for the right words. ". . . she likes to be in control of things."

"She doesn't seem to be very in control of you."

Again James stopped to consider. "No, I suppose not—at the moment."

"You mean she has been?"

"I suppose, in many ways, yes. Not in a bad way . . . it's just she's provided me with some stability, some roots. She's kind of looked after me— I feel safe with her. If I'm being honest, I'd have to admit I wouldn't be where I am now professionally without her support."

"I see," said Chloë. "Do you feel safe with me?"

"No. That's what I love about being with you."

The coke had numbed Chloë's brain a little: at this point his admissions were fascinating rather than painful. "So," she said blithely, "do you think you'll stay together?"

James looked at her. For too long, just as he had all those weeks ago at Louisa's restaurant. There, along with the difficulty of the question, was that same, unstoppable desire. Only now it had more meaning. And danger.

"Chloë, I don't know. I truly don't know. If someone had asked me six months ago, I'd have thought they were mad. Wild horses wouldn't drag me from her. But now . . . I've met you . . ."

"Do you still love her?" My God! She'd asked it!

"Yes, I do."

Even through the coke, that didn't feel so good. "Are you still *in* love with her?"

"No, not after ten years or however long it's been, not in the way you mean."

Go on, Chloë, ask, ask! "Are you in love with me?"

Again he looked at her. "Boy! You're not mincing your words tonight, are you?"

"No." Chloë felt empowered.

"Okay, okay. Yes."

She sat back, vindicated, thrilled. There. It had been said. There was no going back. "Good."

"Good? Is that all you can say? Good?" His eyes were wide.

"Yup."

"So, you pick up my heart, string it out to dry, fuck with my life, do my head in, totally confuse me about my relationship with my wife, let alone my child, and you say it's *good*?"

"Don't be so stupid!" Now she held his gaze. He was making it sound like she'd done it deliberately. "I don't mean it's good for all those reasons. Do you think I feel happy about that? Jesus, James, I might be wicked from time to time, but I'm not a complete cow. No, I mean it's good because I feel the same way."

"Oh," he said, laughing at himself. "I see."

"So, you're not going to leave her, then?" *"Hey!"* She could hear Rob's voice. *"It's only Tuesday!"*

"Chloë." He took her hand. "I don't know. I really don't know. I haven't known you long—there are lots of things to consider. There's Nathan for a start—and things between Maggie and me . . . it's not that simple . . ."

"Right." Although it wasn't the answer she wanted, Chloë did understand.

"Is that what you want?"

Heavens! So two could play at this honesty game. "I don't know," she said frankly. And she didn't. "I suppose . . . I want you to make up your own mind. I don't wish to force you into anything. And I do understand your situation."

"You're very sweet." He stroked her wrist.

"Really? You think so?"

"Um," he said. "In some ways, yeah. Anyway," he signaled for the waiter to bring the check, "that's enough seriousness for one evening. We're here—might as well make the most of it—let's go and dance."

It was nearly two when they arrived back at the hotel, but both of them were still buzzing.

"Let's have another line," encouraged Chloë.

"And open the champagne."

"Oooh, we are so evil! We've got to go to the conference tomorrow."

"Damn it, Chloë. You only live once. Conference, schmonference. We're in New York."

She leaped onto the bed and started dancing. "We're in love!"

"Exactly. Now." He staggered slightly around the room—they'd had quite a bit of wine already. "What are we going to drink this from?"

Chloë jumped off the bed and ran to fetch two glasses from the bathroom. "Here."

He uncorked the bottle with the deftness she'd noted before and poured them each a glass.

"To us," he said. Clink.

"To us."

He racked out two lines. As the sublime I-can-do-anything high hit her again, she took a swig of champagne. Hell, why not?

"Lie back," she said. He did as he was told. She leaned over him, her mouth still full of champagne, and half parted her lips so the liquid gently seeped onto his. He parted his lips. Then she slowly, slowly released all the champagne into his mouth. He swallowed.

She took another swig, this time swallowing it for herself, then another for him.

"Now," she said firmly. "I'm going to blindfold you." She dimmed the bedside light to create a more seductive atmosphere.

"You are?"

"I am."

"What with?"

"This." She produced the black-and-scarlet satin scarf she'd brought with her—there was nothing pastel, elegant, or Fendi about it. She pulled him to a sitting position. "Turn around."

He slid down the white bedspread so his back was to her, and swiftly she tied the scarf.

"I can't see!"

"That's the point."

She undid his shoelaces, pulled off his shoes, then his socks, and threw them recklessly to the other side of the room. "Lie down again," she ordered.

She took off her dress, but kept on her underwear, her stockings, and swapped her dancing sandals for her foxiest shoes. Finally she threw the feather boa around her neck. Wow, she felt so, so horny! Momentarily she was grateful to Rob for making her plan her underwear so rigorously. And she knew for certain that this—not only the stockings and suspenders, but the blindfolding—was one of James's fantasies: he'd said so over dinner last night. Apparently it was something he'd only ever shared with Beth, and that was a long time ago, and he'd had to ask: she'd not initiated it of her own accord.

"Ha!" She ran her hand over his crotch. Judging from the jerking through his trousers, her approach was working already.

"You bitch," he said.

She dug her heels gently into his calves. "Got it in one."

She undid his shirt, slid it off one arm, then the other—he lifted himself up to help her—and ran her fingers down his chest. Lightly at first, then harder. What fun!

"Chloë . . ."

"Bet no one else does this for you, do they?"

"No, not exactly—"

"Or . . ." she unzipped his fly, eased him out of his trousers and boxers, and took another swig of champagne ". . . this?"

She took his cock in her mouth, and swept the liquid over it with her tongue.

"No!" He tugged at her hair. "Mmm."

Now Chloë was completely into what she was doing, her lips wet with champagne and saliva. Submerged in the pleasure she was giving, she could do it for ages, forever, if he liked. Then, to intensify the sensation, as she could feel him get more excited still, she started to use her hands . . .

Finally, inevitably, with a burst like the cocaine high, he came.

"Hmm." She swallowed. (It went with her wicked, wicked mood.) "Nice."

She got up. "My turn." Yet she didn't blindfold herself. Instead she took his hands and tied his wrists together above his head with the feather boa. *So what do you make of this?* She challenged the Vermeer. The old woman didn't seem remotely perturbed.

She removed her knickers and sat astride him, ready to lower herself onto his mouth.

"James, you have to do this for as long as I want you to, and exactly the way I say. So, you can start softly, softly . . . But first"—she got off him again—"here. You need some champagne." She poured a little into his mouth, he swallowed, and she straddled him once more. As he began to kiss her, the liquid made his tongue feel so cool and wet and blissful, she wondered if she'd ever felt so horny before. There was something about the fact that he was so in her power, when she was so in his power—she was so hooked on him—that made it all the more erotic.

Gently Chloë moved herself to and fro, hands propped on *The Lacemaker* for support.

"Harder . . . Harder . . ." His tongue moved, deeper, faster, more assured. "Now, inside . . . In and out . . . Mmm." How she loved this man for doing what she asked. "There, like that, yes, there . . ."

There was something so, so sexy about watching him unable to watch her, and watching herself gyrating on him that slowly, building in the fantastic way the best orgasms did, right from the tippy tips of her toes, up, up her legs and at the same time down from her breasts, in a wave to the peak that was at her core, with a mind-blowing, never-to-be-forgotten rush, she came.

When she'd finished, she lifted herself off and lay alongside him. "Still think I'm sweet?"

"Yes," he said, trying to reach for her but unable to. "You taste gorgeous."

"Guess you have a lot to learn."

"What do you mean?"

"I'll leave you to figure it out," she said, getting up from the bed. "I'm going to take a shower." And she went into the bathroom and turned on the water, leaving James to extricate himself from the boa and blindfold.

22

Thanks to Jean's comforting words, by the time Maggie got back from picking up Nathan, she'd convinced herself things weren't that bad with Jamie. Monday evening she held off calling him, thinking he might go out to some networking dinner. But by Tuesday, after a dreadful night's sleep, she was anxious once again.

It's longer than usual since I've heard from him, she thought. Normally when he's away on business, he calls me a lot—often every day—and it's been three days.

Wanting reassurance, she called him when she went to bed, yet there was no reply from either his mobile or his room. Rather than face increased suspicion, she persuaded herself it was still early in New York, and decided to try to sleep, but it took her ages to drift off, and her fears emerged in a dream.

She and Jamie were each on an island, separated by a strait of very hot water. She was desperate to get across to him, but couldn't because he had the only boat and the water was scalding. She shouted and shouted for him to come and fetch her—she needed to pick up Nathan from school, where he would be waiting for her—but Jamie, surrounded by CDs chaotically scattered in the sand, was too busy listening on his headphones to hear.

She woke in a cold sweat. The clock radio said 4:47, almost midnight New York time; and she really wanted—needed—to speak to him. She fumbled for her mobile on the bedside table and called him on speed dial; once more it went straight to voice mail, so she turned on the light and went and got the landline phone to ring the Paramount again; he was certain to be back in his room now, surely. She didn't have to wait long for the operator to answer, and he said he'd try the room at once.

Again it rang and rang.

Perhaps he's asleep, Maggie kidded herself, although it's unlikely Jamie wouldn't wake up to a phone ringing on his bedside table. Or maybe the operator dialed the wrong room by mistake. Oh, well.

She put the receiver down without leaving a message and turned out the light. But it took her hours to fall asleep again, and as she lay tossing and turning, her thoughts tumbled this way and that, too.

Is it my fault, she worried, am I doing something wrong? Am I being overly demanding? I always try not to be. Didn't Jamie once say it was partly this that caused him to split up with Beth—and the fact I'm less volatile is one of the things he likes about me? So, if I'm not too pushy emotionally, have I been too overt sexually? Though I could scarcely be accused of coming on too strong—the raunchy underwear was a rarity. Maybe *that's* the problem—I'm boring him, being too wifely, not enough of a lover, too wrapped up in Nathan. Perhaps I *should* have found a way to go to New York—sent Nathan to Fran's or something. But how would he have gotten to school? Shere Infants is on our doorstep—it would be a lot to ask Fran to drive him from Leatherhead every day. Perhaps it's Jamie's muddle, then. Still, even if it is, I'm his wife. Shouldn't I help him sort it out?

As the questions mounted, so Maggie's anxiety grew. By the time she phoned early the next morning Manhattan time, she was shaking with nerves. Thank God, he answered the phone in his room.

"Jamie?"

"Oh, hi." Was it her imagination or did he sound particularly rough? By this point it was hard for her to separate paranoia from reality.

"I was just calling to see if you were all right."

"Of course I'm all right. Why wouldn't I be?"

Maggie felt as if she'd been slapped, but she gulped and continued, "It's only I called you last night and you weren't in your room, and it's a few days since I'd heard from you."

"Oh, er, what time was that?"

"I suppose about midnight at your end."

"Ah . . . Well, I turned off my mobile and unplugged the phone in my room. Sorry. I was so tired."

"Right." Naturally, sleep was very important to him. How stupid of her to have been so thoughtless. "As long as you're okay, then."

"Yeah, yeah, Maggie, I'm fine. Look, can I call you later? I should have been at the conference an hour ago but I got held up with calls and stuff—I'm running very late."

Maggie wanted a proper chat to make her feel better; instead he seemed to be hurrying her off the phone. Yet she was loath to say anything that might be perceived as negative, so gulped again and said, "Okay, if you prefer."

"It would be better if we could speak tonight."

"Fine. We'll chat then."

"Yeah, bye, and say hi to Nathan."

As Maggie put down the phone, she had a sudden urge to cry. Don't! she told herself, and swallowed again.

She looked around the kitchen, hoping familiar surroundings might help ground her. She took in the fridge where she'd neatly stuck two of her favorite Nathan paintings, the dresser with its antique blue-and-white china, the stove with its traditional kettle on the burner, and the huge oak table she'd inherited from her grandmother, marked by decades of use . . . It was no good; she still felt anxiety churning in her stomach, so she decided to do something she found extremely hard: ask for help.

Jean's mobile barely rang once.

"Hi, Jean, sorry to bother you. It's Maggie. Is now a bad time?"

"No, no, it's fine—it's nice to hear from you." Although Maggie's call must have been unexpected, Jean's delight at hearing from her was in marked contrast to Jamie's put-out tone. "Is something up?"

Maggie sighed. "It's probably nothing."

"Mm?"

"But I'm, well . . . We were talking about Jamie the other day . . ."

"Ye-es . . ."

"And I know you said I was being silly . . ."

"I don't think that's what I said exactly, but go on."

"Anyway, the thing is, he's still being a bit odd, and I'm rather worried about it."

"Odd in what way?"

"It's hard to explain." Maggie wasn't happy going into specifics, though she knew it would help Jean to understand. "Just more distant, really. He hasn't been calling me like he normally would, and when I do speak to him he's always in a hurry."

"Well, it is ever so frantic here, honey. You know what New York is like. It's easy to get caught up in the mania of everything."

"Oh, I know," said Maggie. "Still, it's not only that. It's how he was before. You remember I said things haven't been that great for a while? I suppose it's over the last couple of months it's gotten noticeably bad. It's meant I'm having real problems sleeping—especially since he's been away."

"I see."

Maggie could tell that Jean was beginning to appreciate how distressed she was. She went on, "It's not simply the child issue. I can't put a finger on it, but he's just not as communicative. He's been busy at work, obviously, and I know when some people get stressed they withdraw into themselves, though with us, I'm the one who tends to do that. Jamie's the expressive one, and he's fine with Nathan. It's me he's different with." She caught her breath. This was so hard to say. "I feel he's not quite *here* for me, really, it's as if he"—another gulp to hold back tears—"he, doesn't *think* about me, or me and him, in the same way."

"I didn't realize things were so serious."

"I was wondering," Maggie hated to ask, "could you have that word with him, soon, possibly?"

"Would you like me to?"

"I think so. I wouldn't normally involve you, but—"

"I'll talk to him today," said Jean briskly.

"Are you sure you don't mind?"

"Of course not. I offered, didn't I? I'd like to do what I can to help. I'm very fond of you both and I hate to hear you so upset. I'll see if I can find out what's up."

"You don't think it's anything major, do you?" Maggie hoped Jean would say no, but was aware the picture she had painted was far from rosy.

"I agree his behavior sounds out of character," said Jean gently, "and if I can help in getting to the bottom of it, then I'm glad to. I very much doubt it's anything to do with you, or you and him. It's probably his stuff— some midlife crisis or something. Though if it is, you've got a lot going for you, and don't ever forget that. You'll get through this, I'm sure."

"Thanks, Jean. You're a good friend."

"Oh, here's another thought," Jean added. "If you're feeling anxious, perhaps it might be worth you having a chat with your GP?"

"Really? What could he do?"

"He could provide a sympathetic ear for starters. Is he nice?"

"Yes, but . . . I wouldn't want to waste his time. Still, I suppose he's always been really helpful about Nathan."

"And you never know, maybe he can recommend a short spell of counseling or something for both of you. Relate or whatever it's called."

"I hadn't thought of that."

"Why don't you call today? I know most doctors are pushed for time, so ask for a double appointment, then he should manage more than five minutes with you—that's what I'd do. After all, better to do it sooner rather than later."

"Before things get worse."

"Maybe worse, maybe better. Who knows? It can't harm. And I speak from experience. Remember how helpful I found my doctor when I was having those anxiety attacks?"

"True." Maggie recalled that Jean's fast-paced life had caught up with her at one point, and she'd become horribly panicked about traveling on the subway.

"Anyway, I'd better go, my dear," Jean said. "I've got some silly damn woman who's probably trying to get through. I'll call you later, when I've had a word. You take care now."

"I will. And thanks again."

Afterward, Maggie was aware that one issue she'd brought up on Sunday had remained unexpressed. She hadn't felt able to ask Jean what she thought because she didn't want to face talking about it, again. Jean hadn't brought it up either. But that didn't mean it didn't exist, or wasn't the key to Jamie's behavior.

Certainly, it's the one thing that would explain everything, the emotional distance, the preoccupation, the absence, the lack of sexual interest . . . No, she squashed the thought immediately. She wasn't going to give head space to *that* possibility.

23

Chloë woke, disoriented. Something was ringing, loud, and as she came to, she realized it was the phone on the bedside table. Even in her hungover state she knew it wouldn't be wise to answer it.

"James." He was dead to the world. "You'd better get that." She shook him.

"Eeuaarghblugh . . ."

"Phone!" She jammed the receiver to his ear. She could hear a woman's voice.

"Oh, hi." At once he was more awake. "Of course I'm all right . . . Why wouldn't I be?"

Oh no, thought Chloë. James wouldn't speak like that to most people. It must be Maggie. She cringed. Even though his wife sounded tinny down the line, it was the first time Chloë had heard her voice and sensed her presence as real. Maggie sounded worried.

If being in bed with her husband didn't make her feel bad enough, Chloë felt terrible—her head was thumping, her mouth was dry. Wanting to prolong the high of pleasure, she and James had consumed all the champagne and cocaine, and Chloë had hardly slept a wink. They'd been up till goodness knows when and, judging from her aching limbs, their sexual exploits had meant using muscles not regularly exercised at the gym.

Plus I've been bullied by Jean into going to the conference, Chloë remembered. How typical of her not to consider vacations sacrosanct. Crikey, is that the time? I'd better phone her.

Chloë was tempted to hide her head under the pillow until everything went away, but she didn't want to listen to James talking to Maggie any longer, so she hauled herself out of bed.

Seconds later he joined her in the bathroom.

"That was quick," she said, squeezing toothpaste onto her brush. It would take a thorough scouring session to remove the ghastly furry feeling in her mouth.

James stood naked next to her at the basin, checking his face to see how rough he looked. "I asked her to call back later. I wasn't really up for a chat."

"Me neither, but I've got to phone Jean." Chloë rinsed her teeth with water and spat it into the sink.

"Where's she staying?"

"The Algonquin."

"Jesus! You're kidding?"

"No. Why? Is it very posh?"

"It's not that it's posh, it's near!"

"Oh, I didn't know. Where is it?"

"It's on Forty-fourth Street, a bit farther east, but still."

"Oops! Guess we've been pretty lucky."

"Mmm." Calming himself, James turned to stand at the commode to have a pee.

I'm sure he'd have been too self-conscious to have done this previously, Chloë observed. We're definitely more intimate as a result of this spell away together.

Chloë showered at impressive speed, given her fragile state, and was rummaging in her suitcase for clean knickers when James emerged from the bathroom. He looked around.

"This room's in a right mess."

Chloë took it in: the empty champagne bottle and the rucked-up sheets were doubtless all in a day's work for a hotel cleaner, but the cocaine-smeared marble tabletop, the discarded underwear, and the ripped stockings were best not shared with the world. And James's attempt to escape from the boa had left black feathers everywhere; it was as if a crow had been massacred. She winced. "We'd better tidy up."

James picked up his watch from the bedside table. "Blast! I'm supposed to be having a breakfast meeting at the Millennium Broadway right now."

"How convenient," she said, a touch sarcastically. "Who with?"

"Adrienne Sugarman, the US special projects director."

"Better get your skates on. You go ahead—we can hardly arrive together anyway."

"Are you sure?"

"Yes." Chloë couldn't afford to waste time either, so she refrained from whining that he could lend a hand, and switched into efficient mode, emptying, picking up, folding, and putting away.

Within minutes James was in his suit and poised at the door. "You're an angel." He kissed her shoulder.

"I'll see you there," she said, turning to peck him on the cheek. That was almost wifely, she thought as she cleaned the table with toilet paper. Then again, given the cocaine smears she was wiping up, maybe not.

Luckily the conference center was just the other side of Times Square, so Chloë was able to finish making both the bedroom and herself presentable and still get there within the hour.

As she pushed her way through the rotating doors, she was thankful for the Whistles suit. The tan skirt and jacket made her appear much more together than she felt.

"Ah, Chloë!" She had barely had time to take in the polished marble, rich mahogany paneling, and sleek leather chairs of the Millennium

Broadway lobby before Jean had breezed over, checking her watch pointedly. "You've made it. We'd better go in at once."

The Hudson Theatre was packed. However lousy she was feeling, Chloë had to admit that it was an impressive venue. It was a proper theater, with a circle and an upper circle. The floral plasterwork ceiling was breathtaking, and the stage, with its sweeping deep red velvet curtains, was enough to make Chloë hanker to be up there speaking herself.

"Come on," said Jean impatiently.

They took two seats on the end of a row and Chloë scanned for James. As the lights dimmed for the presentation, she caught sight of him a few rows ahead, chatting animatedly with a group of older colleagues she didn't recognize. My, she observed, they all look very important. Come to that, in his smart navy suit James does too . . . I thought I knew the work side of him, but this is another aspect of his life where I don't have the full picture.

What a load of nonsense, Chloë griped inwardly as she sat listening to the chief executive banging on about company ethics and "publishing personalities" in accompaniment to her pounding headache. All this corporate stuff wasn't her bag. And in spite of the air-conditioning, with so many people, the auditorium was very warm. She felt her attention drifting, drifting . . . her eyelids drooping, drooping . . .

"*Chloë!*" Jean nudged her. "You could at least have the courtesy to stay awake!"

"Sorry." Chloë felt like a naughty schoolgirl, but the previous night was catching up with her. There was a pointy pen in the conference pack she'd been handed on the way in and she spent the next hour surreptitiously prodding her knees to stop herself from falling asleep again.

At last they broke for a much-needed coffee. "Can I get you one?" she offered, hoping to make up for her unprofessional performance thus far.

"That would be great," said Jean. "I need to have a word with Jamie Slater about something personal, so I'll meet you back here."

"Right." Chloë's heart beat fast at the mention of his name.

"Black, no sugar."

"Fine," said Chloë, but her brain was already racing ahead. Just what sort of "personal" matter does Jean want to discuss with James? Jean is one of Maggie's closest friends, and Maggie seemed distressed when she'd phoned earlier. Maybe she's found out about us, Chloë panicked. Maybe she's told Jean! No, she reassured herself; Jean would never have been so normal just now. Even if she'd been sworn to secrecy, there was no way she'd have been able to hide something so major.

She watched Jean make her way down the steps toward where James was sitting, and gently pull him away from his colleagues, as if she didn't want anyone else to overhear what she was saying. Chloë watched his face. He appeared serious, and nodded, as if to show his tacit agreement. Jean carried on talking for quite a while.

Whatever it's about, it seems she had a lot to say, thought Chloë, flooded with guilt. This doesn't look good. It doesn't look good at all.

24

The doctor's receptionist consulted the computer screen. "Mrs. Slater," she muttered, moving the cursor down. "Ah, yes. Remarkably lucky we had a double appointment." She eyed Maggie as if to say: You don't appear sick; you should be grateful. "Go on up."

The practice occupied a tiny picture-postcard cottage opposite Nathan's school. Ramshackle to the point of tumbling down, it was one of the many houses in the village to which a worn wooden sign DRIVE CARE-FULLY OVERHANGING BUILDINGS applied. Yet despite their low-tech accommodation and the demands made on them, the three GPs dealt efficiently with reams of local people, and over the years of bringing Nathan, Maggie had found one doctor particularly sympathetic. Now she always asked for Dr. Hopkin.

She mounted the creaky stairs, ducking to avoid a beam, and took the last seat in the waiting area. Two elderly women in the corner were sharing a moan about their ailments—a visit to the doctor's office seemed as much a chance for a gossip as treatment. Opposite was a sulky-looking teenage boy with severe acne and an overweight man whose pale, blotchy beer gut was protruding from under his T-shirt. He'd be doing himself a favor if he covered that properly, Maggie decided, her aesthetic sense protesting in spite of her tiredness. Lastly, next to Maggie, a harassed-looking mother was trying to keep her two small children amused with the uninspiring selection of toys.

Of course the practice won't be able to justify the expenditure for new ones, Maggie thought ruefully. It's such a shame everything has been so affected by a lack of funding.

She picked up an ancient copy of *Babe* and began to flip through it, but as she skimmed the pages of tips on fashion, beauty, and relationships, she realized she wasn't taking in a word.

Why I am here? she asked herself. They're so stretched these days in the NHS, and there's nothing wrong with me physically, unless you count the insomnia . . . Though it does seem to be getting worse. She looked down at her hands—they were shaking. Maybe the trembling is a sign of growing older, she thought, something I'll have to get used to?

"Mrs. Slater!" the doctor boomed from down the corridor.

Maggie got up. As she braced herself to speak to him, she had a horrible surge of anxiety. I shouldn't have come, her inner voice scolded. I'm wasting Dr. Hopkin's time. Some people are genuinely sick, and here I am, worrying him over worry itself. I should be able to get over this on my own.

Somehow her feet propelled her into the office.

"Hello. What can I do for you today?" The doctor beamed at her. He was in his fifties, with disheveled gray hair and ruddy cheeks, dressed in comforting elephant cord and brushed cotton.

"I'm not sure," said Maggie, as she took a seat next to his paper-smothered desk.

"Oh." He sounded surprised. Then he looked at her, frowned, and propped his half-moon spectacles up so that he could focus on his computer screen. "I see you have a double appointment." He added gently, "So we've plenty of time."

"Um." Maggie looked down at her hands. They were really shaking now. She could sense Dr. Hopkin looking at them too. He'll probably assume I'm an alcoholic or a junkie or something, she thought. Perhaps the most disabling symptom would be a good place to start. "I'm not sleeping very well. In fact, I've been sleeping really badly."

"How badly is badly?"

"I guess about half the hours I normally would, and this last week even less than that. It's not been right for a while."

Maggie could feel waves of support emanating from the doctor. "I feel exhausted now and I find it hard to concentrate. And I suppose I've been feeling pretty um . . . worried generally." Suddenly she was crying. It was as if she'd released the floodgates on all her pent-up emotions since Jamie had been away, and once she'd started, couldn't stop.

Damn it! How silly of me, she thought, but the tears kept falling. I seem to be crying so much at the moment. What a wimp!

At home before she'd left she'd put on mascara and a little gray eyeliner to make herself look more presentable. She pictured her cheeks covered in smears and her shame mounted. She fumbled in her handbag for a tissue, but her hands were so shaky she couldn't control them. Just talking about her anxiety seemed to be making it worse.

"Here." Dr. Hopkin handed her a box of tissues.

"Thank you." Maggie blew her nose.

"Is there any particular reason that you feel so miserable? Something major upsetting you that's keeping you awake?"

Maggie was silent. It was against her nature to discuss personal issues and she didn't want to be disloyal to Jamie. She took a deep breath. "I'm lonely," she said. Perhaps if she avoided mentioning Jamie specifically, the doctor might be able to help without her betraying her husband.

"Oh?" The doctor sounded surprised again. "I thought you were married. Loneliness is not something I normally associate with happily married working mothers like you." He adopted a more cheerful tone. "They tend to complain that they could do with more time to themselves."

Oh dear, thought Maggie. Deflecting him doesn't appear to be doing to trick. "Well, my job isn't especially sociable. I work from home, mainly."

"I see. I suppose that's different, then. Would you rather be working more with other people around? In an office, perhaps?"

"Um . . ." Again Maggie paused. She knew this wasn't the answer, because it wasn't the main problem. "I didn't used to mind working alone. I tend to be pretty happy with my own company."

"So it's not work, then?"

"No," she said, growing more decided. In the safe haven created by this avuncular figure, maybe she could be more open. "I don't really think that's the solution . . . Though I suppose I would like to write something more challenging." She stopped to consider, and dabbed her eyes. "I'd like that. I could look into it."

"Yes, but you just said you don't think that's the solution. May I ask why you feel lonely now when—unless I misunderstood—you didn't before and if you've always worked from home and enjoyed your own company?"

Maggie squirmed and admitted quietly, "I think it's because I'm not getting on very well with my husband." At once she felt the anxiety lift a little. "We've not been talking as much as we used to, and when we have, we've tended to argue. He's away at the moment, still, it's been going on a while. I don't feel that he appreciates me the way he did in the past, and I'm not sure why. I don't think I'm any different."

"Oh dear," said Dr. Hopkin. Then he added, "Silly man! You're lovely."

"Thank you." For the first time in days Maggie smiled.

"Anyway." Dr. Hopkin coughed, seemingly embarrassed by his own frankness. "I'm afraid I don't have a miracle pill to help you get along better. Might make me a wealthy man if I did—Dr. Hopkin' s Miracle Marriage Mender!" He chortled at the thought.

"No, I realized that."

"Sure you did, sure you did."

"It's just I was wondering maybe about some . . ." now it was Maggie's turn to be embarrassed ". . . counseling or something. My friend suggested Relate. What do you think?"

"Good idea, good idea." The doctor nodded, as if saying things twice would underline how much he agreed. "Many couples find it useful to talk to a third party, get an objective angle on things. Would your husband be willing to go too?"

Maggie hesitated. Would he? She wasn't sure. But not wanting to confess this, she said, "I see no reason why not."

"Sometimes men can be rather less willing to discuss things like this than their wives."

"Mm." Maggie could understand that. Yet *Jamie is normally the more outgoing one in our relationship,* she thought. *If I'm willing to talk, surely he will be too?*

Dr. Hopkin seemed to pick up on her uncertainty, even though she was trying to disguise it. "Well, you have a word with him and see what he says. Remember you can always go on your own initially if need be."

"Can I?"

"Oh yes, of course. And we usually find the men come around in the end. Can't bear to think their wives are talking about them behind their backs. We've sensitive egos, after all."

"Indeed."

"We have an arrangement with the Guildford branch. I can refer you to them through the practice and you pay what you can afford. Here," he got out his pad, "let me give you their address so you'll know where to go." He wrote it down. "I'll write to them now, and you should hear within the next few weeks about an appointment."

"That long?" Maggie was disappointed. Having come this far, she wanted to be able to go along with Jamie as soon as possible.

"I'm afraid there's a bit of a wait. But you should get something in the next month, no longer than that."

"I suppose it's not as bad as some waiting lists."

"No, and maybe you could set yourself a couple of fresh challenges with your work, as you mentioned, to take your mind off things until then."

"That's a good thought." Maggie got to her feet. "In fact, you've given me an idea. I know just the person to talk to about it. She's away on the same business trip as my husband at the moment, but I can have a chat with her soon."

"You do that. Come back and see me in a month, let me know how things are going."

"I will, and thank you."

"Anytime, anytime."

Maggie closed the door to his office and went down the stairs.

When Jamie gets back from New York, I'll talk to him about coming for this counseling, she vowed. And I'll find out from Jean who's working on special projects at UK Magazines—perhaps there's a way I can write some sample pieces for a new magazine as it's being developed. That's how to change things. I'll get involved in something really different and radical again.

She strolled back down the street, smiling at the prospect. She felt more positive than she had in weeks, pleased with herself for taking action. The sun was shining, and even though it was September, it was warm. She stopped for a second to gaze at the river, with its resident white-feathered, yellow-billed ducks. They quacked up at her, hoping for a snack.

There's no doubt that Shere is the place to be on a day like today, she thought. Surely things can only get better from now on.

25

I wish my legs were longer, thought Chloë. Then they'd be able to propel me at a speed to match my current lifestyle.

As she raced back across Times Square and along Forty-fourth Street, she barely noticed the shops full of the latest gadgets, so temptingly priced; the huge billboards advertising films as yet unheard-of in London; the theater posters boasting of the best shows in town. She was as determined to get where she had to go as the locals in their sneakers, and barely checked as she crossed the street to the Paramount.

"Blimey!" exclaimed James, as she whirled into their room. "What's the rush?" He was standing, looking relatively relaxed, loosening his tie.

Panting, Chloë said, "What was Jean talking to you about?"

"When?"

"At the conference. She said, 'I've got to have a word with Jamie Slater about something personal,' and grabbed you. She hasn't found out about us, has she?"

"No, no."

"So, why the grilling? And does she always call you Jamie?" Chloë could barely get the questions out quickly enough.

"Yeah, all my old friends do."

"Really?"

"It's what I was called when I was young."

"Oh." Chloë was winded. Yet again it was apparent that there were aspects of James she knew little about. "Would you rather I called you Jamie too?"

"No, I like you calling me James."

Maybe he likes me calling him something different, she thought. Perhaps he prefers James. She fished, "Why?"

Pushed, James replied, "Because Maggie calls me Jamie."

"Oh." Chloë sat down on the bed, deflated. Yet she was still curious, no matter how much the revelations distressed her. As Rob had often observed, she had a masochistic streak. "So, what did you talk about?"

"Do you really want to know?"

"Yes."

"She wanted to have a word about Maggie."

"Oh." So I was right, sort of, thought Chloë. "What did she say about her?"

James looked torn. It was as if he knew his honesty was hurting Chloë but was aware he wouldn't get away with a fabrication. "She said she thought Maggie was pretty unhappy at the moment."

"Really?" I suspected as much, thought Chloë, hence the phone call. "You don't think *Maggie* knows about us, do you?"

"Not from what Jean was saying."

"Why's she miserable, then?" I hope it's nothing to do with me, she prayed. I never set out to hurt her. It just . . . happened. And now, just as Rob predicted, I've become really entangled.

"Well, Maggie badly wants another baby. And Jean was there when we had this conversation about it."

"Oh." Chloë was shocked. While she hadn't worked out exactly what she wanted from James, it hadn't occurred to her that Maggie might want something else so tangible from him. "You had this conversation recently?"

"No, not that recently. Several weeks ago."

For God's sake, another *baby*, thought Chloë. If James wants a child with Maggie, where does that leave me? Her mind raced back. Was that when he started seeing me? Could that possibly be *why*? But almost before the idea had formulated, Chloë shunned it.

"What did you say?" She braced herself to hear the worst.

"I said I didn't really want one."

Chloë couldn't help but be relieved. "Why not?"

James sat down on the bed next to her and said quietly, "I should have thought that was obvious."

She felt a bit better.

He continued, "But aside from my relationship with you, I had doubts before anyway. I adore Nathan, as you know, but I'm not sure I'm ready to be a father again."

"Really?"

James shook his head.

This was illuminating—even more so than the conversation they'd had the night before. But without the cocaine to numb the pain, it was difficult to take in. She was discovering things about James that she hadn't expected. She already knew he hadn't wanted the first baby initially, and now he didn't want a second.

He's something of a commitment-phobe, observed Chloë. It takes one to know one. But perhaps he and Maggie aren't really suited. At least, it doesn't sound to me like they are from how James has described their relationship.

Then a new realization hit her: What if I want children? If James were to leave Maggie, does this mean he'd never want them with me? She recalled Rob's warning that James might be attracted to her on the rebound. If he'd started seeing her because Maggie was pressuring him to have another child, it looked ominously likely.

It seemed that not only was she gaining new insight into James, she was also discovering new aspects of herself.

Before she could consider more deeply, James collapsed on the bed. "I'm exhausted," he said, clearly wanting to end the conversation.

Chloë was thankful; she'd had enough of revelations. "Me too. Shall we just stay here tonight?"

"That would be great. Let's get a bite to eat downstairs now, then come back and crash out."

"Perfect. I could do with a major dose of carbohydrates."

"You go on down. I'll phone Maggie—I promised I would."

Chloë frowned, not bothering to conceal she was put out.

"Don't worry, I won't be long. I'm starving."

"What are you doing tonight, then?" asked Jean, taking a bite of her sandwich. It was Chloë's second day at the conference and they were eating a stand-up buffet lunch. They'd just been in a seminar on the future of social networking, followed by a discussion of how this would impact magazines. Chloë had to concede the morning had proved far more interesting than the previous day, though maybe it was because she'd had an early night.

Chloë struggled to think of an excuse. A meal with friends wouldn't do again. But it was her last night with James and she was feeling depressed at the thought of having to go home. What's going to happen then? she wondered. Will things be any different? Our relationship can't go back to what it was before. Do the calls from Maggie and the quiet word from Jean suggest that things are coming to a head?

If so, Chloë had mixed feelings. On one hand she could hear her mother's voice: *"I can't believe you're stealing another woman's husband and breaking up a happy home, just like that awful woman your father ran off with."* On the other hand, she believed fidelity to Maggie was ultimately James's responsibility, not hers.

"I've arranged to go out for dinner with Vanessa and I thought I'd ask Jamie Slater too," Jean continued, blithely. "You've met him, haven't you?"

"Er . . . um . . . yes."

Chloë felt her cheeks burning. Fortunately Jean was concentrating on not smudging her lipstick while she consumed a generously filled pastrami on rye and didn't notice.

"Would you care to join us?" asked Jean.

Help, thought Chloë, what a prospect! Dinner with my lover, my ex-boss, and my new mentor. It's almost farcical. Still, given that the alternative was probably sitting alone in the Paramount biting her nails and wondering what the three of them might be saying, she'd better accept.

"That would be lovely." If I can cope with the fiasco at Bloomingdale's I can cope with anything, she told herself. At least this time James and I are forewarned and forearmed.

"I've arranged to meet Vanessa at eight, so we can go back to our hotels and freshen up first. I'm meeting her in a little restaurant on the Bowery in the East Village called Marion's. That'll be nice and easy for you."

Just as Chloë was about to pipe up, "Would it? Wouldn't somewhere in Midtown be better for all of us?" she remembered that she'd told Jean she was staying on Spring Street. "Of course it will. I'll nip back to my friend's place for a shower and see you there."

26

Maggie was still cheerful when Jean called.

"Hold on a mo." She had just gotten out of the bath and was dripping all over the carpet, so she wrapped herself in a towel before taking a seat at her dressing table.

"I must be quick," said Jean. "I'm meeting Jamie and some others from work for dinner and I've got to change, but I wanted to let you know I managed to have a word."

Maggie was suddenly nervous. "What did he say?"

"I think he knew he was in the wrong. He seemed pretty sheepish."

"Really?" Unusual for Jamie, thought Maggie. Humility is not his style.

Jean paused to consider. "Yeah, he was definitely a bit . . . well, sort of *guilty*."

"Oh." Maggie wasn't sure what to make of this. Does that mean he's got something to be guilty about? she wondered. No, she decided. It's because he's not been that nice to me lately.

"I told him I didn't think he appreciated you."

Maggie laughed. Trust Jean not to mince her words! "What did he say to that?"

"I suspect he's aware he's been distant, though of course he wouldn't admit it to me. Although I did get him to agree that he'd try to sort things out between you. He said he'd have a proper heart-to-heart with you when he gets back."

"Good! Just in time."

"Quite. My feelings precisely."

"I was planning to have a chat with him, because I saw the doctor today."

"That was quick."

"I got a cancellation."

"How lucky. What did he suggest?"

Maggie briefly recounted the conversation. "Anyway," she finished, "apparently we should get an appointment with Relate within the next month, so I need to see if he'll agree to come. Sounds like he might, from what you've just said."

"Yes." Jean sounded noncommittal.

"And, in the meantime, my GP suggested that I try to focus on work, take my mind off things. I'd really like to write more challenging pieces. Which reminds me—you don't have to answer this now, but do you know anyone who would be interested in something a bit different at UK Magazines? What I want to do isn't right for *Babe*, so I was thinking more of special projects. Maybe I could help steer the way a magazine covers food and nutrition from the outset, rather than have to fulfill someone else's brief."

"What a great idea!"

"Do you think so?" Maggie was delighted she was enthusiastic. After all, Jean was one of the most successful women in the industry.

"I do! I really do! In fact . . ." Jean hesitated. "Now you've given me an idea."

"Really?"

"Mm. Leave it with me, my dear, and I'll get back to you."

27

Back at the Paramount, James was concerned that he and Chloë might give themselves away over supper.

"You'd better get your taxi to drop you near Spring and walk up the Bowery," he advised her, buttoning his remaining clean shirt.

Chloë was focused on finding something presentable to wear other than her Whistles suit.

"It would be awful if Jean saw you coming from uptown."

"Mm."

"She'd be bound to wonder why."

"I suppose so." If he hadn't been so anxious about exposing their affair, Chloë would have seen the funny side of all the intrigue. Instead she found his jumpiness annoying; it seemed cowardly. She was tempted to ask if it would be so dreadful if Jean or Vanessa *did* work out they were having affair. Obviously it wouldn't be good for either of them professionally. Yet if James was ever going to leave Maggie—and Chloë was increasingly hoping that he would at least *consider* it—they'd have to find out sometime. Otherwise, as she knew from her own parents, this sort of mess could drag on for years.

At half past seven, they caught separate cabs from outside the Paramount. Chloë asked her driver to drop her a couple of blocks from the restaurant. When she arrived, Vanessa, Jean, and James were having a drink at the bar.

"Ah, Chloë," said Vanessa. "You found it."

"And on time," said Jean drily.

"What'll it be?" James asked.

"A margarita, please."

"Salt?"

"No salt." How clever he's being, thought Chloë. She almost forgave him for irritating her earlier.

She turned to look around the restaurant. It reminded her of Louisa's in Soho: it had a similar quirky, casually elegant charm. Yet with its mix of chintz and red velvet, and an assortment of antique plates and old photographs covering the walls, it was more theatrical, in keeping with its Off-Off-Broadway locale.

"This is fab!" she said.

"Do you like it?" asked James.

"Ooh yes. It's just my kind of place."

"I discovered it," he said, visibly pleased that she approved, "then told Jean about it when she came to the conference here last year."

Chloë wasn't surprised. She knew James's taste quite well by now and that the East Village was a favorite haunt.

"Anyway, cheers, girls." James raised his glass. "What a lucky man I am to be out with not one but *three* lovely ladies!"

Hmph, thought Chloë. He needn't sound quite so happy. For all his seeming confusion, perhaps there's a side to him that enjoys having more than one woman.

———

James poured them each another glass of wine.

So far we're doing pretty well, thought Chloë.

She and James were sitting next to each other, knees surreptitiously pressed together under the table. James had steered the conversation away from personal matters, and Chloë had done the same. They were helped by Vanessa's presence; she didn't know any of them intimately.

But then Jean said, "I spoke to Maggie just now," and Chloë nearly dropped her fork.

God, I hope she's not going to have another go at James, she worried. I couldn't bear that.

Jean carried on, "I thought it might help her if I had a word with you two—"

Oh no! Chloë gulped. Is Jean seriously prepared to expose our affair in front of Vanessa?

"—about special projects."

Ah. So "you two" referred to her and Vanessa. By now she was as scarlet as the velvet décor, but luckily the lighting was low. She prayed no one would notice.

Jean addressed Vanessa. "Jamie's wife is a talented food writer. You probably know her stuff—she works under the name Margaret Wilson."

"Of course. She's been around a few years. One of the best in the business." Vanessa turned to James. "I didn't realize she was your wife."

"Yes. She uses her maiden name. Always has." Unless Chloë was mistaken, James sounded proud.

"Gosh. What a small world!" said Vanessa.

"Isn't it?" Chloë reached for her wine. Worryingly small, she thought.

"Well, if you think she's good *now*," Jean continued loyally, "you'll probably be very interested in our conversation."

"Oh?" said Vanessa, James, and Chloë in unison.

"She's keen to write something a bit different, more controversial, features that draw more on her training and passions. She's got a great background, you know. Earned a degree, then trained as a nutritionist and has been contributing regularly to the women's monthlies for a while now. If you think what she does already is okay, I'm sure she could produce some stuff that's *really* stimulating. So, I thought maybe—though God knows why I should help you out, Chloë—you'd be interested in her doing some writing for your magazine."

Chloë's jaw dropped.

"That sounds very interesting," said Vanessa. "Don't you think? Chloë?"

Chloë watched the flight attendants wheeling the trolley down the aisle toward her. Eventually they were parallel with her row, and stopped and proffered her breakfast on a plastic tray.

"No, thank you. Just a coffee." It seems only seconds ago that we had dinner and I can't face food, she decided. It might be six thirty a.m. UK time, but it feels like the middle of the night to me.

She pushed up the blind and bright sunlight flooded in. The plane was high above the clouds; Chloë could see them down below, layer upon layer, from the darkest, rainiest shade to the palest, most ghostly gray.

England, she thought gloomily. I hate it.

Oh yes, she was looking forward to seeing Rob again, and Potato, their couch-loving cat. She would be pleased to be in her own space and have a nice, long bath instead of a shower. She was also happy at the prospect of catching up with her friends on Facebook—arriving on a Saturday morning had some advantages.

And I *had* been keen to start work on Monday with Vanessa, she thought. Although since Jean introduced Maggie into the scheme of things, it wasn't looking like such a brilliant career move—everything was fast becoming so hideously tangled. But it's my baby! she protested to herself. I've spent months working toward this!

The irony that James's wife was now muscling in on Chloë's act was not lost on her. She was too fuzzy-headed to consider all the ramifications right then, so took another sip of coffee and resumed her position, nose pressed up against the glass.

As the clouds thinned she could make out the patchwork fields of Berkshire far, far below. They were nearing Heathrow. If she was going to the ladies' room, she'd better do so now. She squeezed past her two adjacent passengers, but out in the aisle, the trolley was blocking the way. Chloë decided to go up to business class and say hello to James instead.

"Hi," she said, crouching to speak to him; he was on the end of a row.

"Oh, hi!" He ruffled her hair. "Did you manage to get any sleep?"

"A bit. You?"

"A little." He glanced past the man next to him and out of the window. "It seems we're nearly there."

"I know." Chloë was unable to keep the sadness out of her voice. "I don't want to go home."

"You're not the only one." James sounded equally sad. He stroked her cheek. "I've had a lovely time."

"Me too." Chloë could feel tears pricking behind her eyes. She stroked his face in return, a particularly soft bit of skin that she'd discovered on his cheekbone. It's funny, she thought, you get to see a lover's face far more close up than anyone else's. Over the last few days she'd come to appreciate every contour, every line, even the way his stubble grew. "Whatever happens, we've had this time, haven't we? No one can take that away."

"No, they can't." James smiled, then sighed. "I need to have a chat with Maggie when I get back."

"Mm," said Chloë. Did that mean James was going to tell her? Chloë was about to ask what he was going to say, but thought better of it. That was between the two of them, and she wasn't sure that she wanted to know. So she said, "I'd best go," and stood up.

Once she'd been to the restroom, she made her way back to economy class, edged into her seat, and looked out of the window again. The cars were little and rounded, the roads winding and irregular, the houses depressingly suburban and similar.

The FASTEN SEAT BELTS sign flashed on.

After all the excitement, intrigue, intimacy, and romance of the last week, they were coming down.

28

"Is that Chloë Appleton?"

"Speaking."

"You don't know me, but my name's Margaret Wilson, Maggie. I'm Jamie Slater's wife—"

"Oh!"

"—and a friend of Jean's. She suggested I give you a call."

"Yes. So she did . . . Er, could you hang on a second?"

"Sure, sure." A sound of rustling papers, then silence.

Maggie waited. I hate cold-calling, she thought. Thankfully, her professional reputation was well established these days, so phoning this woman whom Jean had described as "phenomenally talented but prone to liking things her own way," was the first time she'd had to do it in years.

After what seemed an age, Chloë came back to the phone. "Apologies for that. Hi."

By now Maggie felt she was interrupting something awfully important. "I'm sorry, is this a bad moment?"

"Er, no, no." Although she sounded as if it was. "It's that I only started in this department yesterday, and things are a bit chaotic around here."

"I can call back if you like."

"It's fine, honestly."

I bet she's thinking, *Blast Jean for getting the publisher's wife to call me*, thought Maggie.

Chloë continued, "I understood from Jean that you might be interested in doing a piece for special projects. What kind of thing did you have in mind?"

"Actually, I wondered if I could come in and show you some of my work."

"I have seen lots of your features over the years."

"You have?" Maggie's heart sank. Doubtless she would already be typecast as a traditional writer of unadventurous recipes.

"Yes—you're very prolific. I'm sure it's not really necessary for us to meet face-to-face."

I bet she's made up her mind about me and already written me off as a waste of time, Maggie concluded.

Yet Chloë continued, "Actually I particularly liked that feature you did, 'Pulling Dishes,' in this month's *Men*."

"You did?" Maggie was pleased. If she was going to be judged on what she'd written lately, at least this was one of her more amusing pieces.

"And Jean speaks very highly of you, so I'm positive you don't need to bother coming in. Tell me more about what kind of articles you were thinking of."

Maggie had spent that Sunday painstakingly putting together a portfolio of cuttings while Jamie, just back from New York, had volunteered to spend the day with Nathan.

Oh dear, she thought. I hate coming up with suggestions on the spot—especially for a new publication. I'd vastly prefer a proper debriefing face-to-face, so I have time to think of something original. I don't want to end up rehashing the same old stuff again.

As she thought about this, Maggie was silent. Conscious of the pause, Chloë said, "Would it help if I gave you an outline of how I see the magazine?"

Maggie hesitated. Oh, what the hell—go on, Maggie, she cajoled herself. Say what you mean. "I'm sure we *could* come up with some ideas together over the phone, but from what I understand from Jamie and Jean you're trying to do something different, less clichéd, quite radical. I believe it would be an enormous help if I could see the dummy, get a feel for who the magazine is pitched at, understand what you're really after, and talk you through where I'm coming from too. So I really do think it would be useful if we could meet up."

"Oh." There was another pause. "Okay, sure, I take your point. When would you like to come in?"

"How about tomorrow?"

"Tomorrow!"

Maggie was keen to get moving. She might not have managed a heart-to-heart with Jamie, yet in comparison this meeting was less daunting. "Yes. I've got to come into town anyway."

This was a lie, but she wanted to appear in demand.

There was more rustling of paper. "Er . . . yes. I suppose that would be fine. Shall we say about twelve thirty?"

"Lovely. I'll see you there."

"Do you know where to come?"

Maggie was more relaxed now that she'd swung things her way and laughed. "Of course! My husband works there."

"Oh, yeah. Silly me. Special projects is on the third floor. Just ask for me, Chloë."

"I look forward to meeting you."

"And me you. Bye."

"Bye." Maggie put the phone down.

Poor woman, she thought. She sounds a bit distraught. Thank goodness I don't work in-house any longer—it's so much more stressful than being freelance.

_____

The next day it was Maggie's turn to take the children to school. After she'd dropped them off, she headed straight out of the village on a run—she'd dressed in her tracksuit that morning.

So, she thought as she ran, how should I dress to meet this Chloë woman? Maybe trouser suit with a pastel T-shirt would be good. I've no idea what she's like, but a cream suit is bound not to offend anyone—it's smart but not intimidating. And if I add that scarf Jamie bought me in New York for a pop of color, who knows, it might even bring me luck . . .

Maggie wasn't looking forward to the encounter; unlike her husband, she didn't enjoy meeting new people, and Jamie had done little to boost her confidence. "Do you really need to schlep all the way into town?" he'd said when she'd mentioned it to him. "I imagine Chloë's very busy—why don't you just pitch your suggestions over the phone?"

I would have thought Jamie of all people would understand why I'm keen to meet face-to-face, thought Maggie. Then again, he's always wanted me to stick with writing the stuff that's guaranteed to make money. Sometimes he can be so unsupportive.

She carried on running round her usual route, and as the surrounding scenery energized her, she pushed her resentment away and told herself to think positively.

And when I've gotten over this hurdle, she vowed, I'll talk to Jamie about going to Relate. I'll feel stronger if I sort this career thing first.

Once home she showered, then spent ages doing her makeup. By the time she'd finished she appeared as if she had very little on, yet her skin seemed clearer, her eyes brighter, and her lips fuller. Next, she carefully selected a flesh-toned bra and knickers that would leave no telltale lines. She put on the suit and knotted the scarf on one side, French-style, around her neck. Finally she put on a pair of white canvas deck shoes and stood back to examine the effect in the mirror.

"You look *okay*," she reassured herself.

Maggie allowed longer than necessary to get into London, so she was early. She decided it couldn't be a bad thing to show that she was keen, and she headed for UK Magazines ahead of time. In the event, it meant that she had to wait in reception.

"I'm afraid Chloë's nipped out for some lunch," explained the receptionist.

While she sat there, many women came and went—some were very glamorous. Maggie was just remembering her sister's observation that there would be lots of opportunity for Jamie to flirt at work, when a dark-haired girl approached her and said, "Hi, you must be Margaret Wilson."

"Yes." Maggie jumped to her feet. "Though people call me Maggie."

"I'm Chloë." She held out her hand.

As Maggie shook it, she thought, She bites her nails. It made her warm to Chloë. A woman who bit her nails must be something of a worrier too.

"I'm sorry, I dashed out to get a sandwich. Have you been waiting long?"

"No, no," Maggie lied.

"Come with me," said Chloë, leading the way. "We'll have to sit at my desk. There aren't any meeting rooms free."

Maggie followed her. The open-plan office seemed very busy and noisy. There were dozens of people, mainly women, and most of them looked rather younger than Maggie. Some were click-clacking away on their computers, others were talking animatedly on the phone, and a few were chatting to each other, whether legitimately "bouncing ideas" or gossiping Maggie couldn't tell. Suddenly her freelance lifestyle didn't appear so perfect after all: her comfortable kitchen seemed terribly quiet and parochial.

I expect I'm very out of touch, thought Maggie. Sometimes I go for hours without talking to a soul. And I've pitched myself as wanting to do something new and different—who am I trying to kid?

When they reached Chloë's desk, Maggie noted that it was smothered in even more paper and magazines than Dr. Hopkin's. I could never work in this chaos, she thought. And didn't Chloë say that she's only been in this department a couple of days? How has she managed to amass so much stuff in such a short time? She's even messier than Jamie.

"Have a seat," said Chloë, grabbing a chair from a colleague's desk and wheeling it over.

Maggie did as she was bid. She was partly relieved to be in a less formal setting than she'd imagined, partly concerned that she wouldn't have the space to show her portfolio.

"Can I get you a coffee?"

Maggie couldn't face the thought of a mug of office instant. "Water will be fine."

"Back in a mo." Chloë rushed off.

Maggie watched her go over to the kitchen area and make herself a quick coffee, then fill a glass from the water-filter machine. As she did so, Maggie was able to get a full view. What a fantastic outfit! she thought. Chloë was dressed in a bias-cut green skirt, a vest that enhanced her cleavage, and an angora cardigan that seemed designed to slip off her shoulders. It wasn't the kind of thing Maggie would ever wear, let alone to the office, and she could see Chloë's bra straps even from this distance, but nonetheless it looked good. As Chloë walked back with the drinks, Maggie observed her shoes.

They're those gorgeous sandals I admired in all the magazines last month, but I knew would make me appear too tall, she realized.

"Here," said Chloë, handing Maggie the glass.

She's very pretty, thought Maggie. Then corrected herself. Well, attractive maybe, not conventionally pretty. She's wearing far more makeup than I ever would, but she's got the kind of face that suits feline eyeliner like that. *And* she's got the sort of naturally tousled-looking curly hair I've always wanted. She reminds me of someone, but I can't think who . . .

Then Chloë said, "So, where shall we start?" and Maggie pushed thoughts other than the strictly professional to the back of her mind.

"I've brought some stuff to show you," she said. The cut-and-thrust environment had made her self-conscious, and she was keen to get her presentation out of the way.

Maggie had had a hunch that Chloë would be the kind of adrenaline-driven young woman she'd met before in magazine publishing—a hunch that, from yesterday's phone call and what she'd seen today, was proving correct. Chloë did look rather on edge, Maggie observed. She's probably stressed.

With this in mind she had put a feature called "Fast Times" at the front of her portfolio. It showed recipes that she'd described as "perfect dishes for the end of a busy day—quick, simple, and full of flavor." She liked the photography as well.

"Mmm, yum," said Chloë.

Judging from her well-rounded physique, Maggie guessed she enjoyed her food. Chloë peered closer and started to read. Maggie was silent. Fortunately the piece hadn't been too hacked by copy editors, and she was happy with how it flowed.

"This is very interesting," concluded Chloë. "I like the way everything can be done in less than fifteen minutes."

"Yes," said Maggie, pleased.

Chloë turned the page. Next, as a contrast, Maggie had put a short and punchy article entitled "Supermarket Spy: The Lowdown on GM." It summarized which stores were still stocking genetically modified products and, although it was far less informative than she'd have wished due to confines of space, it demonstrated her ability to research more topical subjects. "Most people in the business seem to think of me as a home economist, a writer of recipes, but this is the kind of thing I really like doing," Maggie explained.

Chloë flipped over some more pages, pausing to read the occasional spread. Maggie kept quiet, wanting to leave her time to absorb it properly. When she'd finished, Chloë said, "It's a very impressive range. So why do you want to work here in special projects with us? I'm sure you're aware that a lot of what we do in this department never sees the light of day."

"Yes, Jamie said. It's not because I'm out of work—I've got more than I can handle some of the time. It's only that I feel . . ." She checked Chloë's expectant face. Could she risk being perfectly frank? "I feel that women's magazines have gotten stuck in a bit of a rut when it comes to food writing and I'd like to move them on in some way."

"You do?" said Chloë.

"Yes."

"Oh. I wouldn't have expected you to think that."

"You wouldn't?" Maybe she shouldn't have been so honest. "You don't agree?"

"Oh, no." Chloë spoke hurriedly. "I do. In fact, that's been my thinking exactly with this new magazine. It's just . . ." Her voice trailed off as if she was struggling to think of how to express herself. "I'm not sure my involving you would be a good idea."

"Oh." Maggie was mystified. If we see things similarly, why are you giving me the brush-off? Do I appear too conventional? I should *never* have worn this cream suit. I look so different from the rest of these girls. They're all so trendy and interesting—I bet Chloë thinks I'm really old.

Maggie frowned. Maybe Jamie was right—she'd been wrong to come and see Chloë. She wished she could go home and get dressed all over again. But she could only say, "That's a shame. Couldn't you tell me a bit about the magazine anyway?"

"No." said Chloë abruptly. "We have a policy not to discuss new projects with freelancers at this stage."

But I'm the wife of the publisher! Surely you can trust me, thought Maggie indignantly. Still, she didn't want to use her husband's power to get work; she never had before, and wasn't keen to start now.

Chloë continued, "Anyway, I wouldn't want to waste your time." Her tone was brisk.

But she offered to tell me about the magazine yesterday, Maggie recalled. Perhaps she's worried my writing will miss the mark. She had an idea. "If it makes any difference, I could do a couple of pieces on spec? You wouldn't have to pay me unless you liked them."

"Oh, I couldn't ask you to do that."

"I don't mind."

"No, I'm sorry, but it's not company protocol."

Really? thought Maggie. Most editors would jump at the chance of getting articles for nothing. "There'd be no obligation."

"I can't, I'm afraid."

"Oh, okay." Maggie was bitterly disappointed. She took a gulp of water and zipped up her portfolio.

"I apologize, but I really must get going." Chloë stood up.

"Yes, of course." Maggie picked up her things and together they walked back through the office. At the elevator she held out her hand.

"Well, thank you very much for taking the time to see me. And if you'd like me to do anything for you at some later stage, I'd be more than delighted."

Chloë shook her hand. "I'll let you know."

"It was nice meeting you anyway." Maggie smiled. Despite feeling rejected, she wanted to part on a friendly note.

"And you," said Chloë. Then she added, as if she'd thought better of being so dismissive, "You may be right. Just from the little you've said, I do appreciate that we might see things in a similar way. Perhaps we can work together at some point in the future. It's just I don't think now's the right time. I'm very sorry."

Maggie felt slightly comforted. "That would be great."

The elevator arrived, and Maggie stepped in. As the doors slid shut she could see Chloë standing there, biting her lip. She looked lost in thought already.

Oh well, Maggie thought, maybe Jean had hit on something when she observed Chloë likes to get her own way. Perhaps she's not good at sharing things, and doesn't want me or anyone else treading on her toes.

29

Chloë stomped into the kitchen and threw down her bag. Rob was in a familiar attitude, stirring homemade soup at the stove, glass of wine by his side.

"So, what was she like?" His voice had a distinct note of glee, yet it made Chloë uncomfortable—meeting Maggie had been traumatic. She'd tried to persuade Vanessa to see her instead, but she'd had an appointment elsewhere. Then she'd phoned James. "Believe me, I'm as bothered about it as you are," he'd said. "I tried to put Maggie off, though it didn't help. Now I can't think of a way out of it."

How could she sum up her feelings? She hadn't managed to work them out for herself yet, let alone for someone else.

She'd liked her; she'd hated her.

"What did she look like?" prompted Rob.

Pacing around the kitchen, Chloë tried to put her impression of Maggie into words. "Sickening."

"Sickening?"

"Yeah. Stylish, beautiful, tall, slim, great skin . . . you can imagine."

"Blond, brunette, what?"

"Blond." Chloë sighed. "Not mousy like me. Looked bloody natural, too."

"Bet she's not as sexy as you, though."

"Thanks."

"What was she wearing?" Rob had a finely honed appreciation of fashion. When it came to judging character, someone's dress sense was high on his list of priorities.

"Some sort of classy cream suit, posh whiter-than-white deck shoes—all very understated and elegant."

"See? She doesn't sound half so horny. Whoever heard of a sex kitten in white deck shoes?"

"Mm." Chloë wasn't convinced. At the end of the day, Rob loved men. "*And* she was wearing that scarf James bought for her in New York."

"Oh." A pause. Evidently Rob couldn't think of a response to this. "So, what was she like?"

"Actually, she was very nice." Chloë sighed again.

"Nice? You're not supposed to like her!"

"I know." Chloë nodded. "But she was. I wish I could say she was a complete cow, but she was perfectly, utterly nice."

"*Nice?* Who wants to be 'nice'?" Rob snorted. "She can't have any idea about you and James, then."

"Of course she hasn't. There's no way she'd have been that shy and sweet."

"Didn't you say the woman's one of the most respected food writers around? How can she be shy with a career in journalism like that?"

"I dunno, I thought she was a bit. Though, I suppose . . ." Perhaps this was something she could interpret positively. ". . . James isn't shy at all."

"My thoughts exactly. Because neither, my dear girl, are you."

"Maybe . . ." Next to Maggie, Chloë had felt loud and gauche.

"So, what was her work like? Was it as boring as you thought it would be?"

The night before Chloë had stayed late at the office, Googling Maggie to get an idea of her talent and, with the occasional exception, had found to her relief that most of her articles online were more conventional in approach than she wanted for *All Woman.*

"No, it was much better." Chloë sat down heavily at the kitchen table. "Seeing her portfolio convinced me she's a more interesting writer than I'd realized."

"Ouch." Rob wrinkled his nose. "Here. This might help." He handed her a glass of wine.

"Thanks," said Chloë, taking more of a swig than a sip.

It was Maggie's portfolio, paradoxically, that had made Chloë resent her the most. She'd been taken aback by having to meet her so soon after her trip to New York, yet had prepared herself to deal with the face-to-face encounter. At the start of the meeting she'd been charming and friendly, because she'd been convinced that Maggie wasn't going to have anything to offer her. In the first few minutes she'd decided that James's wife was beautiful and polite, a bit shy, and surprisingly sweet. But that only underlines how different we are, she'd thought at the time. Everything that James had said previously had led Chloë to believe this, and she'd not wanted to challenge it. Thus Maggie wasn't right for James, and she certainly wasn't going to be right to work on *her* magazine.

But when Maggie had said, *"women's magazines have got stuck in a bit of a rut . . . and I'd like to move them on in some way,"* Chloë heard echoes of herself in Maggie's words. We've got a similar take on work, she'd realized. This had made her question her assumptions and left her doubtful of her analysis of Maggie's relationship with James, and very unsure of herself. So I was horrid, she recalled. Then I felt guilty for being mean, and briefly, before I said good-bye, was more pleasant to her again. Not that my being pleasant would count for anything if Maggie realized I was having an affair with her husband.

"Hello . . . Chloë?" Rob waved a hand in front of her face. "You're miles away. Come ba-ack . . ."

"Sorry."

"Anyway, bet she can't be such a go-getter as you—you're poised to launch your own magazine."

Bless him, thought Chloë. The great thing about Rob is that although I know he thinks my affair with James is a mistake, he's always on my side.

"You're not going to commission her, are you?"

"Oh, no. I managed to get out of it."

Rob chuckled. "Thank God! Not even you could cope with that."

"What do you mean, 'not even me'?"

"Aw, c'mon, love, you tend to seek out messy situations, don't you?"

Chloë began to chew her lip as she often did when she was uncomfortable. "Do you think so?"

"Yes, honey, I do."

Rob always uses terms like "honey" or "love" when he's saying something I won't want to hear, thought Chloë. I guess he's trying to soften the blow.

"It's the drama queen in you. Still, it sounds as if you handled the situation remarkably well."

"I suppose I did, in some ways. I certainly don't think she had the faintest idea about me and James, and I didn't give anything away."

"And you didn't cause any terrible scenes. Some women in your shoes would have spilled the beans to get things out in the open. Fantastic opportunity, after all, a one-to-one with his wife."

Maybe Rob thinks I'm capable of that, thought Chloë, but I'd never stoop so low. Not in front of my colleagues. Anyway, I'm not that stupid: it might mean I'd lose James forever.

Rob began to set the table. "Shift."

Chloë, who'd been propping her chin mournfully in her hands, lifted her elbows.

"In fact, what with so many crises in one week, I'm quite proud of you." He laughed; clearly he was trying to buoy her. "I mean, it's not every woman I know who could cope with having a lover who's her boss."

"He's not my boss!"

"Okay, a lover who's got some influence over her career, then."

"Not much."

"But you get my point. James gives the go-ahead to your pet project—"

"That was up to Vanessa, not him."

"Okay, okay. Let me finish, anyway. So you resign from your job and secretly go away on a business trip together. Meanwhile your ex-editor is his wife's best friend and you bump into her in Bloomingdale's when you're not supposed to be there, and then she unwittingly suggests you work with the wife, so you end up interviewing the Mrs. to work on your pet project." He paused for breath. "It makes the plotlines of Albert Square look positively mundane! And my point is not everyone could handle that lot as well as you."

"I see what you mean," acknowledged Chloë. Summarized, it sounded a great deal to manage, and she had to agree she'd surpassed herself so far. Yet was this an achievement she should be proud of? *Really?* Was it because she believed in the strength of her relationship with James, or was she in danger of being hurt if she continued putting her emotions through the wringer like this? Should she stick with things in the hope they would get better, or try to get the hell out, if—and it was a very big "if"—she still could? She didn't know the answers, and clearly Rob didn't, either.

There's only one person who can sort this out, she decided, and that's James.

30

Maggie was back from UK Magazines earlier than expected. She had half an hour before Nathan finished school so she decided to see if Georgie was home. As luck would have it, her new friend answered the door and beamed.

"Hi!"

"I wasn't sure you'd be in."

"You must have gotten a psychic vibe. I often have Wednesdays off because I work Saturdays. Come in. Coffee?"

"Lovely." Maggie stepped into the tiny hallway, which seemed even smaller thanks to numerous watercolors smothering the walls, and followed Georgie into the kitchen. "I hope I'm not interrupting?" she asked, seeing books and papers piled high on the table.

"Oh, no! It's always like this. I'm very bad at leaving work at the shop." Georgie reached for a jar of instant. Maggie flinched, but was too polite to say she'd changed her mind and ask for tea. "And I've been trying to keep myself busy—shift my focus." She launched straight into the situation on which Maggie was keen for an update. "Alex split up with me last week." She sighed.

"I'm sorry," said Maggie; she sensed the pain of troubled romance all too keenly at the moment. "Are you okay?"

"I guess." Georgie held her unruly hair off her face and frowned. "It's not as if it had been that long or anything. It's only, when you get to my age . . . Sometimes I wish something would work out. He was very decent about it."

Maggie nodded to herself. Typical Alex, she thought. Nonetheless she could see that Georgie looked paler than usual, she appeared tired, less bouncy. She tried to offer comfort. "He only parted from his wife a few months ago. Maybe it was a bit soon."

"Maybe . . ." Georgie nodded. Then she added, "I just want to meet a nice man who appreciates me. A chap like Jamie, perhaps. I mean, you two seem happy, well suited. How did you do it?"

Maggie was unsure what to say. Her inclination was to respond with something noncommittal, although being frank might make not just Georgie feel better, but herself too. "It's not that great always, you know, being married. Jamie's not quite as wonderful as you might think."

"Really?"

"No. In fact, we've been having a bit of a difficult time recently. Hopefully we'll get over it, but still . . . It's ironic, isn't it—sometimes I envy women like you who have their freedom, who can do what they want, who only have to answer to themselves. Believe me, our relationship is far from one long mutual appreciation society."

"Oh." Georgie appeared taken aback. Then she smiled. "Isn't it funny? We always think everyone else is so sorted, and once you get to know them better, you often find that they're pretty vulnerable, too."

"Indeed." Maggie remembered how she'd come to a similar conclusion when talking to Fran. She laughed with a touch of sorrow. "I've certainly been feeling pretty vulnerable lately."

"You surprise me."

"As you say, people aren't always as resilient as they seem."

Georgie's expression exuded understanding and she said, "Well, I know one person who definitely appreciates you."

"Who's that?"

"Alex."

"Alex!"

"Oh, yes." Georgie leaned back against the counter, more relaxed now. "If you ask me, never mind his ex-wife, I think he's still a mite in love with you."

"Surely not?"

"I might be wrong . . . but whenever he talks about you he sounds so fond of you."

"Oh!" It was Maggie's turn to be taken aback. Yet she was comforted too.

"There you go." Georgie took a large gulp of coffee. "You remember that. I doubt any of my exes still carry a torch for me after fifteen years, or whatever it's been."

I *am* flattered, thought Maggie. But however nice it is to hear my old boyfriend continues to hold me in high regard, the man I really want to appreciate me is Jamie.

As he ran to greet her in the playground, fair hair catching the sun, socks around his ankles, Maggie observed that Nathan had Band-Aids on both knees and both elbows, whereas that morning he'd had only two.

"How did you get these?" she asked, examining his latest wounds.

"Soccer. I scored a goal!" His love of the game never seemed tempered by tripping over, she thought tenderly. He was carrying a large roll of paper. "Here," he said, handing it to her. "This is for you."

"Thank you. I'll have a look in a moment." Maggie tucked the picture under her arm and they set off, Nathan chatting away about his day. They stopped en route to feed the ducks, a frequent ritual. Maggie often had crusts left over from creating breadcrumb toppings for her recipes; she'd brought some in an old Waitrose carrier bag.

"I want to do it," he said, so she gave him the bag and took a seat under the weeping willows by the river. While Nathan busied himself throwing the crusts as far as he could to test whether the white ducks were quicker than the mallards, she unrolled the painting and held it at arm's length.

Mummy, it said, and was signed, with some letters back to front, *Nathan Slater*. She caught her breath. She'd seen Nathan's interpretation of herself many, many times—blond hair the same bright shade of powder-paint yellow, triangular dress, big circular hands with digits carefully attached like rays of the sun, long legs, giant feet. But this picture was different. Normally Nathan painted her with her mouth upturned in a happy semi-circle. Here her mouth was unmistakably turned down.

It didn't take Nathan long to learn that all ducks were equally fast when motivated by food and return to her side.

"But I look so sad in this!" she protested, holding out the painting.

"You *are* sad."

"Oh dear," said Maggie, rolling up the picture. "Do you think so?"

"Mm." Nathan looked down and scuffed his shoes on the path. Clearly he didn't like talking about it.

"Well, we'll have to do something to solve that, then." Maggie slapped her thighs cheerily and got to her feet. "I've an idea what'll make me a happy mummy again. Shall we pop into Nell's Country Kitchen and buy some of their delicious homemade fudge?"

"Ooh, yes!"

Nell's was the tearoom close by on Middle Street. They pushed open the door with a merry tinkle of the bell, and Nathan cantered over to the baskets on the pine dresser where he knew the fudge was displayed.

"Now, let's see," said Maggie, picking through the different flavors. "Which one of these is special magic fudge with Cheer-up Mummy po-tion in it?"

"This one!" Nathan selected the vanilla and nut.

"That'll *definitely* make a happy mummy," agreed Maggie. She handed over the exact change and they went home and had it for tea.

———

That does it, Maggie decided, once she'd put Nathan to bed and sat down in the living room with her feet up and a gin and tonic to await her husband's return from work. Nathan's image of a sad mummy is worrying. Evidently he's aware things aren't right, and it'll be affecting him. And if I'm at the stage of confiding in my neighbors, obviously they're affecting me hugely too. I've got to talk to Jamie tonight.

She took a sip of her drink and braced herself. Just then, an idea came to her.

I know what would cheer me up and give me strength, she thought: a chat with Alex. Get the lowdown on him and Georgie.

"It's me," she said when he picked up.

"Mags! I was meaning to call you. How are you?"

"I'm okay." She didn't want to talk about herself. "More to the point, how are *you*?"

"I'm good."

"I've just seen Georgie," Maggie prompted.

"Oh." Alex sounded worried. "Is she okay?"

"Yeah, yeah." Maggie didn't want to be disloyal to Georgie. "Or, at least, she will be soon, I guess."

"I feel a bit bad," Alex confessed.

"Oh?"

"It's never easy, finishing things, is it?"

Momentarily Maggie flashed back to when she and Alex had split up. She'd just started working in magazines and, consumed by her new job, was unwilling to settle down so soon after graduating, though Alex had wanted to. But she'd never been sure she was making the right decision ending it, which meant, for once in her life, she'd been a little heartless.

"No," she said.

"Probably Georgie was a bit of a rebound thing—you know, after Stella."

"Do you think?"

"Now I do, yes." Alex was always straight with Maggie. "We had a lot of fun, and she's a lovely woman, but I don't feel she's quite right for me. You won't ever say that to her though, will you? I've tried to part from her on reasonable terms, though that's often easier said than done."

"Of course I won't!" Maggie wouldn't dream of being so tactless.

At that moment the front door slammed, and she heard the familiar rustle of Jamie slinging his jacket over the banister.

"Oh dear," she said hurriedly. "That's Jamie. I'd better go."

"Already?"

"I'll call you soon," she promised, hung up, then called out, "I'm in here." A couple of seconds later Jamie appeared at the living room door.

She decided to open with something that didn't involve the both of them. "I saw Chloë today."

Yet even that seemed to disconcert him. "Um . . ." He paused. "How did it go?" He went over to the drinks cabinet, got out one of the decanters they'd been given as a wedding present, and poured himself a whisky.

"Actually, it was a bit odd."

"Odd?" Now he sounded concerned.

"Yes. Well, rather, *she* was a bit odd."

"Really?" He turned away to replace the decanter. Why was it these days he barely ever looked her in the eye?

"You've met her, haven't you?"

"Yes." He took a gulp of his drink.

"Did you think she was odd?"

"No, not particularly." Another gulp.

"Moody?"

"No." He sat down, opting not for the sofa next to her but one of the armchairs. They were at right angles to each other, both with their feet propped on the coffee table, relaxed yet unrelaxed, poles apart.

"Maybe it was me, then."

"Why? What did she say?"

"Nothing I could put my finger on." Maggie frowned, wondering how to explain. "At first she was really friendly, charming even. Then, when she saw my portfolio, she turned cool."

"Perhaps she didn't think your work was right for *All Woman.*"

"Perhaps . . ."

Jamie took a third sip of whisky. He seemed to be drinking it awfully fast. "I did warn you that you might not be of a like mind."

"I know." But years of being the social observer meant Maggie was a good judge of people's reactions, and she was pretty sure that Chloë had liked her work. "You can tell me I'm imagining things, but I don't think that's what it was."

"So, what *do* you think it was?"

Yes, I'm right: he *is* perturbed, Maggie decided. Possibly he's more bothered about what's going on in my life than I've given him credit for.

"Something Jean said . . ." Maggie struggled for words.

"What did Jean say?" Jamie seemed angry now. God, he was so confusing these days! Then again, he'd always been a little threatened by the closeness of Maggie and Jean's friendship.

"She said something along the lines of Chloë not liking to share things . . . so I wondered . . ."

"What?"

"Whether she was being possessive."

"Possessive?"

"Mm, that she didn't want to share working on the magazine project with me or something."

"Really?"

"I can't think of any other reason why she'd be so funny. Can you?"

"Er . . ."

"After all, my work's okay, isn't it?"

"Of course! It's fine. In fact it's more than fine, it's great!"

Now he's all enthusiasm, observed Maggie. She couldn't think of anything to add. "Anyway . . . I didn't want to talk about Chloë."

"Ah?"

"It's no big deal, I suppose. I'll simply have to look to someone else for the kind of work I want to do." Maggie took a sip of her gin for Dutch courage. "I wanted to talk about us." To show she was serious, she tried to look at him directly. But Jamie glanced down at his feet, just like Nathan earlier. Or Nathan was like Jamie. It didn't matter; what mattered was Nathan's upset had opened Maggie's eyes. As his room was directly above, she dropped her voice. "We can't avoid this forever."

"No," said Jamie gruffly.

"Don't tell me you hadn't noticed."

"No. I had."

"Well?" Maggie felt herself shaking again.

Then he surprised her. "I'd kind of thought I should talk to you."

Perhaps this is good, she hoped: if Jamie is prepared to acknowledge things are sticky and wants to talk, surely he'll come to Relate. "What did you want to chat about?"

"To be honest, I wasn't sure what to say."

"Oh?"

"That's why I didn't say anything."

"I see." Though she didn't. He seemed to have lost his nerve.

Silence.

Then Jamie ventured, "So what were *you* wanting to say?"

It occurred to Maggie that Nathan's pictures might be a good place to start. "Hang on a minute." She got up. "I've something to show you." She went into the kitchen and collected the paper roll from the top of the fridge, then returned to the living room. She handed it to Jamie. He looked without saying a word.

"Notice anything?" asked Maggie, finally.

"It's of you."

How selfish that his first concern was for his own standing in Nathan's eyes! Yet perhaps that was significant too: absent-father syndrome.

"Anything else?"

He stopped, and examined it again. "You look miserable?"

"Yes."

More silence. At last Jamie said, "Is that true?"

Maggie was bottling up so much resentment that she didn't know where to start, or how. As she sat there, on the huge Chesterfield, she could feel her heart thudding in her chest, her cheeks burning, the gin glass cold and clammy in her hand. All at once she felt a surge of fury, stirred up by protectiveness of Nathan. Eventually she spat—"You could say I'm pretty fucked off, yes." Then out it poured. "I'm fucked off with you working late. I'm fucked off with you not helping more around the house. I'm fucked off with you not supporting me in public. I'm fucked off with you not calling me from America. I'm fucked off with you for not talking—you've hardly spoken to me since you got back from New York, for God's sake! I'm fucked off with you for making me—yes, *making* me compromise and slave away writing articles I hate, just to alleviate your neurosis about money. And, above all, I'm fucked off with you for not being willing even to discuss having another child."

He could be in no doubt as to the level of her wrath and pain. Yet he merely stared down at his shoes, which made her angrier still.

"You're pathetic," she said.

Jamie was shocked: now at least he looked at her. "Oh?"

"Or, rather," she corrected herself, "your recent behavior is pathetic."

This made him flush, whether with anger or guilt she couldn't be sure. "I just . . ." he stammered ". . . I don't know how I . . . feel about things right now."

"You surprise me," she said venomously. "About what, precisely, don't you *'know how you feel'*?"

He went even redder: "It's not you; it's me."

"Thank you for that insight." She was relieved that he had acknowledged it wasn't her fault, but it was such a hackneyed excuse, and it didn't help her understand things any better—she didn't know what "it" was. The half-formulated belief that he was being unfaithful had remained with her since the day of the exhibition, but she was afraid to articulate it. Instead she asked, "What is it with you? Some midlife crisis or something?"

"Perhaps, I've been feeling a bit claustrophobic lately. I guess I'm not sure quite where I'm at."

"How original." Again she couldn't resist heavy irony. He sounded so juvenile, like a teenager, and she resented being made to feel that she was hemming him in. So she added, knowing it would really annoy him, "Jean was right, then."

"Fuck Jean."

"How dare you talk like that about my friend!"

"How dare you talk to your friend about me!"

"If you won't talk to me, who the hell else am I supposed to talk to?"

"No one."

"No one? Oh, get real, Jamie! I may keep things to myself a lot of the time, but I'm not a bloody robot! We've hardly made love for three months, and when we do I can tell your heart's not in it—probably because you're petrified of getting me pregnant. We've not spoken, you're hardly here, you don't help me, you nag me about money, you go away, you don't call—what on earth am I meant to do? Not breathe a word? Jesus, I had to go to the GP I was so miserable. The doctor, for heaven's sake! And let me tell you, I found him a whole lot easier to talk to than you!"

"You went to our GP?"

"Yes."

"You talked to the doctor about us?"

"Yes."

"Oh, great. So now everyone in the village will know about our marital problems."

Maggie had a flash of guilt about how she'd confided in Georgie earlier, which enhanced her indignation. I wouldn't *need* to confide in these people if he talked to me! she protested inwardly. And, anyway, I didn't say *that* much to Georgie, did I?

"In case it had escaped your notice, Jamie, doctors are sworn to secrecy, so you needn't bloody worry that he'll go around spilling the beans in the goddamn supermarket."

Maggie realized the conversation was not going the way she'd intended at all. I was supposed to be persuading Jamie to come to counseling, not driving a wedge between us, she thought. She was once more conscious there was only the ceiling separating them from Nathan, so she halted to calm down. "Anyway, I think that's the point, isn't it?"

Jamie appeared bewildered.

"I've had to offload to somebody."

"More than somebody. Somebod*ies*."

"Somebody, somebodies, whatever." She moved on, more calmly. "My point is that I'd much rather be discussing things with you." She took a deep breath. "So I wondered, would you come with me for counseling?"

"Counseling?"

Her heart sank; this was going to be hard work. "Yes. Marriage-guidance counseling."

"I don't need bloody counseling."

"*You* might not. *We* do."

"No, we don't." She knew Jamie in this mood. Stubbornness personified. For the time being she was sure he wouldn't budge, but she forced herself to give it one last try. "It's not a bad thing, Jamie. Hundreds of couples do it."

"And we're not one of those couples."

"If we're not one of '*those couples*' who are we?"

"Now you're being ridiculous. I don't want to talk to some stranger about my marriage. All right?"

She inhaled deeply. "Will you at least think about it?"

"No."

Sometimes Maggie wanted to kill him. If I had a gun I'd put a bullet in his brain here and now, she thought. Sitting so smug and self-righteous and self-obsessed on the sodding seat nearby.

"I'd rather sort things out my own way," he said.

He clearly meant in a way that suited him. This convinced her. "Fine. I'll go on my own."

"You can't go on your own!"

"Oh, can't I?" she said. "Just watch me."

31

Summer gave way to autumn and just as a patch of mild weather kept leaves hanging on branches in semi-browned suspension, so reluctance permeated Chloë's mental state regarding her affair. She sensed James was equally unwilling to face the sobering consequences of their actions, thus instead of making demands or precipitating a confrontation, she let their relationship drift on as it had before they'd been away.

"He's having his cake and eating it," Rob cautioned her. "Allow things to slide now, and it's all too easy to do it indefinitely." Heedless of his warning, Chloë continued to see James once a week—twice if she was lucky—but at least this allowed her to focus on work, which might otherwise have suffered.

As well as asking Craig to write a piece on children and divorce as promised, she commissioned one writer with a reputation for investigative ruthlessness to produce a particularly provocative feature, and another known for her soul-searching interviews to go one step further than usual with a star profile. She invited a favorite freelancer to come up with the sharpest, wittiest column he could conceive of, a second to vent spleen with a biting series of reviews, and a third to compose an up-to-the-minute social exposé. "I want you to stretch yourself," she said to each. "Don't hold back. Write as if there was no editor or advertising director limiting what you are allowed to do."

But she couldn't assign all the work out to others and, anyway, she wanted to draft some of the features herself, so one morning she decided she could do with a hand from Patsy. Given that Patsy wasn't employed on *All Woman* and Chloë had no wish to antagonize Jean by stealing her during working hours, she phoned her and suggested they go for lunch.

They met in the foyer. "It's a bit embarrassing explaining this in an open-plan office," Chloë said, ushering Patsy out of the building.

"Blimey! It must be hush-hush—I didn't think you ever got embarrassed!"

"You'll discover what I mean soon enough," said Chloë.

"Tell me, tell me!"

"Patience."

"Oooh!" She could see Patsy was both infuriated and thrilled.

They made their way down Long Acre, crossed onto Endell Street, and headed to Shaftesbury Avenue.

"Where are we going?" panted Patsy; dysfunctional footwear and legs even shorter than Chloë's meant it was hard for her to keep up.

Chloë tapped her nose knowingly. "Aha."

Along Denmark Street, with its music shops that had been there forever, over the pelican crossing on Charing Cross Road, and they were there.

"*Ann Summers!*" Patsy giggled. "Are you sure this isn't something you should be doing with your man, not me?"

But Patsy doesn't know I *have* a man, thought Chloë, momentarily flummoxed. Still, this wasn't the moment to ask what she meant, so she moved on, saying firmly, "No. This is a project, Patsy. Work. Not play. Research."

"You're having a laugh!"

Chloë grabbed a basket and strode purposefully past the underwear, nurses' uniforms, and maids' outfits, and up the steps into the back. Here the lighting was less harsh. She noted there were no lone women shoppers, only couples, and men, presumably buying for their girlfriends or wives. She scanned the shelves—hmm, not the videos or magazines, or the handcuffs, and certainly not the rather tacky "play" whips or masks. (Far more creative to improvise, Chloë believed.)

She halted in front of the biggest display. "This is what we're after."

Patsy was close behind. "*Dildos!*" she whooped.

"Vibrators," said Chloë, mock-sedately. "They call this the Vibrator Bar." They peered at the samples lined up like giant lipsticks before them. There were small pink ones and huge black ones, ridged ones and ribbed ones, ones with curved ends and straight ones, ones with rather alarming prongs, and ones that looked more like massagers. There was even a pretty butterfly-shaped device that didn't resemble a penis at all. Patsy switched it on and jumped back, alarmed, as it sprang to life in her hand. "Now, then," Chloë directed, "let's decide on six different kinds."

"*Six!*"

"Yup."

"Bloody hell, Chloë, I always thought you were a bit of a goer, but six? You're insatiable!"

"They're not all for *me*," laughed Chloë. "One's for you."

"Are you implying Doug's not enough for me?" Doug was Patsy's boyfriend of several years.

"Far be it from me to criticize the prowess of your true love, Patsy dear. I wouldn't dare." Doug was six foot four and built like a rugby player. "No, my friend, this is a little project for girls, *toutes seules*. You know those consumer panels they have in the Sunday papers and *Good Housekeeping*? 'Tried and Tested'?"

Patsy nodded.

"You, my sweet, innocent Patsy are going to head up my specially selected panel for *All Woman* to put six of these lurve machines through their paces!"

"No!"

"Oh, yes. Who wants to know which is the best bottle opener or variety of baked beans? They're hardly the most important thing in a woman's life. And as for stay-on lip gloss and waterproof mascaras, how unadventurous! *All Woman* is going to test those things that you always wanted tested, but were to afraid to ask."

"But we can try them out *here*." Patsy examined one with an intriguing extra prong.

"Not where it counts, you can't."

Patsy giggled. "They'll never let you!"

"Who's *they*?"

"Advertisers. UK Magazines. You know."

"Depends how it's done. Okay, so maybe Estée Lauder won't buy the space opposite, but I'm convinced somebody will. Black Lace novels or Durex, for instance. We simply have to make sure it's written with humor"— Chloë scooped up a mammoth chocolate-colored vibrator called Throbbing Muscle and put it in her basket—"and grace."

They stopped off at Prêt before returning to the office. Perched on high stools at the window so that they could watch passersby, Chloë wolfed a hummus sandwich and Diet Coke at ninety miles per hour, while Patsy picked at a vegetarian sushi.

Partway through, Patsy ventured, "I'm glad we did this."

"I told you, you're in need of a little more buzz in your love life," Chloë teased. "You and Doug have been going out way too long."

"No, not that. I meant I'm glad I've got the chance to have a chat, just us two. There's something I wanted to ask."

"What's that?"

"Are you seeing anyone at the moment?"

Chloë swallowed a large mouthful. She felt herself coloring immediately. "No."

Patsy looked at her carefully. "Are you sure?"

"Of course I'm sure!" That was probably a touch too defensive. "Why do you ask?"

"I thought maybe you were."

"What on earth should make you think that?"

"Lots of things."

Chloë took another bite. She couldn't possibly be seen to be put off her food—Patsy would glean something was up. "Like what?"

"Like . . . talking on the phone opposite me in hushed whispers during your last few weeks at *Babe* . . . your increasingly sexy wardrobe . . . your general glow . . . that mysterious 'vacation' when you wouldn't reveal where you were going or who with . . . Do you want me to carry on?"

And Chloë thought she'd been so discreet. "Mm."

"Look." Patsy took a deep breath. "You don't have to tell me if you don't want to. I have my suspicions but, actually, in this case I'd be happy to keep them to myself." Chloë raised an eyebrow. It was uncharacteristic of Patsy to *volunteer* to keep mum. Normally she'd only do it if asked. "It's just I'm not alone in having them."

"What do you mean?" Now Chloë paled.

"I might as well get to the point. You always were crap at lying. And your every gesture is giving you away. Are you having an affair with James Slater or what?"

Chloë felt her face turn from white to scarlet.

"Obviously you are."

In vain Chloë tried to bluff her way out. "I am not!"

"I've *told* you, I've known for ages that you're seeing someone; I wasn't sure who it was but then Jean said something and I put two and two together—"

"And made five!"

"And made four. You're playing with fire, you know." Patsy looked at Chloë sternly. The effect was diminished by her tiny stature and crazy pixie hairstyle, but Chloë could tell she was genuinely concerned.

What was the point of denying it any longer? It was more important to find out who else knew, and what they knew. After all, if she begged, Patsy *would* keep it quiet. If there was one thing Patsy liked more than gossip it was to be privy to a juicy secret. "You swear not to tell a soul?"

Patsy nodded solemnly. "Cross my heart." She made the age-old schoolgirl gesture.

"And you'll tell me everything Jean said to you?" This was what most worried Chloë.

"My foremost allegiance is to my old features editor, natch."

"Okay . . . Here goes." As swiftly as she could—the minutes were ticking by and they were due back at work—she gave Patsy a brief outline of her liaison with James.

"Well, I'll be damned!" said Patsy, when she'd finished.

"I do really like him," she said quietly. "I like him a lot."

Patsy ignored this. "One question. Then I'll tell you what Jean said, promise."

Chloë checked her watch. "Okay, but only one. I've got heaps to do this afternoon."

"Is he a good shag?"

"Patsy!"

"Ooh, go on, tell me . . . I'm the one who spotted his potential."

"I'm not sure I should reveal that," said Chloë haughtily.

"For goodness' sake!" Patsy jigged up and down impatiently. "You take me to Ann Summers to buy vibrators and then go coy on me."

"Yeah, I s'pose." Chloë felt uncomfortable. Joking aside, she didn't like reducing her relationship to such a low level. She could see that dragging out her colleague on a shopping trip to buy sex toys had done little to enhance her image as an old-fashioned romantic. I want Patsy to understand that we care deeply for each other, she thought. Yet she was too self-conscious to reveal she was in love with him, so she said: "It's great—he's great, if you must know, but that's all you'll get out of me. Go on, your turn. Jean. Shoot."

"Well, so far you're safe. And"—Patsy lifted her chin proudly—"you've me to thank for that. I've batted off every suggestion she makes with a denial."

"Thank you. You're a star."

"Though you ought to be careful. Bloody careful. That woman"—she leaned in close for effect—"has eyes like a hawk and a nose like a bloodhound."

"No need to tell me that. I worked under her editorship. What did she say?"

"Obviously she doesn't have access to your feeble attempts at 'secret' phone calls like me, and she hasn't said anything to me outright. I'm not sure she even realizes that it's James—at least, she's not told me she thinks it's him. Though I don't think she would, what with Maggie being her friend. But she does believe you're seeing someone on the sly. She asked me point-blank the other day but I hotly refuted it—and she *did* see you in New York. She said it was odd you hadn't told her that was where you were going when you knew she'd be there."

Chloë felt rather foolish. "Actually, I'd forgotten she would be. It was all so last minute my going."

"She's getting close to sniffing you two out, that's what I reckon. Only the other day I heard her bitching to Vanessa she didn't understand why on earth you hadn't let Maggie Slater write for *All Woman*. That's how I worked out for sure it was James. I know you; you're a tight cow when it comes to commissions. So I couldn't think of another reason why you wouldn't want to work with someone with such a good reputation who was prepared to contribute free of charge."

"Oops."

"Oops indeed. Anyway"—Patsy got to her feet—"we better go."

They grabbed an Ann Summers carrier bag apiece, slung their empty sandwich packets in the bin on their way out, and raced back up Long Acre.

"Next time she asks, pretend you've found out who I'm seeing, and that it's someone else." Chloë gasped for breath.

"Will do," said Patsy. "Just you watch your step, you femme fatale, you."

Although Chloë's relationship with James hadn't moved on apace, there was one important development: he was going to meet Rob.

Using the well-worn squash-night excuse, James had agreed to come around, and Rob had offered to make a meal. He was a better cook than

Chloë. "If you do it, it's"—he made a slicing gesture across his throat, accompanied by a choking sound—"to your affair. His wife is Margaret Wilson, woman!" It hardly made Chloë feel like donning a pinafore and dusting off her one cookbook.

She ensured she was home at a reasonable hour—if she wasn't permitted to cook, she wanted at least to create the right ambience. On her way she stopped at the big Asda nearby, and bought candles, paper napkins, three bottles of wine—more expensive ones than normal—and some cat food.

The bags weighed a ton. As she staggered home up St. John's Hill in the dusky drizzle, they sliced into her hands, and when she'd finally dumped them on the kitchen table, they'd left cruel red marks on her palms. One of the tins of Whiskas rolled onto the floor and nearly tripped up Rob. He was slicing onions with tears streaming down his face and, glancing down at the offending object, took his eyes off the knife and cut his finger.

"Fuck!"

"Sorry." She winced. "Are you okay?"

"I'll live," growled Rob, running his finger under the tap. "This man had better be worth it."

She was nervous already; this didn't help. Other than her dad and her brother, James and Rob were the two most important men in her life. She tried to cheer him. "So, what are we having? It smells gorgeous."

"Roast halibut with spiced lentils and coriander."

He's making a big effort, Chloë thought.

"I hope he's not going to be late. All this needs timing to the minute."

About this she was confident. "He's never late."

"No, I'm sure every second counts when you've a wife to get back to."

She let the jibe pass. "Do you mind if I freshen up before setting the table?"

"Go ahead."

Chloë headed into the bathroom for a speedy shower. Back in her room, Potato was mewing pitifully at the door, keen to get out for a share of the fish. Ignoring him, she struggled to pull clean knickers on when she'd not allowed herself time to dry. Rummage rummage—where was that top? Ah, yes! Rush rush, quick quick, pull on her shiny black trousers—ugh, they were sticking to her thighs—and those mules, James hadn't seen them before, two minutes on her makeup, a few seconds scrunching her hair with the dryer—it had gone a bit frizzy in the rain—and phew, she was ready.

She panted back into the kitchen and began setting things up. There was just enough space to entertain at the small table if she cleared it of gubbins, so she swept up the piles of magazines and unpaid bills and dumped them in a corner of the living room. She grabbed the broken chair from the hallway and banged the leg back into place—it might possibly take her weight for the evening if she was careful. Next she hunted for three matching wineglasses—in vain. Oh, well, once you've put a folded napkin in each you can't really tell, she decided. She had the same problem with the crockery—theirs was a motley collection of plates. But mix 'n' match is supposed to be in, she persuaded herself. Finally, she ran around the apartment scooping up every tea-light holder she could find and dropped a candle in each.

"There," she said, turning out the main light so that they could have a quick look.

"Wonderful. Almost wouldn't recognize the place. Now, stir this. It's my turn."

Obediently Chloë took the spot at the stove while Rob disappeared into the bathroom. While he was gone her anticipation mounted.

I do so want them to get along, she thought. I know Rob's disinclined to like him, but hopefully James's charm will win him over . . .

Just then the landline rang. With one hand, she reached over and picked up the phone.

"Hello." She tucked the receiver under her chin so she could carry on performing her culinary duties. Well I never, she thought, I'm surprising myself, I am really enjoying this.

"Hi," said a familiar voice, muffled by the sound of a train. "It's James."

"Oh, hi!" Chloë could scarcely contain her excitement. "Where are you?"

"Waterloo."

"Ah, good—you'll be here any minute!"

A particularly loud train thundered past. "I'm afraid I'm not coming."

Chloë thought she must have misheard. "What?"

"I can't make it. I'm terribly sorry."

"Oh." Chloë was so disappointed, she didn't know what to say. There was a long pause. "Why not?"

"It's Maggie, I'm afraid."

"Ri-ight . . ." She knew she sounded pissed off. But, hell, I *am* pissed off, she thought. Gutted.

James elaborated: "She went to see this woman today, and now she wants to talk."

"Which woman?"

"Some marriage counselor or something."

"Oh." Stunned, Chloë struggled to take this in. Does that mean the two of them are trying to work things out? she thought. James never told me.

"I'm sorry, I truly am."

"Yeah."

"I promise I'll make it up to you."

"But we've made everything for you! I've bought the wine! Rob's cooked something specially!" She looked at the beautifully laid place settings, the three chairs, the bottle of white that Rob had put in a cooler on the table while she'd been getting ready. She felt like an absolute idiot. And what would Rob say? She could hear his judgement already.

"I know, I know." Even through the background noise, Chloë could sense his guilt down the line. "Can't you eat it, you and him?"

"No, we can't. Well, I mean we can, or Potato can have it, but it's hardly the same."

"I feel like a complete shit."

By now Chloë was trembling. Should she say it? Yes, fuck it, she would. "Well, you are," she said, and slammed down the phone.

32

The drive into Guildford was so familiar that, although the day was damp and dark, Maggie could focus her thoughts elsewhere.

The last few weeks have been good and bad, she thought. Good because of work: her attitude had shifted and she'd had the courage to approach a couple of editors she particularly respected with feature ideas she believed were genuinely different. Both had been unequivocally enthusiastic (a contrast to Chloë, Maggie noted), so she was currently drafting the first of two commissions. Indeed, she had been so wrapped up in research that she'd been taken by surprise when she'd looked up at the kitchen clock and seen it was time to go, forcing her to leave her notes strewn over the table.

Speeding through the countryside, Maggie's head was still full of the article. She had given it the working title, "Is Your Money Where Your Mouth Is?" and, in order to research it, recently accompanied half a dozen professionals from the food industry on a weekend survival course. There, as well as having to forage for edible berries, mushrooms, and plants in the wilds of Wales, she and the others—who had included a chef, a supermarket buyer, a dietician, and a butcher—had had to kill a couple of fowl and then eat them. Inevitably all bar the butcher were uncomfortable when faced with the stark reality of slaughter.

The experience had tested her too—not only because, after years of eating poultry with Jamie and Nathan, she'd found she couldn't attempt to strangle a live bird so had reassessed her own dietary habits, but also because she'd had to deal with strangers. She surprised herself with how much she'd enjoyed the weekend and it was especially gratifying to leave Jamie and the house solely in charge of Nathan.

That she'd been busy meant to some extent Maggie had been able to bury her worries about Jamie. He hadn't been best pleased when she'd started insisting she was only going to serve them fish, vegetables, and dairy products from now on.

"But I *like* chicken!" he'd protested. "I don't want to eat bloody seafood all the time!"

"Feel free to cook it yourself," she'd said.

Their frequent rows increased Maggie's worries something serious was amiss, but she refrained from asking him outright in case she discovered something she'd not the strength to hear.

Today I'm going to begin tackling this mess, she resolved as she drove into the outskirts of Guildford and dutifully dropped her speed to thirty. I can't bury my head forever. This is not just about me: it involves Nathan too.

Maggie knew roughly where she was headed, so she parked the car on a side street. She got out, checked the front wheels to make sure she wasn't overlapping a double yellow, flicked on the alarm, and walked back onto the main road.

What a vile day, she thought. It can't seem to decide whether it's worth raining properly or not. A gray drizzle hung in the air, getting into her hair and under her skin.

"Three four one, three three nine," she muttered to herself, counting down the door numbers, eventually stopping outside a modern office block with a distinct ring of municipal services about it. She unfolded the typed sheet. Three three five, this was it. She went up the path to the porch.

There, among the signs for voluntary services and family planning, was the word RELATE. "Third floor," it said.

She pushed open one of the wire-glass double doors and looked in vain for an elevator. Evidently she was expected to take the stairs. As she climbed, her navy loafers echoed against the linoleum, and by the time she reached the top she was a little short of breath. How on earth is anyone elderly or in a wheelchair supposed to get up here? she wondered.

On the third floor, there appeared to be only one way to go. Although someone had tried to make it more inviting with potted plants and magazines, the small waiting area had the same cheap but not that cheerful look as the rest of the building. There was a desk with a PC, yet the chair was empty.

All of a sudden Maggie felt overwhelmed with uncertainty and apprehension, just as she had in Dr. Hopkin's office. What am I supposed to do now? she asked herself.

At that moment one of the doors opened, and a woman popped her head around. "Margaret Slater?"

"Yes."

"Sorry," said the woman, nodding toward the empty chair. "Lorna's off sick today. I heard you come in. Is it just you?"

Maggie felt conspicuously alone. "Yes."

"No matter," the woman said warmly. "Give me five minutes and I'll be with you. Make yourself at home."

Maggie didn't feel relaxed enough to sit down so she stood at the window, looking out over a rain-soaked Guildford, worrying about what the next hour would hold. From her first glimpse, the woman was older than Maggie had expected, probably in her fifties. This impression was confirmed a few minutes later when she invited Maggie into her consulting room.

"My name's Nina," she said, sitting down in a well-worn swivel chair that creaked.

There were two armchairs opposite her, one mustard, the other brown.

"Er, where should I sit?" asked Maggie hovering.

"Either."

Maggie plumped for the brown one. Now she could get the measure of the woman better. She had what Maggie thought of as an apple figure: most of her bulk was centrally placed. She had a big bosom and a large tummy, although Maggie could see that she had small wrists and elegant ankles. Her hair was gray and well cut, in a short style that not that many women of Nina's size could take. But Nina had a strong face with a big, broad mouth and good cheekbones, so it suited her. She was dressed equally confidently in a rust-colored bouclé jumper and olive-green velvet trousers, offset by chunky silver and turquoise jewelry that rattled when she moved. The effect was impressive and Maggie thought she looked marvelous, but it did little to lessen her anxiety.

Nina leaned back. "I often think it helps if I start by telling you a bit about how this works."

Maggie was relieved. In spite of her resolution to talk openly, she felt overwhelmed with shyness.

"First, I need to check if this appointment is okay with you on a regular basis?"

"Yes, it is," said Maggie. "I have a son, Nathan, but I've arranged for him to go to his friend's in the village after school."

"Good. And I should explain to you that the session is always the same length—an hour—and we can't overrun, even if you're late, because I see someone directly afterwards."

Maggie couldn't imagine she would wish to prolong the agony of talking about emotional issues, but didn't say so. "I understand that."

"Next there's the issue of funding." She handed Maggie a form. "You'll need to fill in your details and bring this back to the next session. Then we can see if you're eligible for a subsidy, or what."

"Thanks." Maggie took the form. "Though to be honest I doubt it."

"Finally, I wanted to ask," here Nina adopted a more sympathetic tone, "whether it's only today that your partner couldn't join you?"

Maggie found herself blushing. She was both disarmed by the directness of the question, and ashamed.

What will Nina make of the fact Jamie refused to come? she worried.

She might see it as a sign our relationship is beyond hope. Perhaps there's a limit to how many sessions I'm allowed to attend on my own: this is marriage guidance, after all.

The silence seemed interminable. "I don't know," she said.

"Oh?" It appeared Nina wanted her to elaborate.

It was as though Maggie was about to launch herself off a precipice. She was acutely aware that once she'd spoken, she couldn't go back on what she'd said. The questions came thick and fast. If I tell her, will Nina think me disloyal? Demanding? Unreasonable, even? Go on! she exhorted herself. You're the one who wanted to do this!

"Well . . ." She hesitated. "He hasn't exactly been receptive to the idea of counseling so far, no." She gained momentum. "In fact, I suppose it's fair to say that he's been dead set against it."

"So it was your idea?"

"Yes. Or rather it was my friend Jean's suggestion, but it seemed like a good one." She sighed. "We've been getting on so badly, me and Jamie—my husband—that sometimes it seems any attempt I make at communicating is met by a brick wall."

"And how does that make you feel?"

"Desperate." Maggie answered simply. "That's why I'm here." She was silent again. At that moment it seemed as if the room was filled with her troubles, the air heavy with her unspoken fears.

Then something snapped.

Every bit of evidence—in terms of Jamie's emotional and physical behavior—pointed to it. She had known deep down for ages, yet it was only now she was ready to confront it.

"I think Jamie's having an affair."

My God, she thought, I hadn't meant to *say* it. Not in my first session.

But she couldn't bear to keep it in a moment longer. All at once it was as if the blindfold had been lifted from her eyes, and her vision had been restored. Yet it wasn't pleasant, being able to see so clearly. Far from it: it was terrifying.

My husband, *my* Jamie—sleeping with someone else! How could she—the other woman, whoever she is?

Maggie was beyond hurt. She was shaken to her core. In that minute she wanted to die. She felt as if part of her *had* died.

Yet bizarrely, as this ghastly realization took shape, transforming Maggie's world, Nina continued sitting opposite her, plump, capable, and bejeweled. The chair next to Maggie, where Jamie should have been, remained exactly the same, with its worn mustard covers that must have borne witness to a hundred similar heartbreaks. Of course, the whole room was exactly as it had been five minutes before.

Time passed without either of them saying a word. Maggie could hear the clock ticking on Nina's desk. She was acutely conscious of it; that she had only an hour.

"What makes you think Jamie's having an affair?" asked Nina gently.

"Everything . . . Everything."

Then she told Nina how Jamie was out late a lot, how he'd been so odd and elusive when in New York, how he'd withdrawn from her generally. Once she'd started she couldn't stop. It wasn't that it was easy to say—it wasn't—and she was trembling with emotion throughout, but she was burning to get it off her chest. "And we row all the time now," she added, finally.

"What do you row about?"

"Oh, everything. Anything. What we eat," she explained, because it was still at the front of her mind, "the house—his mess. Nathan—how we each are with him. Where we live. His work, my work. Money. Whether or not to have a second child . . ."

"Ah." Nina frowned.

Maggie glanced at her. "How did you know he doesn't want one?"

"I didn't," said Nina.

"Well, I guess he's never been that happy with the idea. In fact, he wasn't that happy when he found out I was pregnant with Nathan. It was an accident, you see. Still, there was no way I could have a termination. I just couldn't."

"Did he want you to?"

"Yes, he did, initially. But it went against every principle I've ever had. I really do believe it was my right to choose. So I said I was going to go ahead regardless. And a few months into the pregnancy he came around. I think it was when he saw the scan . . . At last he seemed able to see it was a little person, a little us . . . Whereas I'd felt like that all along. After that he was completely different about it. And then, when Nathan was born, I suppose he came around so wholeheartedly to being a father—he's great with Nathan, truly great—that I'm sure he'd do so again."

"Maybe he's not so sure," said Nina.

Maggie was shocked: she'd not fully acknowledged this. "Hmm . . . You might be right . . . There is a side of him that's reluctant to grow up."

"Perhaps he doesn't feel ready to."

"Well, I *do*!" said Maggie, vehemently. "I'm nearly forty! And I want another child!"

She began to cry. It was all too much.

Tentatively, Nina ventured, "And now you think there's reason to believe he's having an affair?"

"Yes," Maggie whispered.

"Have you asked him?"

"No."

There was a long pause. Nina passed over a box of tissues that sat on her desk.

"But you're sure?"

Maggie drew her breath. "I'm not *sure*. But I'm not totally stupid. And he's been very preoccupied." She stopped crying.

Nina looked at the clock. It was obviously nearly time to finish.

I'm going to ask him, thought Maggie. She said it aloud, to make it real. "I'm going to ask him tonight."

It wasn't until she was halfway home that emotions got the better of her again. As tears started to fall, blurring her vision, she pulled into a parking lot, fearful she might crash the car. She wept, soundlessly at first, then she began to howl, deep down from the base of her gut, with the pent-up grief of months of worry, with an anguish she couldn't recall experiencing before, not even when she was a little girl.

And she didn't care if the people in the other vehicles in the parking lot could hear or what they thought. She didn't care about anything, except Jamie, and herself, and Nathan, and what was going to happen to them all.

33

"But I'm playing squash tonight."

"Cancel it." Maggie wouldn't budge. I can be as stubborn as you if I want to be, she thought. She might be scared of the outcome, nonetheless she'd vowed to confront Jamie that night, and nothing was going to get in her way. She'd even stood up to phone him to help herself be bolder.

"I can't."

"What do you mean you can't?"

"I promised Pete I'd play."

"Don't lie to me, Jamie."

"I'm not lying to you. Why on earth would I lie to you?"

"I don't believe you're playing squash tonight."

"Of course I am!"

Maggie detected the note in his voice that came to Nathan's when he was caught doing something he shouldn't be. "If that's all you're up to, surely it's easy enough to rearrange? Just phone and tell him you can't play."

"I can't get ahold of him."

"Why not?"

"I don't have his number."

The tension made Maggie's throat so tight that she could barely breathe. Jamie's unwillingness to come home underlined how right she was to distrust him. Presumably he was planning on seeing whoever he was messing around with.

"Jamie, I'm not a fool. Of *course* you've got his number. You must call him all the time."

"I do not." Jamie paused. "He's out at a meeting all day."

His lies were so blatant that Maggie was insulted. Jealousy was eating at her, but she didn't want to confront him over the phone. "Ring his mobile."

"That's the number I don't have—he changed it recently."

"Leave a message at his work."

"He's not going back to the office—he's heading straight to the club."

Maggie found it hard not to scream. "Simply don't turn up, then. Phone reception at the club and tell them to explain."

"I can't do that, Pete's my friend."

"And I'm your wife, Jamie. Your *wife*. Or had you forgotten that?"

"Of course not."

"Say it's a family crisis. If he's such a good friend he'll understand."

"What? He'll understand that my wife's been to see some stupid counselor who's put a whole load of ludicrous ideas into her head? That's a crisis, is it?"

He was doing it again, turning his shortcomings into her failings. "Stop being an arsehole."

"C'mon Maggie." His tone became soothing. "This is a bit melodramatic, isn't it? Why do we have to talk right now? Can't it wait till I get back?"

"No, it can't. You won't be home till midnight—if your recent Thursday nights are anything to go by—and I don't want to sit up waiting for you. Anyway, this isn't the kind of conversation that's going to be over in a couple of minutes. And you're hardly likely to be happy talking till three. Heaven forbid, you might miss some of your precious beauty sleep."

"Can't we talk on the weekend? We'll have much more time then."

How was she going to convince him this was serious? What was he doing that was so important? "Jamie. I. Need. To. Talk. Face-to-face. Now. If you don't come home at a reasonable hour, then you might just find me and Nathan not here when you do."

"Okay." At last he seemed to get the message. "I'll be there."

So, for the first time in months, Jamie was back by seven.

"Daddy!" Nathan ran downstairs to greet him. He was half dressed in a white vest and underpants—Maggie had been poised to put him into the bath.

"Wa-hey!" Jamie took off his coat, dropped his briefcase, and scooped Nathan up in his arms.

Nathan tugged his father's hair as they mounted the stairs. "Read me a story!"

At the top, Jamie set him down. "I'll read to you in the bath," he offered.

Maggie was standing on the landing. Jamie caught her eye for a split second, then looked away.

"Come with me." Nathan dragged him into his room to choose a book.

Doubtless Jamie's glad to have an excuse to put me off for a while longer, Maggie concluded. Yet it tugged at her heartstrings to see the two of them together.

Forty minutes later Jamie had finished putting their son to bed. As she stood in the kitchen, Maggie fondly imagined Nathan tucked under his duvet in his room above her, all clean and pink and shiny. She heard Jamie descending the stairs to join her.

God, give me strength, she prayed, leaning against the stove for support. How shall I start this? If our recent conversations are anything to go by, I've been doing an appalling job of steering things the right way.

"So what's all this about?" he said, entering the room and standing away from her.

"I'll come straight to the point." Her heart was racing. "Are you having an affair?"

"*No!*" he exclaimed without the slightest hesitation. "What makes you say that?"

Maggie drew breath. "Where do you want me to start? It's a cliché, the way you've been acting. Out till midnight a couple of times a week 'working late' or 'playing squash.'" She imitated his voice with acid sarcasm—a manner she was adopting more and more. "Forgetting to call me from New York . . . what do you take me for? You've not been at the office or meeting Pete these last few months, have you? You've been shagging someone else." She spat the word.

Jamie said nothing.

"Haven't you?"

"That's crazy."

"Is it?" In some ways she was desperate for him to say this. There remained a massive part of her that didn't want to know, or better still, didn't want it to be true.

"You're imagining things."

"Oh?"

"Of course you are!"

She was far from convinced, but relieved all the same.

Jamie continued, "You've been spending too much time on your own cooped up here."

Bloody hell! He was doing it again. It was *her* fault.

"Let me get this straight." Jamie was sounding more assured. "What are you talking about? A few late nights and the fact I forgot to call you one day when I was abroad on business?"

Although she was tempted to leave the conversation there, Maggie was damned if he was going to get away with putting a spin on what she was trying to say. "That's only the obvious stuff," she said, struggling not to lose her temper or worse—cry. "What's really made me wonder is how you've been toward me."

"And how's that?"

"Cool. No, more than cool, cold. You've barely touched me since earlier this summer."

"Jesus, Maggie, who's counting? Can I help it if I don't feel like sex at the moment?" Jamie shrugged. "You know I'm not up for it when I'm under pressure—never have been."

That's not true, thought Maggie. Until a few months ago, our sex life was fine. In fact it was often more than fine, it had been great. "You've never been like this before. Not even when you were badly overworked in your last job. We've had the odd patch where one or the other of us hasn't felt much like it for two or three weeks, I agree, but this . . . It's been ages. And anyway," she felt they were focusing on sex, when the real issue ran far deeper, "that's not all. I wouldn't mind about that if you still talked to me."

"Jesus, not this one again. I talk to you the whole time! I'm talking to you now!"

"You know what I mean. Oh, yeah we talk in passing. We touch base about day-to-day things—who's going shopping, who's collecting Nathan from soccer—but we don't talk, properly, just me and you. Other than to argue."

"Hmph." Jamie snorted, though he seemed to relent a little. "Well, I'll try talking to you more.

She pounced. "Will you come to Relate, then? The counselor says it's not too late for you to join us."

"No."

"Why not?"

"I've told you! I just don't want to, okay? Fuck, sometimes I feel so *got* at! I'm simply trying hard to earn money to make a nice home for us, working every hour God sends, and here you are, accusing me of who knows what exactly."

Maybe he's telling the truth, Maggie thought, and it's merely his job causing all this friction.

"Look, it's not my thing, therapy," he was saying. "You should appreciate that. In fact, I'm rather surprised it's yours."

"It wouldn't be, in the normal scheme of things," Maggie continued. "But you simply don't get it, do you? This isn't just about me and you, is it? It's about Nathan. It can't be good for him to have parents who are at each others' throats the whole time."

Jamie appeared to have another touch of remorse. "I'm sorry. I guess I have been pretty wrapped up in my own stuff recently. It's only—you know what it's like—I've never had so much professional responsibility before. I'll make more of an effort, I promise."

"You will?"

"I will."

"Thank you." She smiled at him. She knew it took a lot for him to say this; perhaps he wasn't quite such an arsehole after all.

He smiled back, wanly. Yet it was a smile just the same.

"Shall we have a glass of wine?" she asked, realizing they were both standing there, in the middle of the kitchen.

He let out a long breath. "I think we deserve it."

"We certainly do." Then she, too, relented a little, went over to him, and kissed his cheek.

It seemed to work. "Oh, Maggie," he sounded sad, "I don't mean to be horrible to you, honestly. It's sometimes with the demands of my job I get so stressed . . . and I suppose I take it out on you."

"I know," she said.

"Come here." He reached out and pulled her to him to hug her.

She snuggled into his crisp white shirt and inhaled his familiar scent. "Are you hungry?" she asked, remembering they'd not eaten.

"Not really . . ."

And before she knew it, they were kissing—properly. A thought flashed through her mind that perhaps he'd been doing this with someone else. Ugh. She shoved it away. Gradually, she found herself becoming aroused despite her upset—or maybe because of it. What she really wanted was to be intimate with him again—and it seemed he must want it as well. They grabbed a bottle of wine and the corkscrew, and went upstairs to bed.

In the middle of the night Maggie woke in need of a drink of water. She got up quietly, but on her way to the bathroom she was hit by a sudden, dreadful impulse. She still couldn't shake off her conviction that Jamie had been going to see someone else that evening, even though they'd made love so passionately. The thought of his infidelity sickened her yet again.

She filled a glass of water, gulped it down, refilled it, and left it by her side of the bed. Jamie stirred but didn't wake. Then, as if sleepwalking, she glided down the stairs. Mesmerized, she picked up Jamie's briefcase from the hall where he'd put it down when he'd come in. She carried it into the kitchen, turned on the light, and laid it on the oak table.

Click. Click. She opened the catches.

There it was—his mobile. She hated herself for doing it, but she had to know. She had a *right* to know.

We've only just been making love, for goodness' sake, she shuddered. Is it really possible he was planning to see someone else earlier? That he was going to have sex with her?

Maggie looked down at the object in the palm of her hand. So small and neat, so innocent looking. What secrets did it hold? She had a similar model—a BlackBerry—and knew how it worked. She pressed the menu, scrolled down until she had what she wanted displayed on the screen.

Call history.

Her heart was in her mouth. She wanted to know; she didn't want to know.

She looked for the outgoing call icon. There it was, *0207,* she read. Inner London. Not Jamie's mate, Pete, then: he lived in Wimbledon. She read on, *924,* and tried to remember what part of London the code represented. Someone she knew had the same one. Ah—Jean. Her place was in Battersea. But it wasn't her number. As far as Maggie could remember, they didn't know anyone else who lived around there. She was petrified now, yet couldn't stop. She looked up at the clock. It was five past four, but she didn't care. She pressed *Dial.* Within seconds the phone was ringing at the other end.

Three rings, and an answering machine clicked on. Whoever it belonged to was obviously asleep or hadn't had time to wake up and take the call.

"Hi, this is Chloë," said a voice Maggie recognized. The sound made her retch. "I'm afraid neither Rob nor I can get to the phone right now, so leave your name and number after the tone; we will get back to you as soon as we can."

Maggie ran over to the sink and retched again. She felt hot and cold and sweaty all at once. She puked into the stainless steel bowl, but all that came up was a pathetic remnant of the wine she'd drunk earlier, diluted with water. She thought she might faint. She sat down at the kitchen table, head spinning.

Chloë . . . Chloë . . . Chloë . . .

It fits, she realized. Chloë's strange behavior when I went to meet her a few weeks ago. Her refusal to give me work. The fact that she's a colleague of Jamie's. Didn't Jean even say he went in to see her once, months ago? He claimed he was introducing himself to all the features editors at UK Magazines—I bet he was. How long has it been going on? Jesus, could Chloë have been with him at the conference in New York?

No, she tried to persuade herself. I've got it wrong. Didn't the answering machine mention a "Rob"? Who's he? It sounds as if Chloë is living with someone too.

Then an image of Chloë flashed into her mind. The overt sex appeal. The hourglass figure. She had long suspected this was more Jamie's type. And she must be ten years or so younger . . . How hackneyed. How *obvious.*

Maggie closed her eyes, as if to shut out the truth. She shuddered, then remembered. *That's* who Chloë reminds me of.

If she had any remaining doubts, this made her absolutely sure.

Beth.

The woman before her, who Jamie had been so in love with. She'd seen a picture of her once. She'd insisted Jamie show her in the hope it would make her feel better, but it had merely increased her jealousy, because she couldn't see any physical resemblance between them.

Jamie . . . Jamie . . . And we were making love only a few hours before . . .

Maggie was still so shocked that she was numb.

Eventually, she slipped the phone back into her husband's briefcase and made her way upstairs. Then—at a loss as to what else to do—she returned to bed. Again Jamie stirred but didn't wake.

She edged herself as far away from him as she could, and curled into a tight, protective ball with her back to him. She lay like that for the rest of the night, unable to sleep, unable to move, unable to do anything.

34

When Jamie got up the next morning, Maggie pretended to be asleep. Then in slow motion, she showered, helped Nathan to dress, and took him to school. When she returned home she reached up into the top of the wardrobe, pulled down two suitcases, and began to fill them with clothes. She didn't stop until she'd finished packing.

Around morning break, she telephoned Fran at work. Luckily her sister answered her mobile.

"I'll keep it brief——" she was conscious Fran would be busy "——but I need to get away. Something's happened with Jamie, and I was wondering if Nathan and I could come and stay."

"Of course," Fran said at once. "What's up?"

"I'll explain when I see you." Then, considerate of Fran and not wishing to impose, she added, "I just need to get out of here——have a think. We won't stay long."

"Sounds serious."

If this isn't serious I don't know what is, thought Maggie. Yet she didn't want to create a drama over the phone. "It is," she choked, her voice breaking.

"Do you need us to come and pick you up?"

"No. We'll drive over straight after school, if that's all right with you."

"Can't you tell me what's wrong?" Fran sounded worried.

"I'd rather do it face-to-face."

"Sure. We'll see you later, then."

"Okay . . . And, Fran . . . ?"

"Yes?"

Maggie let out a long breath. "I really appreciate this."

When they arrived, Fran swept Nathan and Dan off upstairs to play, and sat Maggie down at the antique pine kitchen table with a cup of Earl Grey.

"What's happened?" she asked, pulling up a chair close to her sister.

There was little point in dissembling. "Jamie's having an affair."

"I wondered whether that was what it was."

Maggie shivered. Did Fran know already? Did anyone else? She felt so stupid. "Did you?"

"Couldn't think what else would make you leave in such a hurry."

"So you didn't suspect?"

"No! Why should I?"

"Oh, I don't know," said Maggie, not wanting to say, *Because you always know everything.*

"Did he tell you?"

"No." Maggie hesitated, ashamed that she'd had to resort to looking at his phone. But Fran would do the same, she justified. "I checked his mobile."

"Schoolboy error," said Fran—Maggie thought it anything but. "I'm surprised he didn't make more effort to cover his tracks. Maybe he wanted you to find out."

"Do you think?"

"Lord knows. Who is she?"

Maggie flinched. "A girl he works with." She certainly wasn't going to call Chloë a *woman*. That implied maturity, integrity.

"Quelle surprise."

"Why do you say that?"

"Oh, because it's *easy*. Men are so bloody lazy when it comes to affairs. They like it laid on a plate."

Maggie was tempted to ask if Fran's affair was any different, given she'd found her postman on the doorstep, but she needed Fran's support.

"Chloë Appleton, she's called."

"I suppose she's younger than you, too?"

"Yes." The obviousness made it even worse. Tacky. Sordid. "I guess she's sort of up-front looking. Blatant. Displays her assets to the world. Dead trendy. You know the type. Magazines are full of them."

Fran was puzzled. "Did Jamie tell you this? Doesn't seem he likes her that much if that's how he describes her."

"No, of course not. I bet he thinks she's bloody gorgeous. She's exactly his type."

"You don't *know* her, do you?" Her eyes were wide with horror.

"I have met her, yes."

"God! When?"

"I went in to see her to try and get work."

"Did you realize who she was?"

"Not a clue."

"Did Jamie know you were going in to see her?"

The memory stung. That he hadn't stopped her made Maggie cringe. "Yes, I remember him saying he didn't think it was a good idea—"

"I'm sure he didn't!"

"—but I was pretty determined . . ." Maggie frowned. When she looked back on the whole episode, Jamie's behavior was despicable.

"So, how long's it been going on, then?"

Why doesn't she question if it's true? Maggie wondered. Maybe Jamie was a more likely candidate for infidelity than I realized. "I don't know exactly, but my guess is four or five months." Then she explained what had happened the day before, about the counselor, the confrontation, the denial, even the lovemaking—though she shivered at the thought, and she knew it would make Fran judge Jamie harshly. Finally, she recounted how Jamie's mobile had ultimately condemned him.

She had a fleeting concern her sister might think this tantamount to spying, but Fran said, "I have to hand it to you. Well done for figuring it out like that."

So far, her sister seemed behind her all the way. This gave Maggie the courage to ask, "You don't believe this is my fault, do you?"

"*No!* Why would you think that?"

"I'm not sure. I just thought it's never one person to blame for this sort of thing . . . Perhaps I've been boring him, not given him enough attention, or something." Her emotions came in waves: one minute she was strong, fired up by anger; the next insecure, full of self-blame.

"That's bollocks for starters." Fran topped up both their cups of tea. "He hasn't been paying *you* enough attention, not the other way around."

"That's what Jean says. I don't really understand why, then . . ." Maggie trailed off, and blinked away tears.

"Hey." Fran grabbed her hand. "It'll be okay . . ."

"I don't think it will."

"Of course it will! I told you about me and Geoff, didn't I? We went to hell and back."

"You did?" Maggie was surprised. Fran hadn't given this impression before. Although of course Fran was proud, just as Maggie was. She liked to appear to have everything under control.

"Yeah; it was awful . . . awful . . . for a while. Both of us were miserable as sin." For a moment Maggie thought she was going to hear a completely different version of events. "But, I explained before, it came out okay in the end. Look at us now—things have never been better. I'd even go so far as to say that in the long run it was no bad thing."

"Mm."

Fran stopped, seemingly aware she must sound sanctimonious. Maggie was crying, so she asked, more gently, "Is Jamie aware you've found out?"

"No. No. I couldn't face it right away—I simply had to get out. I couldn't get ahold of him at work—I was rather glad not to have to speak to him—so I left a message on his voice mail, saying we were coming here."

"You are going to tell him, though, aren't you?"

"Yes." By now Maggie was sobbing uncontrollably. "Oh—Fran!"

"I know, I know . . ." Fran muttered, standing up and putting her arms round Maggie's shoulders. Maggie hugged her back, hard, gleaning comfort from the warmth of her sister's sweater. She couldn't remember the last time they'd done this; it helped.

When Maggie's tears had subsided, Fran burst forth, "Wait till I get ahold of him! I'd like to chop his prick off!"

Maggie laughed through her weeping. "What do you think I should do?"

"I reckon you should take your time. There's no hurry. First, work out what you want to say. You're welcome to stay as long as you like."

"Thanks. You think I should confront him?"

"Yes, I do. As long as he thinks you don't know, you're stuck in limbo."

Maggie could see what she meant. "Okay. Perhaps we'll go back and I'll do it on Sunday. I don't feel we should stay beyond that or Nathan will worry something's going on."

"It's up to you," said Fran.

"That's what I'd prefer. Hell, though, Fran, how could he do this? Not just to me, but to Nathan. It's not only that he's been seeing someone else, it's all the lies. He completely denied it when I asked him outright! And then he had the nerve to make love!"

"Don't ask me . . . Are you going to leave him, then?"

Maggie's immediate reaction was to grip the edge of the table ferociously and say, "I tell you, if it was up to me, I'd leave now." Then she recalled Nathan's excitement when his father arrived home. "But I can't just walk out. We've got a child. Aside from what he's done to me, I'm not sure I could take Nathan from his dad. Not before trying to get to the bottom of this."

"But you'd insist he finish it?"

"Of course I would!"

Fran nodded. "Then I suppose it all comes down to one thing."

"What's that?"

"Do you still love him?"

Maggie put her head in her hands. Jamie's a liar, a cheat, a selfish pig, she thought. He's been leading me in a miserable dance for months. Heaven knows the full extent of it.

She recoiled at the idea of him and Chloë together. Screwing . . .

Nonetheless, he's the father of my child, she reasoned. My husband. Surely deep down he's still the man I married? Muddled, by his own admission, very muddled; having some sort of midlife crisis. Yet he can't be a total bastard, can he? I swore to love him till death do us part . . .

"I suppose so," she said at last.

35

Chloë was so upset about James that on Friday she threw herself into work with a vengeance. After two cups of coffee and no breakfast, she was racing through the day's tasks. By eleven o'clock she'd chased down the journalists she'd commissioned to find out how they were getting on, seen three photographers' portfolios, had an argument with the art director, and written the introductory paragraph to "A Buyer's Guide to Vibrators." She was in the midst of revising the tear sheets of the magazine when a vibration on her phone told her she'd received a text. She glanced at the screen. It was from James.

Still fuming, she ignored it for a few minutes. She was damned if she was going to do him the courtesy of reading it at once. Eventually curiosity got the better of her.

What can I say? I am so, so, so sorry. I feel absolutely terrible. Please, please forgive me.

She didn't respond.

An hour later: Are you still speaking to me?

She tapped: No!

Almost immediately: Please don't be cross. I can explain. I could come over tonight and make it up to you. I can even stay over, if you'll still have me. J. xx

Maybe they haven't patched things up, after all, thought Chloë, if he wants to see me so soon after a heart-to-heart with Maggie . . .

As she'd drifted off to sleep the night before, she'd had nasty visions of the two of them immersed in conversation. She'd seen James coming around to whatever Maggie was saying, and agreeing they should make a go of it. Chloë had even pictured them making love—until then, she'd bought into James's line that they weren't doing it anymore. Her damaged pride had been compounded by Rob's disgust with James, yet she was still desperate to see him. She texted:

Okay then. But it'd better be damn good!

He's offering to spend the night, she rationalized. Perhaps he's told Maggie he needs space. Maybe they're having a trial split. Or possibly he's told her he's in love with someone else . . .

After all, his text said Chloë could have him if she still wanted him, and he could stay over. This was new—previously he'd always gone home. Had he told Maggie he was leaving her? The thought made Chloë shudder. Was that really what she wanted?

If our affair becomes public, everyone will hate me, she panicked.

No, she convinced herself. He wouldn't write a text with that tone if things have come to a head. His words don't display the signs of a man who's had enough. Thanks to her father, Chloë knew only too well what that looked like.

Fuck it, she resolved, seething again. He can explain tonight, as he said.

In the meantime she made herself another coffee, and got on with her work. Fired up by fury and caffeine, she spent the rest of the day finishing the tear sheets of the magazine, and then, thrilled by how it was panning out and keen to share it, presented it to Vanessa late in the afternoon. Inevitably Vanessa had plenty of suggestions, and by the time they finished it was past seven.

If James has to wait on the doorstep, tough, Chloë thought.

Yet when she arrived home, she was surprised to hear male voices coming from the kitchen.

"Chloë?" called James.

"Is that you?" Rob shouted.

Bollocks. Rob had let James in. The idea of the two of them meeting without her to supervise made her wary. She tried her best to breeze casually into the room.

James and Rob were sitting at the table, an opened bottle of wine in front of them.

"Hi." She was a little embarrassed. "How long have you been here?" she asked James. Judging from the nearly finished bottle, it was a while.

"Oh, I don't know—at least an hour. I thought I'd better not be late. It didn't matter—Rob was here."

An hour! Lord knows what Rob had said in that time. He was rarely backward in coming forward, especially when called upon to defend his friends. He could easily have given James a lecture. She glanced at Rob, hoping to detect a sign of what he'd said, yet his face gave nothing away.

"Look what James has brought you." He nodded in the direction of the sink.

There, standing on the drain board in a globe of water, was one of the biggest bouquets she'd ever seen. The flowers were wrapped in cellophane and hand tied with a huge white bow. Stargazer lilies. There must have been a dozen stems, and each head was larger than an open hand, the stamens a rich, golden yellow, petals tinged with pink. Chloë leaned down into the midst of them and inhaled. They smelt pungent, heavenly.

How romantic! she thought, heart lifting. It's *ages* since a boyfriend has given me flowers. Though if James thinks he can buy me off that easily, he's wrong.

"I'm sorry about last night," said James, coming over and slipping his hands around her waist. That whoosh of desire hit her once more. "Am I forgiven?" he whispered, wiping pollen from her nose.

"Hmph." Chloë pouted. "We made a massive effort, both of us. Didn't we?"

James turned to Rob. "I'm sorry if I pissed you off too. I gather you cooked something specially. You've both every right to be livid. I know I would have been if I was you."

But Rob waved his concern away. "We'll get over it."

Chloë was surprised—James must have been turning on the charm. Speaking of which, his arms were still wrapped around her; his physical presence was making it difficult for her to be cross. Just the scent of him turned her on.

James continued, "So I was thinking, to make it up to you, I'd like to take the two of you out to dinner."

I should put up more of a fight, Chloë thought, or James will think I'm a pushover. Not for the first time, she cursed her body for betraying her—her legs were buckling. If it hadn't been for her yearning to impress Rob, she would have been seriously tempted to drag her lover into her bedroom there and then.

"Never one to turn down a free meal, me." Rob grinned.

"Where do you fancy?" asked James. "You're the chef—you should choose."

"Let's stay local," urged Chloë. "I'm exhausted." She'd been working late on *All Woman* nearly every night.

They went to an expensive Indian restaurant on Lavender Hill which Chloë sometimes went to with her father—Rob loved it but could rarely afford to dine there. The restaurant was bright and boldly decorated, its primary colors creating the perfect backdrop to their upbeat conversation. Chloë's fury with James was blunted further because he and Rob seemed to get along so well. Given the two men came from very different worlds, things might have been sticky—especially because with a few drinks inside him, Rob could be outspoken to the point of tactlessness. But James was at his most relaxed and socially adept—drawing Rob out with questions about his work and his clients. In return Rob asked James about his role as magazine publisher, keen to glean what had attracted him to an environment chiefly populated by women and gay men. He kept well away from difficult subject areas, and appeared eager to entertain rather than provoke. Halfway through their main course it dawned on Chloë as to why.

He fancies him! she thought. And far from being threatened by Rob's sexuality, James appears flattered. I reckon he's flirting back. Well, this is a surpise, she laughed to herself.

By the time they got home, they'd had an awful lot of wine, topped off with brandy, and Rob was on a roll discussing his various sexual exploits. He relished having an audience, especially one as attentive as James, who was clearly fascinated by the number of notches on Rob's bedpost.

"I must say," said Rob, slapping James on the back as they stumbled into the hall, "you're not half so bad as I thought you'd be." Chloë winced. "I wasn't really too sure what to make of you before. What with your being married and having a child." For a split second James looked aghast, yet Rob pressed on: "Although, hey, who am I to judge?" James smiled, if a little halfheartedly. "Anyway, thank you so much for the meal. And now, my lovebirds," Rob winked campily at Chloë, "this is when I leave you to it."

After having to restrain herself earlier and such a successful introduction to Rob, Chloë was on the biggest high she'd enjoyed in weeks, and was horny as hell. With no further ado she shoved James into her bedroom.

The next morning James didn't stay late, leaving Chloë to wonder if he was racing to be home before Maggie after all. Yet nothing could mar the pleasure of thinking about the evening they'd shared, and although she tried to get back to sleep after James had left, in the end she was too excited. Keen to know what her roommate had thought of him, the moment she heard the telltale sounds of the radio coming from Rob's room, she couldn't resist bouncing out of bed, pulling on her dressing gown, and rushing to tap on his door.

"Tea?"

Rob looked at her out of one eye. "You must learn to be quieter," he said sternly. "I can hear everything through that bloody wall."

"Sorry." Chloë blushed.

She made two mugs of tea, carried them carefully into Rob's room, and sat on the end of his bed. By now Rob was sitting up, looking decidedly morning-afterish, his peroxided hair standing in unkempt Tintin tufts.

"So? What did you think?"

"Well, I'd shag him."

She knew it! "You thought he was sexy, then?"

"I'll say."

"What about the flowers and everything? The fact he took us both to dinner?"

"I know." Rob nodded. "Very generous. He seems like a nice guy."

Basking in his approval, Chloë felt confident to push for more. "And what about us? Do you think we make a good couple?"

Rob paused. "Mm." He appeared perplexed, as if wondering what to say. At once Chloë feared he wasn't going to be so positive. "I'm not so sure."

That hurt. "Why not?"

"It's not that I don't think you're well suited. You're great together—I've never seen you that happy with anyone—and he's obviously keen on you. It's only . . ." He sighed. "I don't believe he's ever going to leave his wife."

"What makes you say that?"

Rob rubbed his forehead. It was clearly hard for him to say, but he felt obligated. "I had a rather revealing conversation with him last night."

"When?"

"Before you got home."

After the intense high of the previous evening, Chloë could feel herself rushing headlong downward. "What did he say?"

"It's more what he *didn't* say. I reckon he was disconcerted to find me here without you, and he seemed to feel he had to explain himself a little. Especially since he knew I'd cooked for him. Anyway, I suppose I was pretty cross with him at first. I said something about my cooking not being up to his wife's standard."

Chloë could hear it: Rob was a master of the snide one-liner. "Then he said something about her cooking being amazing, and I said something about how it must make it impossible for him to leave such fabulous home cooking behind."

Oh Lord. "And how did he respond to that?"

"He didn't really say anything." Rob ruffled his hair, causing it to stand up even more bizarrely. "That's what I mean. He simply grunted and said that was probably true. Which, let's face it, doesn't seem the kind of thing he'd say if he was planning on divorcing her tomorrow."

The happiness drained from Chloë's day.

"Then he tried to justify what was going on with you. He was aware I knew about the two of you, and that I must wonder what he's playing at."

"So what did he say?" Chloë had to ask.

"He said he felt irresistibly drawn to you. He asked me if I understood what that was like, and I said I did although I'd never been seriously involved with a married man."

"I see."

"Then he said he felt torn between the two of you, that he'd never done anything like this before, and that he didn't really know how to handle it." Rob appeared extremely hesitant, as if he couldn't bear to hurt Chloë so. "Or how to finish things with you."

"Did he say that?" It was as if she'd been smacked in the jaw. I believed James was on the verge of committing to me, she thought, and he's actually trying to work out how to end it! The pain was all the more intense because it came hard on the heels of such hope.

"Not that I think he *is* going to finish it with you," Rob added. "He clearly cares for you a lot."

"Did he tell you that?"

"In as many words, yes. He said he couldn't just stop seeing you for that reason, and it was even harder because you work together."

Chloë felt tears welling. "So you don't reckon we'll end up together then?"

"I might be wrong." Rob was obviously trying to be kind.

"Do you think I should end it?"

"It's up to you, honey. You've always known what I think. This whole thing's got tragedy written all over it."

Chloë was silent. "I suppose so," she said at last.

36

With a scrunch of gravel, Maggie pulled the car into the drive and turned off the ignition. Nathan was asleep in the backseat; it was past his bedtime, but she'd wanted to be able to tuck him in the moment they arrived so that she could talk to Jamie. She got out and lifted her son into her arms, all floppy and sleepy. The light in the porch came on as she approached the house, and clutching Nathan, she opened the door with one hand.

Jamie heard them and came to help. Unaware of her discovery, he'd clearly been mystified why she'd chosen to stay away the entire weekend, yet she'd refused to discuss anything, explaining over the phone that she wanted to speak in person. "Not *again*," he'd moaned. "I thought we'd sorted it out. Haven't we had enough serious chats?"

The gall! "Seemingly not," she'd said.

"You can get the bags," she ordered without saying hello. As he passed her on the stairs, she'd a good mind to stick out one of her legs and send him tumbling headlong.

Presently everything was safe inside. Sitting on the bed, watching her unpack, Jamie was defensive. "So now what's up?"

"It's not what," her words stabbed the air, "it's *who*."

Jamie flinched. "God, Maggie, you're sounding like your needle's stuck. Can't you leave it alone?"

"Seems *you* can't."

"I don't know what you're talking about."

She hurled clothes into the laundry bin, tempted to turn around and drive straight back to Fran's. But he's in the wrong and I'm damned if I'm going to leave my own house, she thought. And it's not fair to Nathan. "Here's a clue. Her name's Chloë."

"I don't know a Chloë," he said, way too fast.

"Crap! Crap! Crap!" She thumped her books onto the bedside table. "You are one shit liar, Jamie. Have you forgotten that I *know* you know a Chloë? I even know her myself, for God's sake! Though not as intimately as you seem to, that's for sure."

"Where's this suddenly coming from?" The color was draining from his face. "Jean said something to you, didn't she?"

Maggie's stomach lurched. Does Jean know? she thought. Is this common knowledge at UK Magazines? Am I the last to find out?

"Does she know something I don't?"

"You tell me."

"Actually, you gave yourself away with no help from anyone. I found Chloë's number on your BlackBerry while you were asleep. You called her the night I asked you to come back here last week—Thursday."

"You sneaky bitch!" He got to his feet.

"Not half as sneaky as you."

"What does one phone call prove?"

Maggie stopped unpacking and turned to face him. "Do you want me to walk out right now? Because you're sure going a long way toward making that happen. Fran would be more than willing to have me."

"No, don't leave, please. I had to call Chloë about work! She's the editor on a really important project of mine." He sounded desperate.

"Oh, yeah," said Maggie. "Very important project, I'm sure. You had to call her at home, didn't you? In case you've failed to notice, Jamie, I am not a complete dunce. You were going to see her, weren't you, and not going to play squash at all? Then when I insisted you come home, I threw your plans so you had to cancel. In fact," she was really getting going, "I bet you saw her on Friday night, didn't you, to make up for it? That's why you weren't here then when I called."

"You called here on Friday?" Distractedly, he picked up her hairbrush.

"Yes."

"You never left a message."

"Seemed rather pathetic. Wife leaving message while husband's out shagging another woman."

Jamie said nothing and stood tugging hairs from the brush. After a while, with obvious reluctance, he said, "You're right."

Confronted with the truth Maggie didn't feel sick or faint. Instead, she felt a ghastly sense of relief. At least she hadn't imagined it; her judgment was sound, she wasn't going mad. Yet she had to clarify. "Are you in love with her?"

Jamie stared at his shoes. "No."

"Look at me when you answer! I need you to look me in the eyes and tell me that. Because if you don't love her, then I'd like to know why on earth you would want to risk jeopardizing everything you've got. And if you do—" She stopped.

What if he does? What then? She panicked. It might mean that he doesn't love me anymore; then he'll want to leave me, Nathan, our home.

He looked up with those horrible, beautiful, hazel eyes that had cast a spell on her for so many years. To her surprise, they were full of tears. "I suppose I do," he said at last.

Maggie sat down on the bed, afraid her legs wouldn't hold her upright. This was it, then.

The end.

"But I still love you," he added. Sitting down next to her, unsure as to how near was appropriate. "I love you, too." He appeared as if he might take her hand, and thought better of it.

She wasn't sure whether to see this as a glimmer of hope, or as hollow

words designed to soften the impact of what he'd just admitted. A consolation prize. There was only one question left. "Do you want to split up?"

"*No! No!* I couldn't bear it! I love you! I love Nathan! I didn't mean it. It
doesn't mean half as much to me as you do. I couldn't bear to lose you.
Please!"

"What do you mean you didn't *mean* it? Sounds like you bloody meant
it to me. How long has it been going on for? How often have you been seeing her? Is she a good fuck? A better fuck than me?"

"*No!* I told you! It's all been a terrible mistake. Once I'd started I couldn't
seem to stop."

"Was she with you in New York?"

A pause. "Yes."

"Did you see her on Friday?"

"Yes." In a whisper.

"Did you fuck her?"

"Maggie, please."

"Did you?"

"Yes."

"The night after you made love to me?"

Silence. She was acutely conscious that they were sitting, with only a
few inches between them, on the marital bed. Yet they seemed a mile
apart.

She continued, "Can you imagine how that makes me feel?"

There was a long pause, then Jamie cried, "I don't know what got into
me, Maggie, honestly. I've never done anything like this before. It's something that happened, then, before I knew it, I couldn't seem to stop, and
she . . . she . . ."

"She what?"

Jamie seemed at a loss for words. "She was so . . . so . . . up for it."

"Up for it! I bet she fucking was. An older man. Her boss. Someone else's
husband. Every editor ought to do it at least once. Great copy, after all."

"It's not her fault."

"Do me one favor, Jamie. Allow me to hate her. You might be in love with her, but excuse me if I'm not. She's done something I would never have done."

"I know."

"Though see where it's got me."

"I really am sorry," he whispered, his face contorted. He looked as if he hated himself.

"It's not just about being sorry," Maggie said. "It's about trust. I trusted you, Jamie, and you broke that trust. Smeared it over the whole of New York. Jesus—you even allowed me to meet the girl and ask her for work! What a sucker I feel about that now. No wonder she was so odd."

"I didn't mean to hurt you, you know." His voice was so quiet she could hardly hear him.

"But you have, and I don't know if I'll ever get over it. What's more, in the process you've turned me into something I hate—a paranoid, whining, nag of a wife."

"You're not, Maggie. None of this is your fault."

"Well, it's *someone's*. And if I'm not to blame, and neither is Chloë, it's got to be you."

"I agree," he admitted. "I've fucked up."

"You can say that again."

"What can I do? How can I make this better? Is there anything I can do to make you forgive me?"

"One thing is certain. We can't carry on like this." Maggie was amazed at how together she was sounding, how matter-of-fact. Despite this dreadful situation, she was empowered by understanding the full picture. The uncertainty, the suspicion, the anxiety had been worse.

"What do you want me to do?"

He was still sitting there, awkward, unsure. After everything, he was asking her to do the deciding. To Maggie the answer was obvious. She'd had the entire weekend to think about it and for all Jamie's muddle, the options were black and white.

"You have to choose," she said getting to her feet once more to add impact to her words. "It's her or me. You've got to finish it with Chloë and make a go of this marriage, and come to Relate, or that's it between us. Simple."

"And what about Nathan?"

"What about him?"

"You've said yourself this isn't just about me and you; it's about him."

"You should have thought of that on Friday when you were sticking your dick in someone else. It's a bit late to come over all moral on me now."

"He needs a father."

"That's precisely why I'm willing to give it one more go. If it weren't for him I don't know what I'd do. But he needs a proper dad, not a philanderer, someone he can respect, learn from."

"I want to be that for him, Maggie, truly I do."

"Well, prove it then."

"I guess it's one of the reasons I work so hard——"

"There's more to being a good role model than being some professional big shot. Come to that, he needs a mother who's not a doormat, someone he can be proud of, someone with principles."

"Nathan is proud of you," said Jamie quietly.

"Hmph." She was hardly in the mood for flattery. "If we stay together, it has to be on my terms, and we've got to do it properly. I'm certainly not staying around here like some pitiful suburban housewife, letting her husband carry on with all sorts behind her back, purely because she's got a huge house in the country that—heaven forbid—she might have to forgo if what was truly going on came out in the open.

"This way if he ever does find out—which I hope he never has to—at least my son will see that I didn't sit back and ignore everything. No, I've had time to think about this, and I'm absolutely clear. I can't compromise anymore. I feel like I've been letting things slip for ages, and it's more than my sense of self is worth to carry on doing it. If I catch you fucking around with Chloë again—or anyone else come to that—I won't give you another chance. This is it, Jamie. End it. Or this marriage is over, and you'll be the one that has to go."

37

I was used as a punching bag for my parents' rows, the place they'd come to when they needed to get rid of some aggression. One minute I'd have my mum in tears, telling me what a worm my dad was; the next my dad off-loading how Mum didn't understand him. I was ten years old. And I don't agree with people who say children fail to grasp what's going on—they understand more than we think. I knew these demands were making me grow up emotionally in a way most other kids at school didn't have to. Not in a good way—I felt ashamed of the situation at home, embarrassed by my parents' constant arguments. There's a lot more acceptance of divorce these days but when I was young there was a stigma attached. And that hurt. In fact, that's made me very wary of commitment myself—because I associate it with upset and pain. So here I am at forty, still acting the carefree bachelor, unwilling to settle down.

Chloë was at her desk, reading Craig Spencer's article, "Broken Homes, Broken Children?"

It could be me talking, she thought.

So soon after her discussion with Rob, it was like pouring alcohol on an open wound, forcing Chloë to think about Nathan once more.

Is he feeling the effects of all this? she wondered. Is he aware of more than James and Maggie realize? He's only six, isn't he? Poor little boy.

James didn't talk much to Chloë about his son—he probably appreciated she found it hard to hear—but her conscience was increasingly nagging her. Their affair was becoming messier and messier and she was beginning to feel that the good times weren't worth it. If she was honest with herself she knew she should try to cool things, if not finish the affair altogether. Certainly she was aware she should talk to James, yet knowing what she should do and actually doing it were very different. Plus the magazine was making increasing demands on her time; she had been glad of that—it allowed her to procrastinate.

James had responded to the one text she'd sent with the explanation he was also too frantic to communicate at length but that he'd meet her on Thursday. Which was today . . .

"So, how's it shaping up?"

Chloë started; Vanessa had come up behind her. "It needs cutting," she said, unwilling to reveal the article's true impact on her, "but Craig's delivered an excellent piece."

"I gather the research groups are set up for next week. So you're positive we'll have a complete dummy magazine to show them?"

"Yes. This is the last of the features to come in. We'll be raring to go."

"Should be fun," said Vanessa.

Chloë found it hard to imagine Vanessa having fun, but agreed. She too, was looking forward to seeing how readers responded to her baby. Secretly, she was confident. Her love life might be a disaster zone, yet professionally everything was coming together very well indeed.

———

In her heart, Chloë knew that if she was committed to breaking up with James it wasn't wise to meet him at her apartment. It would be less risky to meet on neutral, preferably public, territory. She also knew that she shouldn't have replenished her lipstick, doused herself in perfume, and she certainly shouldn't have put on her best knickers. Rob would have plenty to say about that, she thought.

Still, her roommate would have been proud of the way Chloë kicked off the conversation when James arrived. She sat him down in the kitchen with a cup of tea, not wine, and took a chair opposite, several feet away. She glanced across at him in his familiar navy suit: his shirt needed ironing and the dark hair she loved looked in need of a cut. He seemed worn out.

"I'm beginning to feel all this is a bad idea," she said.

"Oh?" He looked up at her, his hazel eyes mystified. Then he seemed to glean from her expression that she was poised to say something serious and he frowned.

"Yes." Chloë nodded. She'd rehearsed this, to help her come out with it more easily. "I don't just mean in terms of your marriage, but also for me." She bit her lip, then rushed on, "I'm worried about Nathan. I suppose I'm even a bit worried about Maggie. I'm worried I'm going to get really hurt . . ." Yet just when she knew she should say, "So that's it, it's over," she began to cry.

Suddenly the thought of not being involved with him anymore, of not being able to look forward to their evenings together, not having any romance in her life, not having someone to daydream about, share special moments with, laugh at her jokes, banter with, chat about to those few of her friends whom she'd taken into her confidence, seemed too much to bear.

If I break up with him, I'll never go to Louisa's with him again, or share dinner with him in any restaurant, anywhere, she realized. He'll never come around here again. I'll never go to New York with him, go sightseeing, swig champagne. I'll never get to see his face in such intimate close-up. I'll never make love to him ever, ever again . . .

And it wasn't as if she could cut him out of her life, which was how she had handled gut-wrenching breakups in the past.

Instead I'll have to see him every day, she thought. I'll have to work with him—as the launch of the magazine gets closer our professional dealings might well be more frequent, not less.

At last she could see what Rob had warned her about: the situation was too much for her to handle. No matter what she did, there was no way she could come out unscathed.

"Hey, Chloë," said James softly. He leaned over and squeezed her knee. "Please don't cry. I can't bear it when you cry."

"Sorry," said Chloë, sniffing, aware that her eyeliner must be running. She'd always striven not to weep in front of him, knowing how uncomfortable overemotional women often made men feel. "It's just—I hate the thought of not seeing you again, ever—"

She choked, her voice breaking as she fought against the tears. She looked up at him. His face was anxious, concerned.

He's so lovely, she thought. I like him *so* much.

"You will see me," he said. "You'll see me at work all the time."

"That's not what I mean. We won't be close, we won't be able to talk, not in the same way."

"I'll always care about you—you're very special to me, you know that." He took her hand across the kitchen table. "Perhaps we can be friends, do you think?" But his voice cracked as he said the words.

This only made Chloë cry harder. "I don't want to be friends!" she gasped, knowing she should remove her hand but not doing so.

"No, it was a stupid thing to say."

"You never were my friend. I never felt about you the way I feel about a friend—it's different, what we've had."

"I know." James seemed *so* unhappy, too.

"I don't make love to my friends."

"Glad to hear it," said James, and he smiled at her, as though trying to encourage her to do the same. But she was too upset for this to work. Perhaps at a loss as to what else to do, perhaps as a farewell gesture, perhaps to try to heal things, James began to stroke her hand, gently at first, in a way that brought back memories of the very first night they'd spent together, of when they'd first seduced each other in the nightclub on Broadwick Street. And then, of course, he moved up her arm, and she leaned into him, and he kissed her, and soon she climbed onto his lap for comfort, intimacy, to be closer to him again in that unique, special way. And then he wanted to make love and so did she and she knew Rob wouldn't be back till much later, so she whispered this to him, and he lifted her skirt, and she unzipped his trousers, and he pushed aside those newly put-on knickers, and she pulled down his boxers, and they made out like that, in the kitchen, supposedly one last time.

38

The phone rang while Maggie was rereading a printout of "What the People of Britain Really Eat," an article she'd written for the *Observer*. She'd invited an MP, a homeless young man, a model, a doctor, and a single mum living on benefits to keep a food diary for a week.

That's good timing, she thought. I hope it's someone I feel like talking to: I'm ready to take a break.

"Hi, Mags."

Although she could scarcely hear him, she knew that voice at once. "Alex! I haven't heard from you for ages. It's a dreadful connection. Where are you?"

"On the M25. Coming up to junction nine."

"You're really near!"

"I know. I thought I'd call on the off chance you'd be in. I've just had a meeting at a site in Tunbridge Wells, and I was going to go back to the office, but it hardly seems worth it now."

Maggie looked at the clock. It was four fifteen. By the time he'd driven back into London it would be time to go home. "No, no, I'm here. Why don't you stop by for a cup of tea? We've got some cake I made for Nathan's birthday too. I'm sure he won't mind if you have a piece."

"Ooh, goody." Maggie could almost hear Alex's mouth watering through the phone. He had always been partial to her cakes. "I'll be with you in about fifteen minutes."

Perfect. Enough time to run upstairs and make myself presentable, she thought.

It was November, and a bit nippy, so she'd been sitting at the kitchen table in her oldest jeans and a snug red fleece. Casual attire became her, but her rather daft pink slippers with pom-poms would have to go. She pulled on a pair of boots instead, and put on some makeup. She had just dabbed her wrists with Chanel No. 5 when the doorbell rang. She charged back downstairs.

"Hi!" she said, not bothering to contain her pleasure.

"Hi." Alex stepped into the hall. Dressed in a sweatshirt and muddy jeans, with a leaf in his hair, he was as scruffy as ever, she noted fondly. "You look well."

"Do I?" She was surprised but flattered. She'd been worried that the strain of the last few months must show.

"Mmm." He stood back to admire her. "Slimmer? Fitter?"

"I am a bit fitter," she acknowledged, embarrassed. "Though I'm surprised you can tell in this old stuff." She tugged at her fleece.

"You forget how well I know you."

Maggie blushed, flashing back to their intimacy of over a decade ago. All these years later, there was still some sexual chemistry between them. "Tea?" she said brightly, self-conscious about continuing in this vein.

Alex followed her into the kitchen.

"Sorry about the mess." She waved in the direction of the table. There were papers and books everywhere.

"That's not like you," Alex observed. Maggie had been tidy even as a student.

"True. But I was so into this article I've been writing I seemed to forget myself."

"Excellent!" said Alex, going over to her laptop and hitting a key to take it off screen saver. "Do you mind if I have a look?"

"Go ahead." Maggie stretched up to the top shelf of the dresser for the guest teapot. She had a less precious one for everyday use, but Nathan was at a friend's so she didn't need to worry he'd break it.

Alex was silent while he concentrated, and Maggie felt abashed. This was the first time anyone since Chloë had read anything she'd written in her presence. She felt a bitter jolt at the memory, but she was damned if she was going to focus on Chloë now.

As Alex continued reading she took the opportunity to watch him, trying to imagine what it would be like if she was seeing him afresh. He was dark haired like Jamie, and tall, but there the similarity ended. He had a less angular face, with big brown eyes and brows so thick they were almost comical. His sense of humor shows in his mouth, she thought. And while he was naturally muscular and in years gone by had been a great rugby player, these days, thanks to his penchant for puddings and cakes, his physique was more teddy bear than Action Man. He might be approaching forty, but he retained a boy-next-door charm that mothers—including Maggie's own—loved. When I was going out with him I didn't appreciate him fully, she realized. Instead I was attracted to more obvious good looks, like Jamie's. These days I can see what those mature women liked in him. Above all he appears generous, kind.

"Why, this is extremely interesting," said Alex. "I love the exposé of your MP's excessive drinking habits. Very witty."

Maggie blushed.

"It seems quite different from what I thought you usually did though. More of a feature."

"I'm trying to break into something new."

"Oh?"

Maggie went on to explain, concluding, "I suppose I felt I'd lost something since I was a student—my passion, if you like. You of all people should remember what a stirrer I was."

Alex laughed. "How could I forget? You and me, we'd march for any cause that would have us."

"I'm not sure that's entirely fair," Maggie protested, handing him a generous portion of cake.

"So." Alex looked more serious. "How does Jamie feel about all this? I wouldn't have thought revolutionary zeal was quite his scene."

"No, it's not—at least, not when it's me trying to challenge accepted views. It's fine if it's the people he works with," with a shudder Maggie pictured Chloë again, "but I don't think he likes it in his wife."

"I see."

Maggie could tell he didn't approve of Jamie's lack of support, yet she didn't want to focus on criticizing her husband lest it spoil her mood. She changed the subject. "Have you heard from Georgie? I've been meaning to give her a call."

"Not for a while," Alex admitted. "We went out once for dinner as friends, but it was a bit awkward—and it's not like we dated for that long. With hindsight I'm not sure we'll ever be close—though don't get me wrong, I think she's a great woman."

Although Maggie knew she shouldn't be, she was faintly pleased. A month had passed since she'd found out about Chloë, things with Jamie remained far from resolved, and if she'd had to listen to her ex gush about what great buddies he was with every woman he'd dated, it would have been galling. She liked to think their relationship was special.

Alex leaned back in his chair; his weight caused it to creak a little alarmingly. "How are things with Jamie? Any better than the night we came for dinner?"

That had been the last time Maggie had seen Alex. My God, she thought, I've been through the wringer since then.

He continued, "And the baby issue? Has he come around?"

"Um, not exactly." Maggie spoke softly, wondered whether to tell Alex about Jamie's affair. Somehow she couldn't face it. It would take too long, it was too recent, too raw. And anyway, that was past history. Jamie had stopped seeing Chloë weeks ago. She took a deep breath. "I don't want to go into details, but things haven't been that great recently."

"Oh, I am sorry," said Alex, with feeling. She knew he meant this. Sympathy could have been his middle name. "Believe me, I understand what it's like, I've been there." This was true too: Alex had taken the separation from his wife hard. "I don't know if you're aware that one of the reasons we split is that Stella didn't want to have children. Or not mine at any rate."

"No! You never said."

"It didn't seem fair, somehow, to discuss it with the world. I suppose I was a bit embarrassed"—he coughed—"and too proud."

Too proud. I know how that feels, thought Maggie. "Didn't you talk about it before you got married?"

"I know it seems ridiculous now, but no, actually we didn't. Not at any length. We were years younger then and it didn't seem such a burning issue. I guess I hoped she'd come around."

"I see."

"Anyway, Stella's with someone else now," said Alex philosophically. "All water under the bridge."

"Of course." Maggie could see there was pain behind his bravado.

"May I?" Alex reached for the knife to cut himself another slice.

Maggie nodded, happy to provide food in consolation.

"For you?"

She was planning on making something special that night for herself and Jamie. "No thanks, I'm fine."

Alex spoke with his mouth full. "Though you do know, of course, that Stella was convinced that I'd never fully gotten over you." He looked up at her, straight into her eyes. "When we split up, she even suggested I'd be happier if I found somebody more like you."

Maggie was astounded. Although she had cause to believe Alex still had some feeling for her—Jamie certainly suspected it and Georgie had stated it directly—she would never have expected him to come out with it so openly.

Yet Alex seemed unaware of the impact of his words and was hell-bent on making the most of Maggie's culinary skills. "This is delicious." He scraped his plate enthusiastically with his fork. "Would a third slice be out of the question?"

"Yes." Maggie laughed. "I think Nathan might be a bit miffed."

"Oops." Alex wiped his mouth with a napkin. "Of course! How is the little scallywag?" He looked around. "Where is he?"

"He's playing soccer with his friends up on the recreation ground. He does it every week now. They've got a five-a-side team, Shere Tigers."

"Wow, so he's old enough to be on a team!"

"Yes, he was seven last week. We had a party for him."

"How time flies!" Now he'd touched upon his own desire to have a family, Maggie could see that Alex was wistful. She shared his sentiments, yet she could hardly say so: she was in the midst of trying to repair things with Jamie. And when they had, she still hoped against hope that they might try for another child.

39

Although Maggie had just emerged from a productive meeting with a magazine editor she got on especially well with, she was perturbed. Jean had been in touch the night before, and when Maggie had mentioned she would be in town the next day, Jean had said, "There's something I want to talk about; are you free for lunch?" Maggie detected concern in her friend's voice and was worried that she was going to face her with knowledge of Jamie's affair. Maggie was keen to put it behind her.

Sure enough, once they were sitting in Le Pain Quotidien with a bowl of salad each, Jean began. "Maggie, I may be out of turn—"

"It's okay," said Maggie. "I know."

"You do?"

"Jamie's been seeing that Chloë girl who used to work with you."

"Gosh." Jean was winded. "How long have you known?"

"Around a month."

"Really?"

"Yes. We've talked about it. I'm just beginning to come to terms with it all."

"You are?"

"Yes. It's been hard, but I'm getting there."

"Oh. Well, if you say so."

This annoyed Maggie. *Yes, I do say so!* she protested to herself. "I didn't take you into my confidence before because I didn't want to talk about it—and I still don't. It's over now, and Jamie's coming to Relate. He's canceled a couple of times due to work commitments, but even so."

Jean looked at her closely. "Frankly, I'm surprised you're so cool about it. I'd never have put you down as so tolerant, given a situation like this."

"I wouldn't go so far as to say that," Maggie corrected her. "Though we're sorting things out, honestly." Perhaps I shouldn't have agreed to meet Jean, she thought. It's going to be difficult not to explain everything to her: she won't be satisfied until she has the full picture.

"So you don't mind that he's sleeping with someone else?"

Maggie's heart missed a beat. "He's not anymore."

"Oh, shit." Jean furrowed her brow, as if working out whether to carry on, then decided not to, and was silent.

"What?" Maggie went hot and cold.

Pushed, Jean continued. "I saw him in Battersea last week. I was on my way home from work, going up the hill from Clapham Junction. He didn't see me, mind, he was walking ahead of me, but I thought it was strange he'd be around there."

"Was he with her?"

"No, but to be perfectly straight with you, I'd wondered if there was something going on between them—they seemed a touch too intimate in New York, and at the time it struck me as odd that she was there. Then when I saw him walking in the direction of where she lives, I worked out that must be where he was headed. I followed him a bit, just to check."

"I see . . ." Maggie was silent, trying to absorb this information. But perhaps Jean was mistaken. "Which night was this?"

"Tuesday."

Bloody hell—I was at Fran's, Maggie realized. The moment my back's turned he's there like a shot. He was home before her, so it hadn't occurred to Maggie he might have been somewhere first. She began to tremble. He must have gone straight to Chloë's, fucked her, and come straight home. What kind of a person was Chloë to put up with being treated like that? It made Maggie despise her more than ever, and *loathe* Jamie.

So his promises meant nothing, she thought. And as for what he's been saying at Relate, it's a complete sham. No wonder he canceled last week—his conscience wouldn't let him go. Clearly he doesn't want to repair things at all. Or maybe—yet another living cliché—he wants to have his cake and eat it. Either way it's appalling. Weak. Selfish. Cruel.

"I'm sorry to be the one to tell you this." Jean appeared worried. "Believe me, I had to wrestle with myself before I did."

"It's okay . . ." Maggie was surprised by how calm she felt. "Maybe I knew, deep down." She gulped, swallowing her intense disappointment. "I'd have found out sooner or later. Still, he promised me it was over."

"What are you going to do now, then?" asked Jean.

"Ask him to leave," Maggie said simply.

"Gosh, really?"

"I don't mean for good, necessarily, but for a while, yes. I need some space. The thing is, it's not only that I don't trust him anymore, it's that I don't know if I can love a man who behaves like that."

"Bully for you!" said Jean passionately. "I'm proud of you, frankly." Then she added, more soberly, "And you know, my dear, I'm always here for you, don't you?"

Maggie pushed aside her salad; she really didn't feel like eating. "Thanks," she murmured.

Jean reached across and squeezed her hand, and Maggie was grateful. Right then she needed the support of her friends more than ever.

When she got home, Maggie settled Nathan in front of children's TV and went upstairs.

Out came both suitcases from the top of the wardrobe again; in went

Jamie's boxers. In went the T-shirts he wore under his crisp cotton shirts in winter. In went these shirts too—no folding. In went the belts he always removed with that "swooshing" sound. In went socks—never mind putting them in goddamn rows now—then shoes. Who cares that they should be on the bottom lest the other clothes get dirty? she fumed. Good thing if they do. On top of it all she threw the navy suit she loved.

I wonder if he wore it with Chloë? she thought. She sniffed the jacket. Inevitably, she could detect traces of a scent that was not her own.

Once one case was full she moved on to the next. In this she slung the contents of the bathroom cabinet that belonged to him: shaving foam, razor, aftershave, antiperspirant. On second thought, she left that out. It would be good to make him sweat. Next, down to the closet under the stairs: his precious sports equipment. Not much of it would fit inside the suitcase, but she forced what she could within the straining seams. Finally, she added a handful of his CDs.

I should never have married a man who likes Genesis, she thought.

"Mummy, what are you doing?" asked Nathan, catching her in the middle of the hall, case wide open on the floor. Obviously the rumpus had disturbed him. "Are we going on vacation?"

Maggie went over to him and crouched down to his level. She took his arms, and held his gaze. "No, sweetie, we're not. I'm afraid Daddy's going to have to go away for a bit, that's all."

"Again?" He'd missed his father when he'd been in New York. How was he going to find this more prolonged, possibly permanent departure?

"Yes, my love, again. But don't worry, this time you'll be able to see him when he's gone."

Nathan frowned. "How can I see him if he's not here? Where's he going?"

"I'm not sure yet," said Maggie, fighting tears. She hadn't worked this one through. "It's just that Mummy needs some time on her own right now and I think it's better if Daddy's not around."

"Do you still want me around?" asked Nathan, sounding very small and lost.

"Oh, of course I do!" exclaimed Maggie, folding him into her arms. "I want you around very much!" She gently pushed back his head a little, so she could see his face, and tidied his fringe. "You must understand this, darling. No matter what Mummy and Daddy think of each other, no matter what happens, none of this is your fault and we both love you very much."

"What's all this then?" asked Jamie, standing in the hall examining the two suitcases. Luckily Nathan was in bed. Maggie put her fingers to her lips, not wanting to disturb him, and gestured to her husband to follow her into the sitting room.

"I want you to leave."

"Leave?" Jamie raised his voice at once. "Why?"

"Because you're still shagging Chloë, that's why."

"Sorry?"

"Jean saw you."

"Jean! Where?" But she noted he didn't deny it.

"In Battersea, last Tuesday. You weren't with Chloë, but she knows where Chloë lives. They're virtually neighbors, remember? Or perhaps it hadn't occurred to you—you're so wrapped up in your own pathetic little world."

"I tried to end it, honestly."

"*Tried* to, Jamie?"

"Yes." Maggie could almost see his mind whirring as he desperately searched for an explanation. "I couldn't do it at first, but last week, that's why I went to see her."

"What happened to finishing it a month ago? Have you been seeing her all this time?"

"No—I did finish it, then, like you said, but she was so upset and it was hard, with working together . . ." His voice trailed off, his cheeks flushed puce with shame.

"So you went to her apartment and broke up with her on Tuesday, right?"

Jamie nodded, and looked down.

"Pull the other one. If you wanted to end it, you'd hardly have gone to her place. You'd have done it in town, over lunch. Or maybe you'd even have sent her an e-mail—something heartfelt like that."

Jamie blushed some more. "I do care about her, Maggie."

Maggie jumped at the word. "*Do,* or did?"

"Did, do, I don't know . . ."

"So you think that's what I want to hear? That you care about her? Pah! No, Jean's right—you're still seeing her."

"Bloody Jean!"

"Don't you dare take this out on her! You've no one to blame for this but yourself. And do me a favor—don't insult my intelligence. Admit it, you bottled it."

Silence. She knew she had him cornered. Finally he looked up. "I will finish it, Maggie, I will, I promise. Tomorrow— "

Maggie shook her head. "Too late. I told you there are no half-measures as far as this is concerned. I want you to leave."

"But you can't kick me out! I've nowhere to go!"

"Try Chloë's," said Maggie drily.

"I wouldn't go there."

"Why not? I thought you liked it there."

"I just can't." Jamie shrugged. "It wouldn't seem right."

"Right? That's rich! Who are you to say what's right? I don't think you even know what's right anymore. Well, you can't stay here. I can't let this go—not a second time."

"What about Nathan?"

"I've told him you're going away for a bit."

Jamie looked shell-shocked, as if he still couldn't quite absorb it. "Do you want me to leave now?"

"Yes. You can come back on the weekend and see Nathan, though you'll have to take him out. I don't want you hanging around here."

"I'll go to Pete's," said Jamie, sitting down heavily on the stairs. He seemed to realize that Maggie wasn't going to change her mind. "Can I use the phone?"

"Yes, you can stay to make a call, though you could use your mobile. Call Pete, or find yourself a hotel for the night. But that's it, Jamie. No more discussions. No arguing. No pleading. You've ten minutes, then I want you gone."

40

Chloë was excited. For the first time in two years, she was going to see her brother. It was mid-December and Sam was coming home from California for Christmas. Chloë had even taken the first day off she'd had since New York to pick him up from Heathrow.

As she stood waiting at the arrivals gate scanning every luggage label to see if it was from his flight, she was barely able to contain herself. At last his fellow passengers began to trickle through from customs and, after what seemed like an age, she saw a familiar figure, pushing a trolley laden with bags. She was eager to shout but knew Sam would find it embarrassing, so she waited until he'd gotten beyond the balustrade.

"Sam!"

"Chloë!"

They flung their arms around each other, then stood back self-consciously—open displays of affection weren't normally their style.

"So, how are you?" he said. Chloë realized at once he sounded faintly American.

"Oh, I'm fine! I've got *loads* to tell you. But it'll keep. How are you? Flight OK?"

She appraised him. His skin was browner, his hair lighter, he seemed leaner, fitter. He still looked like her little brother—scruffy, with his chestnut curls and his "sticky-outy" ears, as she'd always cruelly referred to them—though his face seemed older, possibly wiser.

"I'm great! I love it there! You should come and stay with us, sis, you really should."

"I went to New York," she reminded him.

"Of course. I got your postcard. Not that it's anything like California, though. What did you think?"

"Oh, I loved it!" Chloe had a pang of nostalgia. "I had the best time *ever*. I'm dying to go back."

"I can imagine. It's just your kind of city. In fact," he reflected, as he pushed the trolley into the Heathrow express ticket area, "I can see it would suit you. Have you ever thought of moving there for a bit?"

"I'd love to!" For a moment Chloë forgot James. "But how could I? It's so hard to get a work permit."

"Tell me about it." Sam was still waiting for his green card.

By now they were at the platform, and within minutes a train pulled in. They struggled aboard with Sam's bags, took two seats opposite each other, and leaned across the table to continue chatting. Uncertain of his response, Chloë held off on telling her brother about James, instead updating him on the magazine. "The research groups came back with *such* positive feedback," she said, "so we're all set to launch in the New Year."

"That's excellent. Now, I've got something to tell you."

Chloë gleaned from his expression that it was major. Oops, she thought, this is the first time I've allowed him to get a word in. "Ooh, what?"

"You know that Couples' Weekend I mentioned months ago? In the end, I went."

Well I never, thought Chloë. Who would have guessed my brother would do something so *Californian*?

"Actually it was rather good, made me see things a bit differently. Helped clarify what's important."

"Really?"

He smiled broadly. "I'm getting married."

"Oh, my God!" cried Chloë, surprised again. "To Michele, I presume?"

Sam laughed. "Of course—who else would it be?"

"Just checking," said Chloë. "You never know." She stopped to think. While on many levels she was delighted—she genuinely liked Michele, and believed them well suited—she felt a touch envious and a whole load of other emotions she couldn't quite place.

So my little brother must have proposed, she realized. Imagine him, getting married, eh? Though I'm older than he is. It should have been me first . . .

She bit her lip. Although James wasn't living at home at the moment, Chloë had not been seeing much more of him as a result. He'd said he needed space, time to consider, and she didn't want to push things, though it made her miserable as hell not to. And now her baby bro was going to be a husband.

Will James ever commit like that to me? she wondered. At once she was struck. If James did offer to commit seriously—or in any way, come to that—would I trust him? she asked herself. He's not as trustworthy as Sam, I can see that . . . I'm biased, of course, but everyone who's met him agrees: Sam's a real sweetie. Oh, well. She pushed these observations aside. Now was not the time to ponder that; she owed it to Sam to focus on what he was saying.

"So where are you going to have the wedding? Here? Australia? California?"

While Sam was sleeping off jet lag on the living room sofa, Chloë caught up on the housework. She disliked doing it, but it had gotten beyond the point that even she could stand it. She put a load of whites in the washing-machine, then set about cleaning the dishes. As she stood at the sink, wrist-deep in soapy water, scrubbing absentmindedly at a casserole dish, she thought once more about James.

Since he had left Maggie three weeks previously, he'd been staying with his friend, Pete, and Pete's wife, in Wimbledon. Apparently, although they had two children, there was a spare room. "So he's not moving in here then?" Rob had asked. The possibility had occurred to Chloë too. "Oh, I can understand why not," she'd said. "He won't want to leap into that straight away," and, heeding Rob's words about James turning to her on the rebound, she'd refrained from suggesting it to him. Nonetheless, she'd been hurt he'd not seemed to consider it himself, which had also made her wonder whether he was still hoping to work things out with Maggie. If he moves in with me it will ruin his chances of reconciliation, she'd realized, yet she was too afraid to ask him outright.

There seem to be more and more no-go areas with James, Chloë admitted to herself. I suppose it's because I'm wary of what he might say.

In truth, now that she understood how vulnerable her own position was, Chloë was terrified. Turning a blind eye was her way of protecting herself. She no longer invited James to spend time with her, just accepted that one or two nights a week was the most he could give. She didn't ask him if he loved her, as she was petrified that now he was potentially available, he'd say he wasn't sure. And she hadn't even asked for details on his split with Maggie.

"So his wife found out about the two of you?" Rob had been keen to discover.

"No idea," Chloë had replied. "All I know is they had a huge row and he walked out."

The notion that Maggie might despise her, and that people would perceive her as the villain of the piece, made Chloë shudder.

Nor had she told her friends what was going on: a sure sign that she was uncomfortable with her own behavior. She'd never put Sam in the full picture either, although she normally confided in him, and she'd certainly not told her parents. So the only person who was aware that James had left his wife was Rob. And there was no avoiding telling *him*, thought Chloë.

At that moment her brother emerged from the living room, rubbing his eyes and yawning. "Blimey, what's gotten into you?" He looked at the pile of clean dishes, stacked precariously on the drain board.

She'd been so preoccupied, she'd accomplished more than she realized. "Impressive, huh?"

"You'll make someone a good wife yet. Any chance of a cuppa?"

"Of course." Chloë jumped to attention. "Tea? Coffee?"

"Got anything herbal?"

"Really?" Chloë was surprised. Her brother used to like his drinks laced with sugar and caffeine.

"Yup. I'm on a bit of a health kick."

Inwardly, Chloë smiled. On the train earlier Sam was scathing about the West Coast obsession with the body beautiful, yet he appears to be embracing the lifestyle even so, she thought.

Cup of decaf in hand (it was the best Chloë could do), Sam returned to his spot on the sofa and edged his feet back under the duvet. Potato shifted grudgingly to make room.

"How's your love life then?" he asked.

He was bound to ask eventually, Chloë acknowledged. She hesitated, wondering where to start. "Bit of a mess actually . . ."

"You seeing more than one bloke?" Sam teased.

If only! thought Chloë. But at least here was a way in. "Not exactly . . . It's more like the other way around."

Sam appeared perplexed. "You're seeing some guy who's seeing someone else too?"

Chloë nodded. "You could put it that way."

"Do you mind?" Sam examined her face closely. "Yes, you do. You're too old for the double-dating game. Why don't you tell him you want to go out together properly, or knock it on the head?"

"He's married," Chloë said, then hurriedly looked away.

"He's what?"

"Married." Chloë was conscious of his gaze but unable to return it. Then she added, hoping it might sound less dreadful, "Though now he's not living with her anymore."

"Now he's not—you mean he was?"

"Er . . . yes," Chloe admitted, coloring. She might deceive herself, but she couldn't lie to her brother. "Until last month he was."

"How long has this been going on, then?"

Chloë cast her mind back. "About six months." Her cheeks were burning; she felt horribly ashamed. Although Sam was younger, she desperately needed his approval. They'd always looked after each other, particularly when their parents had been preoccupied with their own misfortunes.

"Are you telling me he left his wife for you?"

"Oh, I'm not sure about *that*," Chloë said rapidly. "I mean, he'd probably have left her anyway."

"Hmm. I suppose next you're going to tell me he has children."

Chloë squirmed. "Only one," she whispered.

"He? Or she?"

"He."

"How old?"

She could barely say. "He's seven, now."

"Oh, *Chloë*!" Disappointment emanated from Sam's every pore. "How could you?!"

"But I really like him! You haven't even allowed me to explain! You don't understand!" I love James, thought Chloë. Sam's only being so self-righteous because he's about to get hitched.

Yet Sam was stern. "I think I do. Where did you meet him?"

"At work—he's the publisher at UK Magazines."

"You mean he's your *boss*? Blimey, sis, what were you thinking of? This spells disaster!"

"James is not my boss—Vanessa is!" Chloë began to cry. She reached out for Potato, picked him up, and cuddled him close to her. He might be fat and lazy, but at least he wouldn't judge her.

"Hey, I'm sorry. I guess that was a bit harsh. It's just I'm surprised, you know, after everything Mum and Dad went through, I wouldn't have expected you to be a marriage wrecker yourself."

A marriage wrecker? What a dreadful phrase. Chloë had rarely felt so small. Still looking downward, stroking Potato with one hand, she began to chew her nails on the other. "But they're fine now. They're both very happy. It was good they split up, in the end, don't you think?"

"Yeah, yeah. Still, don't you remember how much we hated Julia? Ghastly woman."

"But it wasn't her fault!"

"Mm." She could see from Sam's face that he was far from happy.

"So, do you reckon I'm truly awful, then?"

"Not necessarily. I haven't met the bloke. I know you're nothing like Julia, actually, and if you say things between him and his wife were bad already, and their marriage was over anyway, who am I to judge? It's just, you're my sister . . ." his voice went gruff ". . . and I'd rather see you with someone available, someone without baggage. You deserve to have a nice time with someone who'll treat you well." He paused, seeming to appreciate that maybe Chloë thought she *was* having a nice time. "How much are you seeing of this James, then?"

"I suppose we get to see each other once a week or so."

"Oh, so it's not that serious?"

"No, it is," she countered. Nonetheless it forced her to consider: if James was serious, shouldn't he be keen to be with me more often?

By now she felt the lowest of the low—unscrupulous, unwanted. She sniffed loudly. "Oh, I don't know, Sam. That's what I meant—I've got myself into a mess, haven't I?"

41

Christmas was the hardest. Maggie didn't feel able to refuse Jamie's request that they spend it together as a family, so she allowed him to come home for a few nights, insisting he stay in the spare room. For Nathan's sake she put on a brave face, and prepared a huge dinner as usual. She invited Fran, Geoff, and Dan, in the hope additional people would ease the tension between her and Jamie. She even roasted a turkey, and made do with a rather unsuccessful nut roast for herself.

At the event it was pretty depressing. Fran was so angry with Jamie she could barely be civil to him, and Geoff overcompensated with forced joviality. Nathan and Dan seemed to pick up the vibes, and jumped down from the table the moment they'd finished the main course, refused pudding, and galloped away to play in Nathan's room.

"I'm losing respect for him," she'd whispered to Fran as they carried the dishes from the dining room after dinner. "I get the sense that we're going in different directions, growing apart. It's as if the more I regain strength in my own convictions and become confident about what is right, the more woolly and muddled Jamie grows."

"Or perhaps that's just how he seems to you now," Fran had responded.

"What do you mean?"

"Maybe he's always been like that but this situation has allowed you to see it, highlighted this difference between you. It could be you who's changed."

"Possibly." Maggie had nodded, scraping the leftover bread sauce into a smaller bowl and putting it the fridge. "Yet the trouble is, for me there's no going back. I can't compromise so much anymore. It's why I changed the work I was doing, and the same goes for our marriage. For me, now everything is out in the open, it's an issue of right and wrong, and while I suppose I wish Jamie would appreciate where I'm at, I don't see much evidence."

What she'd refrained from saying to Fran was that she couldn't shake the image of her husband with another woman, that being in such close proximity to him made her skin crawl.

I'm so disappointed in him, she'd acknowledged to herself once they'd gone. I'm not sure I'll ever feel the way I did before.

This was compounded by her certainty James was continuing to see Chloë. She'd asked him directly and he'd said, "Not really." Which means he is, she decided. In some way I might understand better if he'd run into Chloë's arms more assuredly; it would hurt hugely, but at least it would suggest the angst we've been through had a purpose, genuine passion, underlying it all.

Instead his halfhearted "not really," coupled with his repeated pleas over Christmas that she let him move back into the family home permanently told Maggie that he was still torn and cared for them both, and when he left on Boxing Day, she heaved a huge sigh of relief.

New Year's Eve promised to be more fun. Jamie had offered to look after Nathan, and Maggie's friends William and Liz were holding a dinner party with around a dozen guests. They preferred to entertain at home, having recently had their baby, and so it was agreed that Jamie would stay in Shere with Nathan, so that Maggie could stay overnight with them in Twickenham.

It was strange socializing on her own, but as the evening progressed and Maggie had a couple of drinks inside her, she began to enjoy herself. Anyway, she argued, I knew William and Liz long before I met Jamie, and the other guests have never met me before, so why shouldn't I let loose a little?

At about nine o'clock, when Liz was muttering that they couldn't wait any longer and would have to start eating without him, Alex arrived. "Sorry I'm late," he said. "Peace offering." He handed over not one but three bottles of champagne.

Liz had organized the seating so that Maggie and Alex were next to each other: as the two "single" guests it seemed an obvious move. The irony of being planted next to her ex did not escape her, and Maggie was pleased. It gave her a chance to update him on the situation with Jamie without having to yell it across the table, and also, as she rapidly realized, it made it easy for them to flirt.

By the time it reached eleven o'clock she was warmly, but not uncontrollably drunk and at ease, though not so much so that she didn't appreciate the spark developing between Alex and herself. Over the hour the chemistry became more marked, until eventually Alex leaned in close and asked, "Hey, Mags, d'you reckon you'll get back together with Jamie, or is there any hope for an old flame like me?"

Maggie couldn't think what on earth to say. Just then, as she was sitting there with her mouth opening and shutting like a goldfish, the countdown to midnight began.

"Ten!" shrieked William, poised at the head of the table, with one of Alex's bottles in hand, his wrist tilted to face him so he could see his watch.

"Nine . . . eight . . . seven . . . six!" Everyone else joined in, standing up in the excitement. "Five . . . four . . . three . . . two . . . ONE!"

"Happy New Year!" There was the crack of a cork and champagne flew everywhere other than into the glasses. At that moment Alex grabbed Maggie's hand and led her out of the dining room into the hall. "Only this once," he said, "for the New Year. May the next one be better for both of us than the last."

And then he kissed her.

To Maggie's amazement, it was fantastic. Gentle and soft, but oh, so sexy. Had Alex always kissed like that? She was sure he hadn't. In fact, once it had started she didn't want it to stop, and were it not for a vague awareness that someone might emerge from the dining room and catch them, she would happily have stood there, in the corner of the hallway, kissing him, so deliciously, for the next few hours. She felt her whole body come alive, as if what was happening to her lips was a magic key, unlocking her entire being.

Suddenly, she thought about Jamie, about how she'd been judging him, about how she'd implied to Fran only a few days previously that infidelity was such a clear-cut issue. Was this what had gotten into him? Was this what it had been like with Chloë, so tantalizing, so irresistible?

She pulled away. "Oh, Alex . . . I'm not sure we should be doing this, should we?"

"No, we probably shouldn't," he said, but he didn't sound as if he meant it, and merely started kissing her again.

Lord, it was so good!

He felt different from Jamie, smelled different. Yet he felt and smelled familiar too, and briefly Maggie was taken back to her youth, to the years they'd spent together. How comforting, reassuring. And then again as they continued embracing, touching, she grew increasingly aware that Alex wasn't the man he'd been then, that he was different, somehow, somebody exciting, new.

"Maggie, you do know I still care about you, don't you? I care about you an awful lot . . ."

"And I you," she said, realizing that she did, though unsure whether it was quite to the same degree. And as she was swept up into his kisses once more, and felt the solidity of his body against her, she was filled with yearning for him, for his uncomplicated kindness and humanity.

"Where are you staying tonight?" he murmured a few minutes later. "Have you got to go home?"

"I was supposed to be staying here," Maggie whispered, "with Liz and Will . . ."

"Why don't you come back with me?" He pulled away from her a little, and started stroking her hair. She remembered how he'd always loved her hair, how soft and beautiful he'd said it was. "It's not far . . ."

Maggie frowned. If I go back I can guess what will happen, she thought. I'm far too turned on not to have sex with him. Then there won't be the clear distinction between my behavior and Jamie's anymore. It's only been a month since Jamie moved out and I haven't sorted my feelings about him, let alone another man . . . But then, she argued with herself, would it really be so bad? She'd been so goddamn *good*. Wasn't it time she had some fun? And at least with Alex she knew he cared . . .

Ultimately, what swayed her was curiosity. As far as she remembered— but it had been over fifteen years since she'd slept with him—Alex hadn't been *that* great a lover, at least not as good as Jamie, and she wanted to see if this was still true. Because if these incredible long kisses were anything to go by, he had changed . . . He had changed, a lot.

"Okay. What the hell? It's New Year's Eve . . ."

"I'll tell them you don't feel so good," said Alex, appreciating without her saying that she'd want to be discreet. "I'll say I'm going to drop you home after all."

"Thank you." She smiled up at him. He's generous, she thought.

And so, an hour later, she found herself in Alex's apartment in Putney. He poured them each a nightcap, and sat down next to her on the sofa. Maggie felt self-conscious all over again.

What *am* I doing? she thought. Is this really such a good idea? Won't it ruin the chance of a reconciliation with Jamie once and for all, or are we beyond that anyway?

Alex seemed to pick up on her doubt. "It's okay." He took her hand. "I'll look after you, I promise. You don't have to do anything you don't want to do. And you're not to worry—I've no expectations beyond to-night."

Yet as he said that, Maggie knew that she did want to—that she more than wanted to, she *needed* to, and she needed Alex to want her very much indeed. It was as if the lid had been lifted off all the unexpressed passion she'd harbored for months, and now she had an outlet for it, with someone who reciprocated her desire.

What started as a little tentative hand-stroking rapidly developed into more; within minutes Alex had slipped his hands into her bra and was stroking her breasts. Soon they'd tugged off each other's clothes and she'd pulled him on top of her. Then they threw the cushions off the sofa and—laughing—tumbled onto the floor. Maggie could feel the carpet scraping her back, but she didn't care. Far from it—there was something about the mild discomfort that turned her on even more. With one foot, she pushed away the coffee table so she could lift her legs, allowing him to penetrate more deeply.

Bloody hell! she thought, I am quite, quite convinced Alex did not do it like this before . . .

Halfway through he stopped and withdrew from inside her, then very gently put two fingers into her, pushing slightly toward her belly, then away as he did so. Jesus, she said to herself, I've not had that experience, ever—maybe it's the G-spot I never really believed existed . . . And then he started to kiss her body, pausing to suck on her breasts—mmm, she'd *always* liked that. He continued kissing her lower down, so she wasn't sure what was what or where, only that it felt so good.

She opened her eyes and looked down at him, and as she did so she could see him tenderly watching her, seeing if she was happy.

"Are you okay?" he asked.

It made her long for him all the more. She nodded. "Alex, come back inside me now . . . I want to come with you . . ." So he stopped what he was doing and did as she asked. "Can you feel it?" She breathed. "Can you feel I'm about to?"

"Yes," he whispered, and paused, so he could feel the pulse of her. He began to move rhythmically again, and digging her nails into his back, she came with a fantastic shudder. Sensing her do so, he gave in to his own desire also.

42

On February 14, the first issue of *All Woman* was launched. The day the magazine hit the newsstands, its controversial subject matter and provocative tone, offset by typography, illustration, and photography that were stylish and groundbreaking in equal measure, caused a Twitter storm, and Chloë found herself asked to talk about it on local radio and television. The first time she had to do so, she was nervous, but having done it once, she discovered she took to center stage rather well.

"You're more of an actress than you'll ever know," Rob had observed, after watching her on the TV. "Must be the theatrical family background—you put this particular drama queen to shame."

The main event of this frantic week was the launch party, due to be held—at Chloë's insistence—at the Café de Paris in Leicester Square. While it was no longer the trendy nightspot it had once been, Chloë believed its opulent faux-Baroque interior would provide the perfect backdrop for a fancy-dress extravaganza. Guests were invited to come as historic figures they felt were "all woman," and as word spread that it was a media event to be seen at, invitations became highly sought after, with style and news correspondents fighting to get on the list.

Rob couldn't contain himself when he heard. "You're going to have all these straight journos turning up in *drag*!"

"Exactly." Chloë nodded. "They won't be allowed in otherwise. It'll be a scream, don't you think?"

"Ooh, I *wish* I could come." He pouted.

"I'd love for you to, but it's not really up to me, I'm afraid. Everything's organized by our PR department."

Inevitably Chloë took ages to decide what to wear. She was determined to look unique, so she rejected rental shops, yet in the end she left it so late that she was forced to assemble the outfit herself, running round the wholesale outlets of Soho's backstreets to piece it together.

"Well, what do you think?" she asked Rob when she was ready, twirling into his room.

Rob looked at her, mystified. He took in the white sheet swathed around her hour-glass form like a toga, exposing not unattractive amounts of curvy flesh. Her dark curls were gathered up like those of a Greek goddess, with a few tendrils framing her face becomingly. Her eyes were emphasized with copious black liner. Her wrists jangled with gold bangles, and on her feet were thong sandals. The final touch, which she was proudly brandishing in front of her, was a large box.

"Totally divine," he acknowledged. "Though who the devil are you?"

"Open it," she ordered, thrusting the box into his hands.

He read the carefully handwritten label, *A Gift from Zeus*, and lifted the lid. Startled, he jumped back as half a dozen springs popped up, narrowly missing his face. Yet where one might perhaps have expected there to be a jack-in-the-box, on the end of each spring was a different object: the figure of a little devil, a lipstick, a miniature bottle of tequila, a packet of condoms, and a scaled-down copy of *All Woman* . . . He scratched his head. "Evil things . . ." he muttered. "So you're wicked . . . but not Eve . . ."

"Ye-es?"

"Hmm?"

". . . a box . . ."

"You're Pandora!"

"Appropriate—don't you agree—that I should be single-handedly responsible for bringing all the troubles into the world?"

"Ideal for the editor of such a contentious mag." He nodded.

"Thank you," said Chloë, as the doorbell rang. "Eek, that's my taxi!" She snatched back her most crucial accessory.

"Knock 'em dead!" shouted Rob, as she bolted out of the door.

On arriving at the Café de Paris, Chloë helped herself from the silver tray laden with glasses of champagne held by a waiter in the foyer and downed it in one to steady her nerves. Then she moved on to a second waiter for another and pushed open the double doors into the main body of the nightclub.

The first thing she saw, straight ahead of her, was a giant poster of the *All Woman* front cover. Chloë flushed with pride; at what must have been twenty feet high, it took up the entire stage, spanning the lower and upper levels of the club. She moved toward the edge of the balcony, where two symmetrical staircases swept in golden spirals to the main floor below, and looked down.

She'd made sure not to be too early, aware that waiting for guests to arrive would only make her anxious, especially as she was one of the hosts. When she and Rob entertained at home she had no choice in the matter, but here, at a work party where everything was set up already, she didn't have to sit around biting her nails. The bar area thronged with people. Despite the dim, ultraviolet lighting, from her vantage point Chloë could see many familiar faces. There was Jean, dressed as . . . yes, Anaïs Nin. How typical of her to choose someone so literary. There was her co-host, Vanessa—or Morticia, rather—she'd barely had to dress up at all. And there, surrounded by three male Marilyns, clearly relishing an invitation to assess their fake cleavages, was Patsy—Holly Golightly to a T. Chloë scanned the rest of the dance floor. There was a very masculine Nell Gwynn, a couple of Madonnas, a chubby Mata Hari, half a dozen Cleopatras—three of each sex—and a riot of other amusingly costumed guests. Yet where, among all these people, was James? Chloë couldn't see him, so she decided to go down and have a thorough look.

No sooner had she reached the bottom of the stairs than she was cornered by Jean.

"Chloë! Long time no see!" She was tipsy already.

"Yes," said Chloë, feeling at once that she was to blame. Despite working in the same building, she'd not been in to see her old boss in weeks. Although she knew it was advisable to keep on the good side of a woman as influential as Jean, she'd hardly had a moment to spare. Also, since Patsy had warned her of Jean's mounting suspicions all those months ago, she was concerned that Jean would jump at the chance to delve. James had told her that Jean knew, and was furious with them both. Rather than face her, Chloë had opted for her default response to matters emotional: avoidance. She said none of this, but simply muttered, "I've been swept off my feet."

"So I gather. Whenever I've caught sight of you, you've been awfully preoccupied."

Was Chloë being paranoid, or could she detect an underlying jibe? "Well, you know what it's like, launching a new magazine—never enough hours in the day."

"Not with a life as full as yours, I imagine." Now she was in no doubt: this was barbed. Especially as Jean then drained her glass and added, "Love the outfit—how very risqué." Her eyes were fixed pointedly on Chloë's exposed bosom, as if to say, And unseemly. Chloë scanned the venue for an excuse to talk to someone else. She had witnessed Jean's tendency to vent spleen when tipsy before. Out of the corner of her eye she could see Patsy giggling with the three Marilyns. How she longed to join them at the bar! Yet Jean was on a roll. "I wanted to congratulate you on not one but two impressive achievements."

"Oh, yeah?"

"First the magazine. I must say, it's marvelous." Jean swayed slightly, then took hold of Chloë's arm to steady herself. "Goddamn marvelous. No, I mean that. It's very different, thought-provoking, great fun. I love it."

Chloë blushed. "Thank you."

"You've achieved everything you set out to do, and I'd like to congratulate you on a job well done." Jean clinked Chloë's glass.

"I'm glad you like it."

"And the other thing," here Jean leaned close, dropped her voice, and spoke with thinly veiled sarcasm, "is that I want to congratulate you on breaking up what, until you came along, was one very happy little family."

Shit. I knew it, thought Chloë. I just knew it. What on earth am I supposed to say to that? There was no time to answer, however, because Jean hadn't finished.

"I gather Jamie's had to move out of the family home—away from Maggie and Nathan. I also understand that you're still seeing him. Though at least I hear he's had the sense not to move in with you immediately. Well, I hope that's what you wanted. Driving a father away from his son, a husband away from his wife. I hope you're satisfied."

Still Chloë couldn't respond. She experienced the same stomach-churning guilt that she'd had on occasion when talking to Rob about James. Only this time her guilt was more pronounced, as it had been when she'd spoken to Sam at Christmas. Her old boss and her brother: their moral judgment was more formidable, less compromising. It weighed on her hard. Her shame was compounded because she had not had the courage to shift the status quo. She'd neither finished the relationship, nor tried to move it along; she'd been paralyzed. I've had so much on my mind, she protested inwardly. It's such a bad time to deal with something so difficult and potentially painful.

"Maggie told you?" she asked, finally.

"Who else but Maggie?"

"Oh." This was the first time Maggie had been mentioned directly by Jean in this context. It sounded strange, hearing her name, coming from a friend; someone who actually knew this woman, doubtless had heard her side of the story. It made Maggie seem more real, less remote, and exacerbated Chloë's discomfort. "Jean, I'm not sure this is the right place to talk about this."

"I'm sure it's not. But where is? Indeed, there are plenty of people who would consider it quite inappropriate to mention it, but I'm not one of them, I'm afraid. You know me; I have to speak my mind. And I'm not sure if you realize, Chloë—sometimes you can be quite naive—but I've done a fair amount of listening to Maggie over the last few months—a lot of picking up the pieces. She's been to hell and back, you realize."

"I know," said Chloë, stifling a desire to scream. *So have I.*

"I also don't know if you're aware of quite what a woman she is, how remarkable."

"Hm." Though surely, thought Chloë desperately, if she was *that* remarkable, James would never have been attracted to anyone else, would he? He wouldn't have walked out on someone truly right for him?

Then, like a spear plunging directly into Chloë's heart, it came: "I think Jamie wants her back, you know."

At once Chloë began to shake. She felt her world with James, her vision of the future crumbling. "Does he?"

"Yes, I do think so." Jean seemed determined to put Chloë straight. "Maggie tells me that he phones and hints heavily at moving back in all the time."

"But, but . . ." Chloë was horribly confused. "He's the one who walked out! He could just go back—if that's what he wants?"

A waiter, dapper in his white dinner jacket, was hovering with a tray of freshly filled glasses, oblivious to the shattering dialogue close at hand. Jean reached for another drink and Chloë, keen to take the edge off all these harsh words, followed suit. In the background she thought she caught a glimpse of James, glancing in her direction and rapidly looking away.

"So that's what Jamie told you, is it? That he walked out on her?"

"Yes."

Jean sighed. "Sometimes I wonder about him, I really do. He surprises me. Seems to be telling you each a different story. I wouldn't have put him down as so duplicitous, but I suppose I shouldn't be amazed at things people say when they're caught in the middle like that." She shook her head. "I guess I've not heard his side of it, and I probably never will. But if that's what he told you, it's not true. Maggie found out about the two of you—otherwise I'm not sure he ever would have told her. When she found out, she made him promise not to see you anymore, and to try to work things through with her, and he didn't stick to that promise. When she discovered he was *still* seeing you regardless, she told him to leave."

Chloë's mind was racing, trying to work it out. I honestly believed James was the one who chose to go, not the other way around, she thought. I understood it was a positive decision, albeit one made in anger. She could hear Rob's voice: *"This only underlines how unsure James is about what he's doing. He'll probably go back to Maggie eventually—if she'll have him. He'll never commit to you, didn't I say?"*

Seeing Chloë look so crestfallen, Jean appeared to appreciate there were perhaps slightly extenuating circumstances. "How ironic," she said, scanning Chloë's ensemble once again, less critically this time. "Pandora, eh?"

"Oh, you know me . . ." Chloë faltered, feeling humbled. "Nothing but trouble . . ."

"Hey." Jean nudged her. "Look, I realize you're not really that wicked. You must understand, this hasn't been easy for me, knowing you both like I do, being so fond of the pair of you. And I'm very fond of Nathan, too. Hell, I'm even fond of Jamie, in many ways . . . But I worry for you, Chloë, genuinely I do. I wouldn't want to see you come unstuck in all this. You've got such talent, and I know that more than anyone. It's not just a passing thing, it's rare. I meant what I said about the magazine. It's great. You ought to be very proud." She drew breath. "Anyway, I've said my bit. I don't want to spoil your evening completely, so I'll shut up now. Off you go, Chloë, scoot. This is a very special night for you. Enjoy it."

Chloë needed no further encouragement to take her leave. James was deep in conversation with someone she didn't recognize and, anyway, she certainly couldn't approach him *now*. She noticed that he hadn't bothered to dress up. Probably thinks he's all things to all women simply like that, she bristled. Instead she headed straight for the bar, and Patsy.

"Oops," said Patsy. "That looked heavy. You okay?"

Chloë exhaled. "Only just."

"Here. Let me get you a drink." Patsy drew herself up to her full height in a bid to get her presence noticed behind the counter.

"Margarita," she ordered. "No salt."

On top of three glasses of champagne, Chloë knew this probably wasn't the best idea in the world, but she needed it.

"Thanks."

A few minutes with Patsy and the three Marilyns and Chloë had put a bit of space between her and the ghastly confrontation. Within an hour she was on a more even keel.

"Ah! Here's the woman I was after!" exclaimed a familiar voice. It was Vanessa. "Chloë, here's someone who's dying to meet you. Adrienne Sugarman, Chloë Appleton."

Chloë wished her mind was less fuzzy. She recognized the name, though she couldn't place the woman before her.

"Hi!" enthused Adrienne, shaking her hand with the iron grip customary in confident Americans. "Special projects director. US Publishing."

Ah yes, of course. Adrienne's golden touch was well known throughout the whole organization. Aside from the aura of success that surrounded her, with her deep honey-toned skin, wild Afro, and sensational curves, she oozed sensuality. Although she held the equivalent position on the other side of the Atlantic, she was the antithesis of Vanessa physically, certainly, and quite possibly in temperament too.

"Fabulous magazine, Chloë. *Fabulous*."

"Thank you." Chloë warmed to Adrienne at once.

"Can I get you a drink?"

"No, thanks, I'm fine."

Vanessa moved off, leaving them together. "Gee, if I'd known, I'd have gotten dressed up like you guys, but I only flew in today and Vanessa invited me along. Anyways, I had to say, I so *love* what you've done with the magazine! It's so refreshing! So challenging! So very . . . zeitgeist." Chloë was feeling better and better. "Speaking of new," continued Adrienne, "I think us guys should get together while I'm over. Just you and me, off the record initially, of course."

Chloë raised her eyebrows.

"It's only an idea, but if the magazine does as well here as it looks set to do—and I believe we'll know pretty fast—have you thought about launching a US edition? I could see it going down *fabulously* well." Chloë couldn't believe what she was hearing, but Adrienne left her in no doubt. "What I'm trying to say is, would you ever consider coming to work with me at US Magazines in New York?"

43

Chloë picked up Potato and cuddled him to her. "How would you feel if I went to New York?" she whispered into the furry triangle of his ear. "Would you be okay if I left you here with Rob?" Potato purred. "And what do you think I should do about James, my fat friend? You think I should finish things, don't you? You never liked him—always on your bloody sofa." Potato purred some more.

With a sigh, Chloë put him down and watched him make his way back to the dent in the cushions that was the hallmark of his snoozing spot. He doesn't give a fig, she thought. She hunted for her handbag, located it under the kitchen table, and cast her eye around the apartment, allowing herself a moment's nostalgia as she recalled the good times she and Rob had shared there. It had been her haven (albeit a messy one) virtually since the day she'd left college, and she wasn't sure how she felt about someone else moving into her room, even though it was set to be a good friend of Rob's whom she also knew. Then there was Rob. Would he be okay without her? More to the point, would she be okay without him?

Hell, thought Chloë. I'll never know unless I try it.

She caught the bus to work as usual, and took her favorite seat on the top deck.

What a few weeks it's been, she acknowledged as the double-decker crossed the Thames. *More than I could have dreamed for careerwise seems to be coming true, and this will be one of the last times I'll travel this particular route . . .*

She'd not breathed a word about her transfer to anyone at the office other than Vanessa until it was all signed and sealed—even James didn't know. They'd gotten together a handful of times at her apartment since the party, but with uncharacteristic patience she had held off on mentioning anything until she'd an offer in writing. Two days ago her contract had finally arrived, so today she was due to break the news. She'd chosen neutral territory and arranged to see him during her lunch hour.

They met in Soho Square. It was a bright, spring day; the daffodils were out. And although they needed to keep their jackets on, it was warm enough to sit on the grass with their sandwiches.

"You wanted to talk." James unwrapped his panini and took a large bite. He sounded faintly worried.

Confronted with this situation, Chloë couldn't think where to start. Several voices were fighting to be heard in her head.

There was Jean, reminding her that Jamie probably still loved Maggie.

There was Rob, despairing because James had shown no sign of being able to decide between the two of them.

There was her mother, all those years ago with her theories of rebound relationships.

There was Sam, who seemed so disappointed that his sister was selling herself short.

And there was also another set of voices: Chloë's own voices.

There was the hedonistic voice of the rebellious teenager, which said, *"Hey, but you've had such a good time! Surely you're not going to give up all that fun?"*

There was the romantic voice, which recalled the flowers, the lovemaking, the passion.

There was the intellectual voice, which made her question whether she'd ever enjoy such sparky conversations with another man.

There was the lonely voice of the little-girl-lost, who didn't want to be on her own.

And there was the voice of doom, which said she'd never get over it, that if she finished it with James she'd never meet anyone, ever again.

But the voice that finally spoke was none of these. It was the voice of self-belief, the voice of resolve, the voice of a grown woman. "I'm leaving you," she said.

James stopped mid-mouthful. He swallowed, hard. "Oh."

Chloë knew she needed to explain more fully. "I mean literally leaving you."

James looked puzzled. "Literally?"

"Yes. I'm leaving. Going away."

"On vacation? You're having a break? You deserve it."

Chloë laughed, slightly bitterly. "You couldn't be more wrong. I'll probably end up working harder than ever. I'll have to learn a whole different market."

"I don't understand." His mouth was contorted.

"I've got a new job."

"Oh? Gosh." He sounded surprised. "But these first few issues of *All Woman* have been such a success. I thought that was what you wanted; it's your baby. Would you really want to go and work on another magazine? And, anyway, even if you did, why does that mean you're leaving me?" She noticed he'd stopped eating altogether.

"I'm still going to be working on *All Woman*. But they've asked me to go to New York. Set up an American edition there."

"What?" James was clearly stunned. In the normal run of events, as the publisher, he would have been aware of such a move.

"I asked them not to tell you, or anyone, till I'd thought it through." Chloë went on, beginning to find the conversation harder now. He was plucking at the grass, little tufts of unspoken emotion. "I know it was a bit out of turn . . . but I didn't know what else to do."

"I see." James looked up, into her eyes. He looked so wounded, so hurt, so adrift, like a small boy. It was a look she'd seen before, all those months back, in the Paramount in New York, just after he'd spoken to Maggie. The day before he told me he loved me, she thought. Her gut wrenched. Oh God, this was so unfair!

"I'm sorry," she said softly.

"Are you definitely going to go?" He was hoarse.

She nodded.

"Do you want me to stop you?"

"No, not really. I don't think it would be a good idea."

"It's me who should be sorry," he said. Bloody hell—he was crying. "I know I've been . . ." he stumbled over the words ". . . pretty useless, really."

"No . . . no more than me, you haven't."

"Can't I come and see you? You know, I come over to New York a lot."

"Well . . ." She hesitated, but then a voice reminded her of what she had pledged to do. "By all means say hello, put your head around the door of my office, or whatever . . . maybe even go for lunch. But as for more than that, no, you can't."

"Oh." James made the word sound like a cry of pain. "I suppose you're right. It wouldn't be a good idea."

"It's just . . ." Chloë was getting tearful too, but fought against it, crazily aware that she had no tissues. "I need to give myself another chance, you know, of meeting someone else." Her resolution grew stronger again. "Someone who wants me, and only me."

The sadness of his expression suggested he was far from enthusiastic about the idea of her with another man. "So when are you leaving?" he asked in a whisper.

"Monday." It was Friday. "Vanessa's taking over the running of the magazine here, and I'm going to liaise with her from New York for this next edition. Then next month they've got a new editor here in the UK. Someone I know actually—she's very good."

"But she's not you." The miniature pile of grass was getting quite high now.

"No, she's not. But I'm not Maggie either."

"No. That's why I loved you."

"I know." Chloë sniffed. "But you love her too—and I don't want only half of you." Then she added, generously, "You could go back to her, you know."

"I'm not certain she'd have me, even if I was sure I wanted to . . ."

"But you're not sure."

"I don't know. I don't know what I want anymore."

And although Chloë felt terribly sad, this convinced her that she was doing the right thing. "You're not sure you want me, my love, either."

James was silent then said, "I hate good-byes." Right then he seemed a million miles from the successful, confident publisher she'd first met less than a year before.

Suddenly Chloë felt old and wise. Philosophical, even. "They don't matter. It's what's gone before."

"It's what you're telling me can't come after. Nothing. No more us."

"Yes." She paused, pained. "That is what I'm telling you."

"I should never have become involved with you, dragged you into such a mess."

"But I knew what I was doing, James, really. I knew you were married when I went into this. I walked in with my eyes open. I may not have liked what I saw, I may have blinded myself. I don't blame you, honestly. It's just . . . in a way, in a funny way . . . you've given me a taste of what I could have, had things been different. And now I want to see if I can find that properly. And it's easier for me—and it'll be much easier for you—if I can do that without you around, constantly reminding me." She leaned forward and very softly, kissed those still-contorted lips. "I'm going to go now," she said, standing up and dusting off her skirt. "And please don't phone me or e-mail me or anything. Just let me go and do this my own way." She looked down at him one last time, sitting there on the grass of Soho Square surrounded by all the other people with their sandwiches, enjoying their normal, everyday lunches. "Part of me will always love you; you know that. And I know that part of you will always love me. But part of you is not enough for me now. I want more—maybe I want too much, who knows? Still, I've got to give it a try, because I've only got one life . . . And I know this might sound melodramatic, but I want to be able to live with myself as I live it. So this is it. Good-bye."

And before he had a chance to say any more, to protest, to beg, to tell her he loved her, to promise that he'd make a go of things with her, she picked up her handbag and turned and walked away.

Once her back was turned she started to cry. Yet she kept walking, determined, back for her final afternoon at UK Publishing, all woman at last.

44

They were standing on the edge of the soccer field together, watching the Shere Tigers versus the Godalming Lions. It was a typical March afternoon—neither warm nor cold, cloudy nor sunny, though it was windy, and gusts kept catching Maggie's hair, swooping wisps in front of her face.

With only five minutes to go, the Tigers were losing one-zero, and Nathan was standing scuffing the turf with his boots, bored. The game had been focused down at his team's goal end; as a striker, he'd had little chance to play. Suddenly, one of the Tiger's defenders snatched the ball in a rare moment of aggression, and kicked it away from the goal mouth, toward him. Startled, Nathan realized he had an opportunity at his feet.

"C'mon, Nathan, my son!" shrieked Jamie, caught up in a wave of excitement.

The Godalming defense, having had it easy the entire match, were taken unawares. Quick as a flash, Nathan shot down toward the goal, dribbling the way his father had taught him, with virtuosity surprising in a seven-year-old. He nipped around the defender. Now, other than the keeper, there was only one player between him and the goal.

Maggie couldn't contain herself. She jumped up and down and squealed, "Oh, my God!"

"You're on side!" bellowed Jamie. "Go for it!"

And with a decisive *thwack,* Nathan kicked the ball past the keeper, through the posts, and scored.

"*Hooray!*" his parents yelped, and caught up in unanimous pride, threw their arms around each other just as Nathan's teammates rushed to do the same to him.

A few seconds later, flustered, Jamie and Maggie broke apart, shocked at the first physical contact they'd had in months.

Maggie took a step back. "He's very good, isn't he?"

"Brilliant," Jamie enthused. "That was a magnificent shot. He's far better than I ever was."

"Surely not. I thought you were the best in your class."

"Hmm." Jamie shook his head. "I think he's got a perfectionist streak that I never had." He turned to look at her. Her hair was still blowing in the wind. She'd grown it over the last few months, and it was longer than it had been in years. She'd been told she looked different somehow, younger. "Must have gotten it off his mum."

Maggie blushed, but there was truth in his words: she was more of a perfectionist than Jamie, an idealist, even.

"I miss him, you know," said Jamie.

"I know."

They stood watching their son in silence.

Presently Jamie said, "I'm not seeing Chloë anymore."

Maggie looked at him, saying nothing, but her face must have expressed her skepticism.

"I appreciate you've heard me say that before," he added with some urgency, presumably conscious that the game would finish in a few minutes.

Again Maggie was silent.

"This time it's different. It really is over."

Maggie sighed. Part of her so wanted to believe him, still wanted things to work out, if not for her sake, then for Nathan's. "Why should I believe you? What makes it different this time?"

"She's leaving." explained Jamie. "Going away."

"Oh." Maggie felt a mix of emotions. Part of her was glad that at last this woman would be out of her life. Yet regardless of her relief, part of her still refused to give in to her desire to make up with Jamie, to reunite as a family. She realized that this was what he was asking her to consider— he'd pretty much said so before. Yet deep down something prevented her from feeling at ease. She tried to put a finger on it, and in the hope of gaining clarification, asked, "Where's she going?"

"To New York. She's been invited to set up an American edition of *All Woman* there."

"I see . . . So when does she go?"

"Tomorrow."

There; there it was. That was what was bothering her. Maggie was sure she could hear regret in his voice. It was so subtle that someone who knew him less well might not have heard it. "Tell me, Jamie, did you finish it?" She paused. "Or did she?"

Jamie looked down at his shoes. "I suppose . . . she did." He must know this wasn't the right thing to say; that it meant he would lose her, yet perhaps at last he was sick of lying.

Maggie tucked her hair behind her ears so she could see him properly. "That's it, Jamie, don't you see? It was all I ever asked of you, for you to decide for yourself. And you never could. That was all I wanted—for you to come back, to try to make a go of things, of your own accord. But you couldn't do that, and even now that it's over with Chloë, you weren't the one to decide. The ceaseless fluctuating . . . Never knowing what you wanted . . . Always reacting to me or her, never taking the initiative. You must see that I can't take you back. Not on those terms, not now."

"Mm." His voice was small, disappointed, but resigned. "I kind of thought you'd say that."

Again she sighed. "I guess maybe it's because I'm a perfectionist, like you said. But that's the way I am and try as I may, I can't change it. I wouldn't be being true to myself." She fought back the tears, struggling to express what she meant, yet be kind. "That's the irony—it might be one of the reasons you love me but . . . I don't know. Perhaps we're too different in that way. Your ambivalence, your pragmatism . . . I understand it, but living like that, it was killing me, all that compromise. And I ended up putting all my idealism into the wrong stuff—stupid things, shallow things—an immaculate house, the perfect bloody soufflé . . . I'm sorry, but I've fought so hard to get it back . . . who I really am. It's not that I don't still love you, it's that I can't love you like I used to—or at least be with you—not in the same way, not anymore."

At that moment the referee blew the final whistle and the boys came running off the pitch. Nathan charged over to his parents, pleased as punch with his performance, happily unaware of the significance of their conversation. He bounced along between them, and they made their way back across the recreation ground.

When they reached the car park, Jamie headed for his vehicle as if to drive straight up to London.

"Hey." Maggie touched his shoulder as he turned to go. "Why don't you come back with us for a bit? Have some tea and biscuits?" This was her white flag; her way of saying he was still a part of her life with Nathan, regardless of whether the two of them remained husband and wife.

"Really?"

"Of course," said Maggie. "You'd like to have tea with Daddy, wouldn't you, Nathan?"

45

Chloë got out of the yellow cab and checked her watch.

Damn. She was early. It was only twenty to eight, and she was meeting Adrienne Sugarman at Nobu on the hour. She took a peek through the double doors of the famous restaurant. Every table was packed, but the bar was empty. It was in the center of the room and she'd be conspicuous, especially as she hadn't brought anything to read.

To kill time she strolled a couple of blocks down Hudson Street. Soaring ahead of her against the clear sky of the late June evening was the new World Trade development; on the corner was a tavern, Puffy's. Small to the point of poky, it was seedy in comparison with the impressive bamboo chic of Nobu, but a great deal less intimidating—several people were sitting at the bar.

Chloë pushed open the door and squeezed herself in at the counter.

"What'll it be?" asked the bartender.

"A margarita. On the rocks. No salt." That'll help my meeting go with a swing, she thought.

As the bartender prepared her cocktail, the guy sitting next to her caught her eye. "Are you English?"

"Yeah."

"Been here long?"

"About two months."

"Not on vacation, then?"

"No." Chloë wasn't really in the mood to talk.

He leaned forward and smiled. "So you're here a while?"

"As long as it takes," said Chloë, and thought, to get over a broken heart. She was silent for a moment, contemplating how hard it was to be so far from home. She missed Rob and her friends and family, but at least Facebook allowed her to stay in touch with them on a regular basis, and Rob instant messaged her often to chat online. No, the person she really missed was James. She'd stuck to her resolve and had not been in touch with him, and it was getting easier as time passed, just as Rob kept assuring her it would be, but it was testing her newfound self-control to the max. She knew this was for the best, yet it was often when other men chatted her up that she missed James most keenly—they never seemed as special as he was, somehow.

"Huh?" The guy next to her interrupted her thoughts, sounding puzzled.

She realized her responses—or lack of them—must appear odd, so explained, "I've come for work."

"What kind of work?"

"To launch a magazine."

"Really?" He appeared genuinely interested. "Cool."

There was nothing like flattery to bring Chloë out of an introverted mood. She beamed proudly. "I'm meeting my new business partner at Nobu in a few minutes. She's bringing some potential advertisers."

"*Nice,*" said the guy. "Hey, I'm Peter." He held out his hand.

As she shook it, noting his firm grip, she took him in properly for the first time. She judged he was a few years older than she was, and his clothes suggested that he wasn't short of a dollar or two. Indeed, he was pretty nice-looking in an Italian-who-likes-the-good-life kind of way.

Peter continued, "And these are my friends—Ben, Brad." Two men leaned around the counter and shook Chloë's hand in turn. They were decidedly leaner and scruffier than Peter. One looked like a dissolute rock star, while the other—if his paint-splattered hair was anything to go by—must have been an artist of some kind. Yet all three had one thing in common.

They were gorgeous.

At once she felt better still. "I'm Chloë." She grinned.

Then, for a split second, she wondered what it would be like to have sex with them all. Simultaneously. Better than the boys in the gym back home, that was for sure. Though maybe they were gay. This *was* New York. And before she could stop herself, she said, "So, are you straight, or what?"

Peter, the Italian-looking one, laughed. "Now, there's a direct to-the-point kinda girl. Far as I know to date, yeah, we are."

She smiled wryly. "Married?"

Each shook his head.

Wonders will never cease, thought Chloë.

She took a generous gulp of margarita.

What the heck?

Perhaps she was just *beginning* to get over James, after all.

46

"I suppose it's time to say good-bye," said Maggie, checking her watch. She looked around the room. With its view over Guildford glistening in the summer sun, it seemed less shabby to her than it had the previous autumn, more comforting, homely. It was a retreat she would miss, just as she would miss Jamie and their house in Shere. But she was ready to leave it behind all the same. "I wanted to thank you for everything you've done for me. You've been brilliant, a great help."

"Do feel free to stay in touch," said Nina, "let me know how things are going. I'd like that."

"Oh, I will." Maggie nodded, knowing she would, in the same way she would stay in touch with Georgie; even if she only ever sent a Christmas card. She was good that way, loyal. "It's a bit far to come every week, now that Nathan and I are moving closer to London again."

"I quite understand."

"And I feel we're moving on in other ways, too, so I ought to draw a line under this whole affair, try to put it behind us."

Now it was Nina's turn to nod. Her jewelry rattled accordingly. "Good luck." She got to her feet and held out her hand. "I hope it all goes well for you."

"Thank you." Maggie shook her hand. It seemed strange, such a formal gesture, after everything she'd shared with this woman over the last few months. So, impulsively, she reached forward instead, and gave Nina a swift hug around her broad shoulders. "Thank you," she said again and turned and left the room.

Back in her car she rummaged in her handbag for her mobile. She checked her messages. There was one from the *Observer*, giving her the go-ahead on an idea she'd put to them that morning. That was a fast response—they must have liked it. There was one from Jean—very excited Maggie was going to be living closer to her again, and offering to lend a hand with packing. And there was one from Jamie, asking if he could have Nathan on Saturday instead of Sunday and take him to a game. He wondered if it was possible for Nathan to spend the night with him. Now that he was renting his own apartment this was a viable option.

Maggie hit *Call back.*

"About Saturday," she said when he answered, "that's fine. In fact, it's helpful. I fancied doing something myself so that makes it easier."

"Great! I'll look forward to it."

She hung up without getting drawn into a long chat but before starting the engine, decided to make one last call. "Hi—it's Mags. Can you talk?"

"Sure."

She felt a bit funny, flustered even. "I—er—you said you wanted to see me this weekend? Maybe go away somewhere?"

"Yes?" Alex sounded hopeful, and a little nervous too.

"Well, it's fine. Only for one night, that's all I can manage. But I've decided I'd like to. Come with you, I mean."

"I'm so pleased. I'll look online, see if I can book us in somewhere special. Anywhere you've a hankering to go?"

"Surprise me," she said.

ACKNOWLEDGMENTS

A big thank-you to family, and especially my mum, not just for her direct advice about this novel but also for her support over the years.

I also wish to thank Rachel Leyshon for helping to develop the idea in the first place and for her editorial expertise; my publisher at Orion, Jane Wood; and my agent, Vivien Green, who believed in this from the off; plus Donna Brodie from the fabulous Writers' Room in New York.

My friends Debbie Fagan, Margaret Heffernan, Jenny Lingrell, Julie Miller, Paula Morris, and Michele Teboul deserve special mention, as do my very own "Robs," Bill Graber, John Scott, Patrick Fitzgerald, and Karl Miller. And as for the J/J-like guys I've known in my time, well, have a margarita on me.

I'd also like to add thanks to my UK editor, Francesca Main, who helped hone this revised version; my U.S. editor, Sara Goodman; photographer Madelyn Mulvaney and designer Jonathan Roberts for their work on the new cover; Pauline Amaya-Torres for helping with typo-spotting; and my other half, Tom, for being nothing like this novel's James.